LYNN YVONNE MOON

the

Devil's

between

the

Beads

The Devil's Between the Beads

Lynn Yvonne Moon

ISBN 978-1-953278-579 Hard Back
ISBN 978-1-953278-586 Soft Back
ISBN 978-1-953278-593 E-Book

Published by

INDIGNOR
— HOUSE —

Chesapeake, VA 23322

I to die, and you to live. Which is better God only knows.
— Plato —

*The world is a dangerous place, not because of those who do
evil, but because of those who look on and do nothing.*
— Albert Einstein —

The best time to make friends is before you need them.
— Ethel Barrymore —

You can hide from the Devil, but he'll always find you.
— Allen Iverson —

Based on the true story of a young girl raised within the walls of a coven, do you dare to read?

One

AS THE PRESSURE grew and the sensations darkened, Winifred closed her eyes and prayed, the familiar stench of rotting eggs filling her with dread. Glancing over at her sleeping friends, she took a deeper breath, releasing the stale air with her heart's ever-increasing rhythm. Accepting her fate, her skin filtered through the pain like sand through a bloody sieve, pushing her soul deeper into the evolving depths.

Flames flickered, taunting her nakedness, shaming her to consent. The shadow of the bull's head grew larger and with each sensation, she begged for a release, that pleasurable release taught at such an early age, but what also filled her soul with regret.

As he entered her, she held back a scream. Hot and wicked, the heat soared up her spine and into her chest. Closing her eyes, the warm ooze dripped across her bare breasts, sizzling, scorching. With each thrust from the demon lord, his heat expanded, the pain spreading deeper. Remembering her friends and the mother who promised to protect her but never did, Winifred screamed, and for the first time, she slapped and kicked.

Winifred had finally fought back. "No! For God's sake, no!"

The demon raised his hand. Large claws ripped across her stomach, his fangs digging deep into her flesh. A warmth, different from the sensual heat, ran down her sides, leaving a trail of blood.

"No!" she yelled again. "This is not real ... not real!"

Winifred was born during the early fifties when people talked across wires and not through the air. A time when mothers gave birth in hospitals and where fathers paced in different rooms. Cookies were not purchased in clear packages but made from scratch with raw flour and soft butter. Adolph Hitler, the evil one, had died only a few years earlier but was still considered a threat. It was a time when smoking was acceptable, meaning that a person was *hip*.

First communion was one of Winifred's earliest memories – a fleeting vision of her desecrated past. The church was called a mission, because according to her parents, the buildings were erected by the missionaries. When she visited many years later to bury her grandmother, the pink, cinder block wall where she had waited for her first communion was still there. When she was only so tall, the *thing* towered above – intimidating and powerful. Hidden somewhere on the other side was a secret garden that housed a statue of a beautiful lady. A lady, Winifred eventually grew to admire. During her youth, the mission was where she craned her neck to pray and where she bruised her knees for penance.

It was on a very hot Sunday, not unusual for Southern California, when her new and shiny, black Patent-leather shoes pinched her toes, along with the frilly white socks that nipped at her ankles. She hated the dress – a white itchy thing that gathered just under the arms and clung to her knees. Dark, curly hair fell to her waist because it was a sin to cut. However, the long locks continuously pulled and tangled under the fake flower headband to which her mother had stitched a long, white veil. The guidance given was to not dirty a *thing*. Therefore, Winifred stood, playing with the white gloves – stiff material that pinched her tiny fingers.

Winifred's life on this wobbly world had existed for only five years. A life that consisted of a small house where the rooms changed frequently, where a younger brother lived with whom she fought on a daily basis, and where a father had disappeared into the night. Therefore, it was on her grandmother's farm where Winifred found solitude and where the wild pigs gave her comfort. During school, she wore a blue checkered jumper, knee socks, and stiff, white and black saddle shoes. The ones that never stayed tied. And it was a time when her grandmother wore a long, black cape with a dark purple lining. A robe she and her cousins were never allowed to touch, not without permission.

The children entered the mission which dubbed as the church, following the child in front. Two lines, one for the girls and one for the boys. Winifred didn't know the boy who walked by her side nor did she care. She just didn't want to enter that building where the thin, red carpet gave neither cushion nor comfort. Her short stature didn't allow her to see much other than the shaking veil that bounced in front. To the side, people smiled as if offering the children freely to the demon god who sat up front.

Guided to a chair where only a child would fit, Winifred watched. One by one, each child stood before inching closer to the creature lurking inside a huge, golden chair. He sat proudly on a red velvet cushion. The man, if it was a man, wore a thick, white robe embossed in gold that draped to the floor. He also wore a very odd-looking hat. She wanted to laugh because the thing reminded her of a party hat she once wore at a girl's birthday party – tall and pointed. But this hat was not colorful – just white. He held a long, golden staff that he gripped tightly in his right hand while offering his other to each child.

Her teacher, a nun and wearing a black habit, harshly touched Winifred's shoulder. "Winni," she stated, "it's time. Stand up."

Winifred stood as she had practiced and followed the older girl. Every step felt as if she was inching closer to a cliff's edge. An edge that fell into the unknown pits of Hell. They were taught that each step inside a Catholic church moved a person deeper into their faith. But Winifred had no idea what a *faith* was or if she ever possessed one to begin with. To her, it was just a word – a funny word. Dripped in gold and adorned with stark statues, the church was supposed to draw one closer to God. As for Winifred, it meant something completely different.

The girl in front, Winifred's thin veil of safety, knelt and kissed the creature's large, green ring. The girl nodded before walking away, leaving Winifred alone. The *thing* was not human, the face almost invisible. The *thing,* wearing the funny hat, was now right in front of Winifred – only inches away. He was taller than a house. He was larger than her mother's car. And *he* stunk, reminding Winifred of something between rotting hay and stale eggs. Winifred rubbed her nose with the back of her glove.

The nun pushed Winifred from behind.

Winifred took a step, and between the creature's thick, white robe, a bony hand sprang out. Fingers without skin and boasting a large, green ring, flashed before her eyes.

Winifred froze. Her heart pounded and her head spun. She screamed. She screamed over and over again as the demon was about to devour her.

The bony hand disappeared, and a strong arm grabbed her around the waist. The rhythm of the man's jogging only reinforced the idea that nothing was real and that life was simply fake for little Winni. The veil fell from her head, and the flowers bounced across the aisle. As her hair covered her eyes, Winifred screamed again.

Two times two was supposed to equal four. That was easy to calculate because Winifred had ten fingers. But having to write a sentence dictated by her instructor was something she always failed at. Words never seemed to calculate. Who cared whether 'i' came before 'e' or the other way around?

School would simply teach Winifred to never forget how to spell *squirrel*, since she spent a lunch period once, writing that word over and over again. It wasn't so much that her stomach had growled but that the other children had laughed. Embarrassment seemed to hurt Winifred more than the hunger pains.

Every summer, she spent four months with her grandparents, working the farm. There were eleven cousins who were more of what one would call unpaid laborers than actual grandchildren. Eleven cousins who obeyed and worked hard.

It was on a hot Sunday morning when a rooster decided that Winifred was a threat. While walking to the old farm truck, the darn thing attacked. The rooster's spur struck just behind the back of Winifred's foot, only an inch above her heel. Blood soaked the clean white lace that was stitched perfectly for a little girl of six.

The rooster, whose spur was now, what she believed, permanently embedded in her foot, flapped wildly to free itself.

Winifred screamed.

The creature flapped several more times, yanking on her foot, making Winifred fall into the dirt.

Grandmother grabbed the animal, ripping him from the child's leg. After ringing the bird's neck, the woman simply tossed the dead thing into the pigs' pen. As for Winifred? Grandmother cleaned the wound with a smelly, clear liquid before wrapping the foot and replacing the bloody sock. It was either a trophy or a lesson learned, but Winifred wasn't sure which. They just had to hurry as time was running short, for it was time for church.

At the ripe old age of six, a child's job as a grandchild was to rid the farm of rats – rats as large as her grandfather's arm. Grandmother would wrap each child in torn flour bags, before tying a thin rope around their wrists and ankles.

"Keeps the rats from crawling into your clothes," Grandmother would say.

The children were then dropped into the silos along with a large potato sack. Grabbing a rat by a tail was a tricky job. If not timed just right, one would learn rather quickly how sharp a rat's tooth could be, and bleeding on the corn was never a good thing to do.

Growing up on the farm made a person mature rather quickly. When she was nine, it was Winni's job to pluck and cut the chickens for frying. Then it was her job to drive the tractor while towing a huge trailer of food. She would stop at the end of each field where the workers would gather. When she reached the end of the line, Winifred simply turned around and headed back the other way, picking up the dirty plates left at the side of the road. For the rest of the afternoon, it was her responsibility to wash and dry the dishes.

For five years, Winifred worked on the farm as an innocent child. For five years, she also learned how to survive. At first, it was exciting to be away from her mother and little brother, and from age five to nine, her cousins enjoyed each other's company. Especially when the moonshine was a cooking. With a small tin cup and a teaspoon of sugar, capturing the foam from the outside of the still made for an excellent dessert. Not to mention, it calmed those hyper kids down – way down.

But everything changed when Winifred turned ten. Life seemed to flip against her. Winifred's brothers were no longer her brothers, but an obstacle to overcome. Her friends were no longer her friends, but the competition. As for her cousins, they were in the same situation as Winifred, just a little more advanced or a little more behind. But they were all in the family together.

"Winni!" Grandmother's call was never pleasant. It meant she was either in trouble or about to be handed another chore. "Winifred June!

I'm not calling to hear myself talk." Grandmother was wearing her black robe – not a good sign. A robe Winifred once admired but soon learned to fear.

Two men she had never met stood at her grandmother's side. They were also wearing black robes. One was a little taller than the other. They remained silent as her grandmother reached out a hand.

"It is time for you to learn, child," Grandmother stated.

Winifred stared at the woman who was probably five times her age and was more of a stranger than family. The woman stood tall, always in complete control. Grandmother was a beautiful woman. A little over five and a half feet, her long, black hair streaked with gray naturally curled around her shoulders. A slender waist with blossoming breasts attracted every man she met. With a heart-shaped face, slender nose, and deep, brown eyes, the woman outshined any other who dared to challenge her beauty.

Grandmother nodded to the men. The one with the gray hair held Winifred's hand. She obeyed and followed the trio. They left the safety of the old house and entered the yard where a black car idled. Winni sat on a seat next to the stranger with the gray hair.

During the fifties, no seatbelts were installed in cars, but Winifred did enjoy the tuck-n-roll style of upholstery. Often, she would run her hands over the many hills and valleys, pretending she was at the ocean and that each roll was a wave. A wave that would whisk her away to a reality that never existed – at least not for her.

No one spoke as her grandmother drove. No one paid Winifred any attention as the countryside disappeared and the small town filled the windows. The white structure where they parked was nothing fancy, but the lot was deeply shaded by the other buildings. It was chilly in the shade and Winifred shivered. Glancing in the direction of the setting sun, the old mission's steeple stood tall against the dimming light. The bell was just visible over the other buildings, hanging silent and cold.

The man took her hand, and they entered through a single, black door. Tall curtains that draped from the ceiling created a shadowy kaleidoscope they had to traverse. A large room with an odd painting on the floor grabbed Winifred's attention. She had never been to this building before, never knew it existed.

No windows and no other doors from what she could or could not see. They passed through the large room with the strange floor to a smaller room in the back. Still, no words were spoken.

Several people who were patiently waiting were also wearing black robes. They turned and nodded as the trio entered. Grandmother acknowledged each one who cautiously backed into the shadows, before raising their hoods.

Chanting – chanting voices filled the air as Winifred was pulled into the middle. With walls and a ceiling painted blacker than a midsummer's night, she shivered as her clothes were removed, one by one, and slowly. At age ten and only partially developed, Winifred felt abandoned and forsaken by a truth that always seemed to betray her.

On that warm summer day, several men stripped what little humanity Winifred owned – what little dignity her religion allowed her to enjoy. Screaming wouldn't help since a rag was shoved inside her mouth and a black bag covered her face. Only darkness comforted Winifred that day as she was ripped and bruised and abused by so many.

Winifred woke in a bed on her grandmother's farm – the attic if she remembered correctly. Again, no one paid her any attention. No one said a word. Walking was a struggle as each step brought a pain more powerful than that stupid rooster had brought four years earlier. She continued to bleed for what seemed like weeks. While her grandmother read the scriptures, Winni would stare at her cousins and grandfather, wondering how they had survived. The thought of why she had to suffer alone never entered her mind as this was Winifred's life – her summer routine – until she escaped at age seventeen.

"Coming to the game tonight?" Clarisse asked.

"Not sure," Winifred replied.

"Come on, Winni, seems like you never want to do anything anymore. Something wrong at home?"

Winifred glanced at the field where the boys were kicking a ball. Several birds flew overhead, and the warm sun felt inviting. "Just don't feel like it. Besides, I think Grandmother is picking me up tonight."

"Oh, yeah, it *is* Friday." Clarisse shrugged. "Farm chores." The girl laughed. "What're you doing for your birthday? You're gonna be fourteen on Monday."

"Nothing special," Winifred replied. "Mom'll probably bake a cake, and they'll sing, but other than that, nothing."

Clarisse shrugged as the small buses rolled to a stop. The girl rode bus 42 and Winifred rode bus 108. They waved as they climbed into their respective coaches.

"Hey!" It was Billy Stanton. A boy Winifred despised. He was about her age, maybe a year older, but definitely a year stupider.

"What?"

"Wanna ride the waves?" By waves, he meant the hills behind her house. Every fall, once the grass died, a flat cardboard box became the perfect sled. One could ride the slopes, praying not to fling over the edge and into the lemon orchard.

"Sorry ... grass all gone." Winifred shook her head. "It's November and my uncle plowed already. You know that the grass is always gone by October."

"Oh, yeah, forgot."

The kid sat backward on the bus all the way home, staring at her. Her stop was the second and his was last. Winifred breathed in deeply as the yellow *thing* rattled down the road, puffing out a dark cloud.

Winifred's house was built in front of a huge hill. At the top, her uncle grew avocados. An uncle she was never allowed to visit. The man owned hundreds of beautiful trees that seemed to run for miles. Between those trees and on God's warm Earth, Winifred often escaped. The long rows of green seemed to mesmerize her, pulling her into a peaceful world of make-believe, and a place where the orchards grew more fruit than a person could count. Her uncle's fields also grew lemons that were larger than Winifred's hands. One never thirst for lemonade nor begged for an avocado sandwich when practically living inside his orchards.

Standing near the foothill, she stared at her aging house. The green roof was on its last leg. Several windows were missing, and the front door was actually a large piece of wood nailed to the frame. But it was home. The dirt puffed as she scuffed her feet into the powdered soil. No rain since last fall and none was expected anytime soon. Rounding the corner of her yard, Winifred froze. Grandmother was standing near the garage, talking to Mother.

"Winni?" Grandmother waved. "Ready to go?"

Weakly, Winifred waved back.

"Come on, child," Grandmother yelled. "We have *things* to do."

Winifred stared at her mother who refused to make eye contact. The woman simply puffed on her cigarette several times, which made the end brighten in the growing shade. Taking a deep breath, Winifred shrugged as she scooted onto the front seat of her grandmother's blue station wagon.

"See you Sunday, Mom," Winifred's mother stated, refusing her gaze to fall in her daughter's direction.

Grandmother nodded as she started the car. "I'll bring over the material you wanted for that new dress, Morise."

Winifred's mother waved as they backed out of the driveway.

"Tonight is *training night*," Grandmother whispered.

Winifred cringed.

As Winifred entered the old farmhouse, Glenn Miller's band played *In the Mood* from the record player and television combo. Three girls she had never met sat on the ugly, yellow couch. Long, wavy hair fell across their shoulders, reminding Winifred of dripping chocolate on a white layer cake. Only one was a blonde.

"Girls …" Grandmother stated after closing the front door. "Introduce yourselves while I gather the things."

Winifred's eyes followed her grandmother into the kitchen. *Things? What things?*

"I'm, Diana," the blonde stated.

"Winni." She smiled.

"Short for Winifred?" Diana asked.

Winifred nodded.

"Hi, I'm, Deborah, you can call me Deb," the girl sitting next to the end table added.

Winifred nodded again.

"I'm, Pam." The last girl lowered her eyes.

"Hi." Winifred sat on the red velvet armchair. A place where she often ran her fingers, enjoying the soft, fuzzy material.

"Okay." Grandmother handed each of the girls a rather large banana.

They stared at the long, slender fruit not understanding what to do.

"In order to entice, you must first learn how to please." Grandmother held her banana, pulling down a peel.

"Please what?" Pam asked.

"Why, a mortal, that's what." Grandmother laughed.

"I don't understand," Deb replied.

Grandmother sighed. "Peel your bananas and suck on them until there's nothing left. However!" She held her fruit a little higher before breaking it in half. "Never shall the shaft break … never!"

The girls made eye contact. Pam shrugged. Deb smiled. Diana wiped a tear from her eyes. Winifred froze.

"You are fourteen now," Grandmother stated. "It's time you learn more than just how to spread your legs. Why, a cow can do that. And … you're no cow."

Winifred's insides crawled as they each peeled their fruit. She held the sticky thing between her fingers, wishing to be anyplace else. The idea of sucking on a banana in front of the others grossed her out.

"Go on," Grandmother coached.

Carefully and cautiously, the girls practiced. That night, Grandmother taught them how to lick and suck and slowly ease into a rhythm in order to not bruise the delicate fruit.

Just before hers was half eaten, Diana's banana broke. "Oops." She giggled, picking the piece off her lap. "Mine broke."

Grandmother grabbed a cane from the side of the couch and slapped Diana across the back of the head. Diana flew off the couch, her forehead slamming into the coffee table. Blood dripped into her eyes as she inched herself into the corner, covering her head, preparing for the second blow.

"I told you bitches not to break your damn bananas!" Grandmother yelled.

Boom and another strike, only this one hit Diana across the face. Her lips now bled as did her hands.

"You will start over!" Grandmother yelled.

Winifred stared at the girl who now cowered between her knees. As her shoulders raised and lowered, she wiped her face with the back of her bloody hand.

"Here." Grandmother held out another banana. "This one you will not break."

Diana reached up a shaky hand, accepting the fruit. Cautiously, she peeled it. As her bloody lips covered the tip of the banana, Winifred's heart broke for this pitiful child. *Why is she being punished for breaking a stupid piece of fruit?* Winifred honestly didn't understand.

It was well after midnight before the girls finished *practicing* on the bananas. Winifred had no idea what they were practicing for, but they were practicing. With tired jaws and full tummies, they were told to share the room with the twin beds. Four girls, one at each end. Slipping between the covers, Winifred wondered what her little brother was doing at home.

Using an old blanket for a pillow, Pam whispered, "You okay, Diana?"

"I think so." Diana gently touched her swollen lip.

"Shh," Deb whispered. "She may come in here."

"What are we practicing for?" Winifred asked as softly as possible.

"Are you stupid or what?" Pam asked. "Shit, I can't believe any of this."

Winifred sat up, pulling the blanket closer to her chest. She glanced out the window and sighed, staring at the full moon that greeted her gaze. "Perhaps, I am stupid."

"A man," Diana whispered, loudly. "We're learning how to give blowjobs."

"Blow what?" Winifred repeated.

"You really are stupid," Pam replied. "Our part is to lure men into the coven."

"Why?" Winifred asked. "What for?"

"Oh, lord," Pam whispered. "Sacrifice, you dumb bunny."

Winifred again glanced at the moon, her bright smile fading. She wasn't sure what there was to smile about because she didn't know any men to lure. How would she ever find one? Pulling the covers a little closer to her chest, Winifred's mind flipped to her little brother and his little cars.

T<small>wo</small>

THE GIRLS WERE fast becoming friends. Close in age, they seemed to share a common bond – *fear*. Diana's face eventually healed with time as nothing was broken except her inner spirit. Pam and Deb now whispered whenever Grandmother was near. Something, Winifred couldn't blame them for.

It was a Friday, and Grandmother had picked Winifred up after school. Again, the girls practiced on that stupid fruit, which gave a person a whole new perspective on the food pyramid.

It had only been about a month or so when they were awakened early for chores. Winifred was assigned to feed the pigs. Deb raked the stalls. Pam and Diana were directed to kneed about a hundred biscuits for the farmhands.

By mid-noon, they stood by the blue station wagon, waiting for Winifred's Grandmother. Today, the girls wore long, black dresses that pinched at their waists. The material itched almost as much as the communion outfit she had worn years earlier. It was an awakening experience standing in that cool air. Clothing was just as much an involvement in her life as was her religion. Winifred was assigned special clothing for school, for church, and now for Saturdays.

Grandmother stepped out of the old farmhouse, wearing the black robe with the purple lining. A color, that to this day, Winifred despised. The screen door banged a couple of times before settling in the frame and Grandmother smiled. "Inside the car with you." She slid behind the wheel.

The ride to the white building where Winifred's sanity was stripped from her soul felt oddly uncomfortable. The place was packed with strangers. Any female under the age of eighteen wore a black dress. Everyone else wore black robes, including the men. Hoods covered most of the faces, and therefore, Winifred had no idea who anyone was.

"Blessed be Satan," Grandmother said as they passed several who stood watch at the door.

Pam mouthed the words, *'Blessed be Satan?'*

Winifred shrugged.

The girls followed Grandmother as if they were her little ducklings. Again, the black curtains blocked their path, but this time, low murmurings echoed between the drapes.

"You four, stand over there." Grandmother pointed to the back of the room.

Together the girls inched through the darkness as various candles flickered, casting deeper shadows against the walls. Several hooded heads seemed to follow as if questioning who they were.

Grandmother stood at the altar. Behind her, a tall, black triangle stretched to the ceiling. The woman opened a large, old book, before raising her hands.

Winifred couldn't see what the book was, but it almost covered the podium.

"Today," Grandmother said, shaking her hands in the air, "we pay homage to Satan, our father and ruler of our worlds. The month of March, the time of the great crossing when Saturn passes our Earthly plane. The deepening realm that separates our time from their space, our cold from their warmth, our work from their labors."

Double doors, not far from where the girls stood, slowly opened. Someone taller than the doors knelt as he entered the room. Wearing a long black robe that hid his body, a bull's head flared, loud and clear, as to who was truly in charge. Huge, red globes adorned the creature's ears. Horns that curled around a black, top hat, seemed completely out of place for such an event.

Several people stood along the walls blowing on horns that were longer than Winifred was tall. Behind the bull walked a man. He too wore a black robe, but he was carrying something. Something small. Something that moved.

The girls strained to see what it was, but the room was just too dark. It wasn't until a shy cry echoed that they understood.

Pam grabbed Winifred's arm. "My god!" she whispered. "Is that a baby?"

"Whose baby is it?" Diana asked.

"Shh," Pam warned. "You'll get us in trouble."

The doors closed behind the men as if on their own, and the dark couple made their way to the altar and the large table that was in front of the triangle.

Grandmother stepped in front of the podium and raised her eyes and again her hands. "Hail, Satan!"

The other individuals repeated the words. "Hail, Satan!"

Winifred couldn't count the number of worshipers because the room was too packed. Only the path to the front was left clear.

"Glory be to Satan the father of our worlds!" Grandmother declared.

The group repeated her words.

"And to Lucifer our guiding light and to Baphomet who walks between our worlds."

Again, everyone repeated her words.

"Do *we* say anything?" Deb whispered.

"Shh," Pam warned again.

"And to Lilith the queen of the night!" Grandmother yelled.

And again, the group repeated the words.

The bull stood behind the table, staring down at the crying baby who thrashed its tiny arms and legs.

"The baby's naked?" Diana asked.

"Shh," Pam whispered.

"As it was in the void of the beginning, is now and ever shall be!" Grandmother yelled.

The man who had carried the baby had disappeared somewhere in the crowd. But the bull was still up front. He raised a large, glowing knife over the crying baby.

"Satan's kingdom!" the bull shouted, clasping the knife with both hands. "World without end." The bull thrust the knife into the baby's chest. Blood hit the bull on the face and his hands dripped red. "So it be done." He had hit the child with such force that a deep thud echoed through the room. Now holding something the size of a large apple, blood dripped down his arm.

Grandmother knelt.

The group chanted in a language Winifred didn't understand. The baby didn't move. The bull held up the knife and the still pounding heart, shaking blood everywhere. Grandmother was on the floor, and Winifred couldn't see what she was doing, there were just too many excited people.

The chanting or singing seemed to go on forever. But eventually, the robed people left, not saying goodbye or speaking a word. When the room was almost empty, the girls inched their way to the table. Walking close together, their shoulders touched and their pinky fingers hooked. Flickering candles surrounded the dead child. The dull eyes stared into an imaginary heaven, the mouth slightly ajar. Blood was splattered everywhere. The stench was overwhelming. A large gash in the child's chest gave Winifred a moment of thought as she studied the now silent heart that rested on top.

Winifred had to look away. At the same time, she thought about her younger brother. Was he playing with his cars? Was he climbing a tree?

"Disgusting," Diana whispered.

"Why all this?" Deb asked, wiping her tears.

"This is the bond that holds us together," Grandmother stated from behind.

They jumped at her words, neither wanting to look at the woman who had just guided the murder of an innocent child.

"Our spiritual father grants us the vision, the wisdom, and the guidance. Through this child's blood, he protects us."

Still walking side-by-side, the girls exited through that single door. Waiting by the blue station wagon, no words escaped their lips. Their eyes simply stared into the empty back seat. Nothing could justify what they had just watched. Nothing could explain what they were feeling. And all Winifred could think about was whether they were next to be on that table.

Saturday was a day of darkness and death, and where her grandmother dressed in black.

Sunday was the day for holy worship. A sacred ceremony where priests walked in white robes and incense filled the room.

"The Lord be with you," the priest said from up front.

The congregation responded with, "And with your spirit."

It was supposed to be the congregation's way of affirming they were in the presence of their god. But what about the baby from yesterday? What about him? Was he with their god right now?

The congregation sang hymns, knelt for prayers, or participated in holy communion. Inside the mission that also dubbed as a church and for a little over an hour, they chanted their praises to their lord.

Grandmother would nod at her friends or shake the priest's hand who would then kiss hers. Winifred stood next to her mother who always wore her Sunday suit and who never spoke a word. Every woman and little girl wore a frilly hat. It was more of a handkerchief, actually. A headband with lace and ribbons, but it was mandatory.

Pam, Diana, and Deb stood by their parents. Each wearing a frown. Sometimes, the girls waved at each other. Sometimes, they ignored each other. On a typical Sunday, Winifred left with her mother but today would be different.

"Winni … girls!" Grandmother ordered. "Follow me."

Winifred glanced at her mother who of course acted as if she didn't exist.

Pam, Diana, and Deb were waiting by the side door. Their parents had already left. Together, they entered the secret garden that hid behind the mysterious wall. A beautiful sanctuary with a round fountain and an exotic lady who stood in the middle. Her hands clasped as if telling a secret to our lord.

"You girls get out your rosaries," Grandmother ordered. "Kneel here."

They did as instructed, the brick patio cutting into their knees, knowing better than to protest or complain.

"Ah," Father Hurley said as he passed, cuddling his bible. "Paying penitence, are we?"

Penitence? For what? Accessory to a murder? Winifred sighed.

"Recite the rosary until I return," Grandmother ordered, pointing at the statue. "Do not leave. You are being watched by our Holy Mother."

Pam glanced around but Grandmother slapped her across the head. Immediately, their eyes landed back on the beautiful lady who seemed to be crying.

The girls gave the sign of the cross and recited, "In the name of the Father, and of the Son, and of the Holy Spirit. Amen."

Grandmother left and the old, wooden gate banged behind her.

It wasn't until dark that Grandmother returned. With bloody knees and swollen ankles, the girls sat in the old woman's blue station wagon, wishing they were dead.

How could they worship a devil on one day and a god the next? Didn't the two spirits ever speak to each other? Several weeks after their knees had healed, Winifred found a blue pacifier in the room behind the double doors. The doors that opened into the central chamber with the pentacle painted on the floor. Without anyone noticing, Winifred shoved the little thing into her pocket. When she returned home, a loose board in her room opened into a secret hiding spot. And it was there, between the studs, where Winifred hid her treasures.

At fifteen, she once tried to count the pacifiers, but had to give up for there were just too many – white ones, pink ones, blue ones, and several with little flowers. Each represented a soul that had returned to Heaven so that Winifred's grandmother could continue her reign of power over the small town where they lived.

The spring county fair was in full bloom, and the girls were excited. The four now spent every weekend together at the farm, working or practicing. Some days were better than others. But this weekend was gonna be the best.

"Rides!" Diana said. "I can't wait. I want to ride every one."

"Girls …" Grandmother yelled from the other room. "Come here."

The girls glanced at each other briefly before following the order.

"Good, good." Grandmother studied what they were wearing. "Tight tops, no bras, tight jeans, this is good."

The girls nodded.

"Grandfather will drop you off when he takes the animals to the fair. You will leave in a little while." She handed each girl a small white pill and a larger red one.

"What are these for?" Pam asked.

"The white one is for you. Take it as soon as you get there. Always carry a cola with you. Always." Grandmother handed each girl several dollars. "Go play, have fun. And when you are no longer enjoying the rides, you each find a man. Not an old one, but a younger one. Not a child either."

Diana nodded.

"Get that red pill into them, unknowingly. Have them follow you back to your grandfather. He will take it from there."

Pam nodded.

"Do not fail me." Grandmother held her cane high in the air, shaking it several times.

The girls rode in the back of the truck with the wind lashing at their hair. Hands were just not enough to keep the strands in place. Laughing and giggling, they smiled as they jumped from the back.

"You girls do as you were told," Grandfather stated. "I'll be here waiting."

"Jim?" A man in overalls waved from the next stall.

The girls took off, popping the small, white pill into their mouths, the red one in their pockets. The rides were thrilling and fun. No fear. Just pure freedom. Several times, they spotted different men taking notice as they ran and laughed. It wasn't until the sun sunk below the ocean waves that the rides became scary. During the last one, Winifred screamed and banged on the cage to be set free. With tears in their eyes, they stood between the Ferris Wheel and Spider Crawler and shook.

"What happened?" Pam asked. "We were having so much fun."

"Not sure," Winifred replied. "Everything is so scary now. Almost as if it's more real."

"The pill," Diana added. "That pill made us fearless. I'm sure of it."

"That means it's time," Deb said, glancing around.

Not feeling confident on how to find a man to lure, the girls walked, holding their small cola bottles. They took a sip before sitting on a bench.

"I'm tired." Deb sighed, dropping the red pill into her bottle.

"Me too," Winifred said, doing the same.

"Well, hello there, you beauties." Two men, probably in their early twenties, were leaning against a tree with folded arms. "What are you beauties up to?"

"Nothing." Pam dropped her pill into the bottle.

"Wanna hang out?" Diana asked, slipping in hers.

"Of course," one of the men replied. He sat next to Winifred, wrapping his arm around her shoulders. "You girls *are* sweet!"

"Wanna drink?" Winifred asked, holding up the bottle.

"Name's Bill." He gulped the soda, before tossing it into the weeds. "That there is Dicky. Let's have some fun, girls."

Diana smiled. "Yes, let's." She wrapped her arm around Dicky's waist before handing him her bottle.

He gulped the soda, tossing the bottle next to the other one.

The girls aimed for the stalls as the boys finished off the last of the soda. The evening air was cool and a slight breeze was picking up. Several cows mooed. A goat bleated from somewhere inside the shadows.

"I've gotta sit down." Bill seemed a little wobbly.

"Me too." Dicky wiped his eyes.

"You guys okay?" Winifred asked.

Grandfather stood by his truck, smiling. The girls held the men's arms as they walked.

"You can sit here." Pam pushed Dicky to the back of the truck.

Several men jumped from the shadows. They grabbed the two and shoved them onto the truck's bed, tying their hands and feet before stuffing rags into their mouths.

The girl's eyes widened as they watched.

"Get in." Grandfather glanced around.

The girls climbed into the back, keeping their eyes on the men's eyes. Grandfather and three others sat up front, two in the back with the girls. As for the truck, it aimed for the white building.

The ride was short, only a few blocks. The men were out cold by the time they arrived. Several others wearing black robes were standing by the door as if expecting their arrival. The girls watched as the sleeping men were carried inside.

"You wait here," Grandfather ordered. "You are not to be seen … understood?"

The girls nodded.

The black door to the white building closed. With no windows, the parking lot became eerily quiet.

"Now what do we do?" Pam asked.

"Let's take a walk," Deb suggested.

"We're not to be seen," Diana stated.

"But it's not even nine yet." Pam shook her head. "Who cares if we walk the streets at eight? Besides, the park isn't far."

Winifred shrugged, jumping from the truck. "I'd rather walk than just sit here."

The white building was on a hill that overlooked City Hall. The girls wandered down the sidewalk, enjoying the late afternoon. The stars were just starting to sprinkle through the evening sky. Several cars rushed past in small groups. Otherwise, the town seemed deserted.

"Guess everyone's at the fair?" Pam asked.

"Probably," Winifred replied. "Should we go back to the truck?"

"Not yet." Diana ran across the street.

They entered the park and sat under a large tree. Far away in the distance, ocean waves danced. Rustling leaves announced that small critters were emerging to search for dinner. It was the sound of freedom for the girls, titillating in a foreboding sort of way.

From inside the darkened shadows of that old tree, they watched as couples kissed, dogs ran, and cars passed. It all seemed so innocent but also somewhat sinister.

"What did they want those guys for?" Deb asked.

Pam stood, brushing off the back of her jeans. She sighed and grunted before aiming for the street.

"Was it something I said?" Deb asked.

"Winni?" Diana shrugged.

"I don't think it's for anything good," Winifred replied. "Come on, let's go."

As they stepped into the parking lot, a bright light flashed, centering just on them.

"Halt!" a stern voice stated.

"Cops!" Pam yelled. "Run."

The girls darted down the hill. A driver slammed on his brakes as they ran across the street, back to the park. Sirens blared from somewhere in the darkness. The girls exited the park on the far side that led to the high school, the only one in town.

"Follow me," Pam yelled again.

Up another street and between several houses, a large vacant field with grass taller than an average man's waist filled their view. Once in the middle, they hid, not moving.

Winifred giggled. "This is kinda fun."

"If they don't find us … now be quiet," Pam ordered.

Lights flashed across the tall grass just above their heads. "I don't think they went this way," a man's voice stated. "We must'a lost 'em."

The girls remained still for what seemed like forever before slowly standing. All was quiet and dark. After tripping several times over old tractor parts, they finally made it to the road.

"We'd better take the back streets." Pam crossed the single lane.

"Sounds good to me," Diana replied.

After inching their way through several backyards, avoiding dogs, the girls stood next to a large cinder block fence.

"How do we get over this thing?" Deb asked.

"Stand here," Pam said to Deb. "Hold out your hands, rest them on your knees."

Deb did as told.

Pam hoisted herself up. "Help the others."

With Winifred and Diana safely on the other side, Pam pulled up Deb. The four now stared at the empty truck that was parked next to the large and quiet white building.

"Follow me," Pam whispered.

They inched around to the far side of the building hidden from prying eyes. Stacked crates created long shadows that felt colder than the rest of the town. Near a single white door, that blended perfectly with the brick wall, a small table and chair waited. Pam reached under the table, pulling out a single key. She waved it in the air before inserting it into the lock. The door clicked. After placing the key back into the little holder, she slowly inched the door open.

"Be very quiet," Pam whispered.

"How'd you know about the key?" Deb asked.

"A fairy told me," Pam replied.

The long, black drapes hid them perfectly. Silently, the door closed, and Pam twisted the lock. A slight click echoed and the girls froze. Muffled voices sounded from the large room with the painting on the floor.

"Be very, very quiet," Pam whispered again.

They followed the wall to the back stairs. Slowly, they climbed. At the top, a long narrow hallway opened onto a balcony with several rows of theater seating. The girls picked the seats on the top and in the shadows.

The men were lying on tables, naked. Their wrists and feet were tied by what looked like black cloth – no rope. Robed people stood around the men who struggled to get free. From above, the girls could easily tell what was painted on the floor. Two gold circles encased a five-pointed star with the picture of what resembled a devil in the middle. Odd symbols were on each point. One robed individual held the large book that Grandmother often read from. When a person turned around, the lining of their robe glowed in the candlelight – it was purple.

"That's Grandmother," Winifred whispered.

The bull-headed creature stood between the two tables. He held a knife in each hand and recited something in a language the girls didn't understand.

A hand reached out from under a robe with a red lining. The hand caressed one of the men's private parts. That hand worked diligently but gently, and just like the girls had practiced on the bananas, the robe head lowered over the man. He remained still for a while as another person did the same on the other one. The first man started to moan and turned his head from side to side. As his legs trembled, the bull-headed man aimed the knife directly into the stranger's heart. The robed person with the red lining stood back, wiping their mouth. The same thing happened to the second man.

At only fourteen, the girls had no idea as to what was happening. Television and movies only went so far during the sixties, such as to show couples entering a room and closing the door. The girls understood intercourse. They experienced it several times a year, laying on those same tables. But they couldn't comprehend how to match the fruit exercise with what these people were doing.

The girls' hearts pounded and their minds froze. It was Winifred who motioned for them to leave in the same manner they had entered. One at a time, they crept down the stairs, each waiting for the next to appear from out of the shadows. The door clicked and opened. Pam found the key and locked the door.

They ran to the truck and jumped inside. No one said a word. They refused to look at each other. As the moon rose over the distant mountain ridge, several large birds soared through the clouds. A coyote howled from somewhere and dogs replied.

The single door finally opened, and Grandmother and Grandfather stepped out, carrying two large trash bags.

A county garbage truck slowly entered the parking lot, and the girls watched as the workers gladly accepted the bags. Grandmother pointed to the black door, and the workers waited for others to bring out more bags. A tall man, way over six and a half feet, stepped out of the building. He looked just like any other man except his build was exactly the same as the bull-headed man. He tapped on the side of the truck bed, winking at Winifred before climbing into his expensive-looking sports car.

"Are you ready to return home?" Grandmother asked, making them jump.

"Yes," Winifred replied. "We're tired.

"Fair fun?" Grandmother asked.

"Most definitely," Pam replied.

"Good." Grandmother climbed into the driver's seat.

"Enjoy the show?" Grandfather asked as he scooted across the passenger seat.

The girls remained quiet on the ride to the farm. Did the grandparents know of their snooping? And who was that tall man who drove the fancy car? And were the dead men inside those trash bags, and if so, why was the trash truck picking them up as if on schedule? Too many questions for just four fourteen-year-old girls.

Three

SUMMER HAD ARRIVED and in California that meant more heat and dryness. Not much rain ever hit California in the sixties. Although time was a changing, not much else was, except for those who worshiped Satan and eager for the summer celebrations. A couple of the girls, Pam and Diana, enjoyed their fifteenth birthdays. But Winifred and Deb wouldn't enjoy theirs until the school year started.

Tomorrow was June 21st, a huge celebration of feasting, but not with food. A day the girls were not looking forward to. Inside the mountains of Southern California were long, deep valleys filled with boulders and dead trees. In some valleys, water flowed. In others, only a dried riverbed wandered.

The valley owned by the coven was one of the wetter ones. It was wide, several miles at the center. At the end where the mountains met, a tall waterfall fell into a huge, natural pool. In some places, it was over ten feet deep. Many a night, the girls were allowed to camp at the falls by themselves. Grandfather would pitch a tent, start a fire, and leave. They would enjoy the cool night, splashing until their energy died. Then they would eat until they could eat no more and sleep until Grandfather came to fetch them the next morning.

But today, and although the tent was pitched, would be no fun. No excitement of frill or gaiety.

Grandfather had placed their camp not far from the stream. With only a short jaunt, having to wash dishes or themselves was rather easy. The water was just down a short embankment.

"Change for the ceremony, girls." Grandmother pointed at the tent.

Four purple and slender dresses with no sleeves and a bowed neckline were waiting for them on the cots. Each dress had a slip of paper with the girl's name on it. Pam pulled hers over her head.

"Nothing underneath," Grandmother yelled.

Pam hesitated before slipping off her panties. "Tonight's gonna suck."

"Shh," Diana whispered. "We'll get into trouble."

They stepped out with the slender material clinging to their bodies, barely reaching their knees.

"You look beautiful," Grandmother said, holding a brush. "Let me do your hair."

She combed, creating long, wavy curls, with a few fresh flowers here or there. Now, they looked sweet and innocent. No makeup, but a little clear lip gloss. Apparently, they were too young for face paint.

The girls followed the voices to the center gathering. June 21st of each year was the summer solstice. The night for sexual activities and blood rituals, and it would be their private parts that would be sacrificed.

"Who are those girls?" Pam asked, motioning to several dressed in the same slender outfits, only green.

"Or them?" Diana asked, pointing to a group wearing blue.

Several others wearing yellow, red, and black huddled together. The girls stepped up and smiled.

"You're from the Kalevala coven," a girl wearing yellow stated.

The girls smiled.

"Which one of you is the High Priestess' granddaughter we've heard so much about," a girl wearing red asked.

Winifred took a step and raised her hand. "I'm Winifred."

"Well, so the almighty is finally showing her face?" the girl wearing yellow replied.

"Watch it, Sara." A girl wearing blue grabbed the girl's arm. "No need to be found floating in the cold water tomorrow with your throat cut."

"What are your coven's names?" Pam asked.

A tall and beautiful, black girl stepped up and smiled. "I'll help here," she said. "I have them memorized. I'm Keeshia by the way."

The girl was much older, maybe seventeen or so. If she was eighteen, she wouldn't be wearing these outfits. She would be wearing a robe. Her long, black braids seemed almost alive with a beauty held by no other. Dark-set eyes decorated by deep lashes made her face shine. Naturally red lips gave her a seductive stance that felt almost unnaturally luring.

"Kalevala, means *Daughter of Death*," Keeshia said, "and you're from Southern California. We're from central Nevada, we're called the Bellona Coven, which means *Goddess of War*."

"You're not all that." The girl wearing blue stepped forward.

"Shut up, Kelly," Keeshia replied. "Aamon Coven is from San Diego and it means the *Hidden Ones*."

"Hidden ones?" Pam repeated.

"Weird, I know. Then there are the others, but I don't know from where. They're Adam, Adder, Kali, Gorgon, and … Euryale. They're mostly from other states, like Oregon and Washington. But the one from New York, that's the Abigor Coven. They wear yellow and are arrogant." She glanced at the girl in yellow. "Each High Priestess' lining will depict their coven. And their girls, well, we wear what we're wearing, same color."

"Okay, is this stuff written down anywhere?" Pam asked.

"Nope, just gotta memorize it," Keeshia replied. "There are others, some from overseas. You'll figure it out."

"There's a lot of people here," Winifred stated.

"More is coming," Keeshia replied. "Some stay in hotels and will arrive later. When it's darker."

"Wow," Diana replied.

"I'd like to hear you say *wow* at midnight." Keeshia laughed. "Hungry? Might wanna eat now while you have an appetite."

The four, along with Keeshia and another girl wearing yellow, aimed for the food tent. The others disappeared into the growing crowd. After filling their plates, they sat to talk.

"I was four when they pulled me in," Keeshia said between bites. "My mom's sister, my aunt."

"Did your mom object?" Winifred asked.

"Yep, and she's dead now." Keeshia shrugged.

"My mom knows everything," Winifred stated. "Never says a word."

"Good thing," Keeshia replied. "Keeps her breathing."

A whistle blew and the girls glanced around. When a man with a bull's head stepped in surrounded by various men wearing black robes, everyone grew silent. The tent, with about twenty rows of tables, was now filled with people, some wearing the required colored dresses, some wearing robes, but many were just wearing street clothes. Those cooking stopped to raise their hands. Many bowed.

The man with the bull's head was wearing nothing but a white loincloth. His muscular and tanned chest shined with the falling sunlight. He must have been coated in oil. But why?

"Young sisters of the night," a robed man stated, "enjoy your feast as you wait for the evening rituals to begin."

Grandmother boldly stepped through the crowd, pushing past the man with the bull's head. She aimed straight for the girls. "Parden me,

Bellona sister," Grandmother said to Keeshia. "I need my girls with me now."

Winifred sighed, finishing off her burger.

Pam stood along with everyone else.

"Winni," Grandmother said. "Let's go."

They followed Grandmother through the crowd and past the bull. Winifred glanced up and noticed that the head was just a mask made from paper mâché. She smiled, averting his gaze.

They entered the tent and sat on the cots – there were six.

Grandmother handed each girl a yellow pill. "You take this at the start of the ceremony. You understand?"

Each girl nodded.

"It will help you cope."

"Cope with what?" Pam asked.

"This is your first ceremony of the feast." Grandmother seemed somewhat angry.

A loud wail echoed through the campsite, and the girls glanced around as another scream blasted out from somewhere.

"Those who are giving their souls," Grandmother said. "Ignore them. Why don't you hike up to the pool and waterfall? Just enjoy yourselves."

Something in the woman's smile bothered Winifred although it only lasted a brief moment. The woman who had helped to birth Winifred in her mother's matrimonial bed was no longer a person of comfort but a person of fear. Winifred picked up the yellow pill and placed it in her herb pouch that hung around her neck. The other girls did the same. Without another word, they walked out, leaving the old woman alone.

Screams echoed as they inched along the well-worn path. Each step took them deeper between the canyon walls. The running water sounded peaceful and serene. As another group of girls passed, Pam paused. It was as if she was waiting for the girls to disappear between the struggling trees.

After glancing around one last time, Pam grabbed Winifred by the arm, pulling her between the shrubs. The other girls followed. When they entered a small clearing surrounded by several large boulders, they sat.

"What's up?" Winifred asked.

"Shh," Pam whispered. "Our voices will carry."

Diana picked up a stick and drew a face in the dirt.

"This is all wrong," Pam said. "Who brought you in, Deb?"

"My father," she replied. "He divorced my mom a long time ago."

"What does he do for work?" Pam asked.

"He's an attorney for the state," Deb replied, "why?"

"Diana, who brought you in and what do they do?"

"My aunt," Diana replied, "started out as me babysitting for her on weekends. My mom never asks."

"And what does she do?" Pam shook her head.

"Chief of police," Diana replied.

"Winni? It was your grandmother, correct?" Pam asked.

Winifred nodded.

"Farming?" Pam added. "Retired from the Farm Bureau, right? And my mom, she's the head of the local hospital. Very important people in our community with a lot of power."

"And?" Deb asked with a shrug.

"Do you not get it? That guy standing next to Mr. Bullhead? He's our mayor and behind him was the governor. It's just too convenient. This is all wrong."

"What can we do about it?" Winifred asked.

"I'm not sure yet," Pam replied.

It was dusk and time to return to camp. The girls followed the trail behind another group wearing black. Those girls seemed much older. The center of the camp was huge and not far from the gurgling stream. An altar of a large goat with human feet now stood behind several men wearing robes. Winifred counted the heads and ended at thirteen. Someone pounded on a drum as the High Priestesses entered. Each sporting a robe with a different colored lining. The women were of all ages and nationality. No two looked alike. Each carried a large staff that matched their colors, symbolizing their covens. Grandmother's was a large, purple owl.

The girls gathered at the sides, according to their colors. As the air thickened but cooled, they shivered. However, Winifred was sure they were shaking more from what was to come.

The man with the bull's head stepped out from behind the altar. He raised his hands. After reciting a short prayer to Satan, he relaxed and glanced around. Everyone bowed.

Winifred nudged Pam who nudged Deb who nudged Diana. The girls placed the small, yellow pill onto their tongues and swallowed. The bonfire blared and the drumbeats grew louder. The summer's colors brightened, and the air felt somehow alive.

The man wearing the bull's head walked in front of the girls, studying each one. He stopped on the four wearing purple. He reached out and took Winifred and Deb by the hand. They followed him to the altar.

Winifred's heart pounded. Was this their end? Would they be stabbed and their hearts removed? Tears filled her eyes as she contemplated the pain. And what about her little brother? Who'd take care of him after she was dead?

But the man with the bull's head didn't stop at the altar. Instead, they continued walking down a dark path lit only by candles to a large tent draped with black cloth. The place seemed to be melting.

They entered, and he motioned for the girls to each take a glass filled with something red. Winifred and Deb obeyed, taking a sip. The liquid was warm, tasting bitter.

"Drink all." He pulled off the large mask.

The man was tall and had the muscles of an animal. As Winifred placed her empty glass on the table, the man reached for her hand. Pulling her dress up over her head, he studied her slender fourteen-year-old naked body.

"Nice," he stated.

After pulling off Deb's dress, he tossed the material onto a pile of blankets.

He pushed the girls to the bed with their feet dangling off the edge. Kneeling, he gently spread Winifred's legs, and with his tongue, licked her as she had licked the banana. After some time, her mind twirled, and she shivered with a delight more pleasant than life that exploded throughout her body. As she slowly recovered, he started on Deb.

The girls remained quiet on the bed, not sure of what to do.

The man stood by the tent's entrance. Someone handed him a large bowl without entering. Winifred watched and her mind reeled. She wasn't sure what was happening. He placed the bowl on the table and reached for Winifred. He sat on a chair, pulling Winifred to his lap. With his hands on her waist, he moved her up and down. As his eyes widened, a wicked smile creased his lips. He exploded inside her, yelping several times.

Tossing Winifred on the bed, he walked back to the table. And with what looked like a long tube, dipped it in the bowl. After licking his fingers, he returned to Winifred, shoving the tube between her legs. She moaned as something warm engulfed her, making her feel as if nothing was real.

Deb moaned as he pulled her from the bed. He sat in the chair again, but this time, pushed Deb to her knees. Placing a hand on each ear, he shoved her face into his lap. Deb, remembering her training, treated him like a banana.

Winifred remained on the bed, her eyes glued to what her friend was enduring. The room spun, but her body remained still and warm. Her insides burned as if a fire was raging, but no flames surrounded her. It seemed like forever before her friend was by her side again.

The man, using the same long tube, pushed the red liquid into Deb's mouth. She gagged but swallowed. Her eyes rolled to the back of her head and she remained still, too still.

Winifred tried to sit up, but the man pushed her back down. He took what was left in the bowl and slowly poured it across their chests. The warm liquid felt as if it was seeping into their souls.

Time passed, and with each violation of their young bodies, Winifred tried to place the puzzle pieces together, but nothing fit. It was the bull-headed man, but then again it wasn't. Several times, it looked as if the goat was on top of her, but then again it wasn't. At one point, a woman was licking between her legs, biting and nipping. But then again it wasn't.

Winifred opened her eyes and the room was lit with only a few flickering candles. Several people were on the bed with her, all naked. The bull-headed man was in the chair, smiling that wicked smile. Winifred and Deb were being violated in every possible way, however, no pain, no sensation. Just a pleasant wave of warmth and satisfaction that held her inside a trance she could not escape.

Winifred woke in her own bed in her own home. She glanced over at her bother's bed, but it was empty. After sitting up, Winifred gently ran her hands down her nightgown. No blood. She stood. No pain. Winifred didn't understand.

Entering the living room, the house was quiet. All seemed normal, in fact too normal. Her stomach growled. On the kitchen table was a ham sandwich and a glass of lemonade. Taking a small bite, her hunger exploded, and she gulped down the small meal.

"Feeling better?" her mother asked from behind.

Winifred turned and stared at her. "Where's William?"

"Outside playing." She sucked on a cigarette.

"How did I get home?"

"Your grandmother dropped you off."

"Who changed me?"

"Changed you?"

"My clothes?" Winifred replied.

"You came home, I spoke to my mom for a few, you took a bath and went to bed. I'd say you changed your own clothes. You okay?"

"I'm fine." Winifred glanced out the window and watched as her little brother drove a hand-size tractor across the dirt.

"Pam called earlier," her mother stated. "Told her you'd call her back."

Winifred nodded.

"I have some errands to run. Keep an eye on your brother?"

Winifred nodded again.

As the phone rang, Winifred searched her brain for anything to remember, but only darkness filled her memories.

"Hello?" Pam said into the phone.

"Hey, what's up?" Winifred replied.

"Winni? Are you alone?"

"Yes, what's up?"

Pam sighed. "Do you remember *anything*?"

"No, I don't. Just woke up in my bed, all clean."

"I'm telling you, something's not right."

"Let's meet up later tonight," Winifred stated. "I'll ask my mom to drive me over. Call the other girls. Today is what?"

"Thursday," Pam replied.

"Grandmother wants us tomorrow, so let's try for tonight."

"You got it." Pam hung up.

As she scanned the room, Grandmother's satanic bible sitting on the coffee table grabbed her attention. Picking it up, she smiled.

"Thanks, Mom," Winifred yelled as her mother drove away.

The four girls stood in Pam's living room not saying a word. They just didn't have anything to talk about after what had happened to them, which most, was a complete blur.

"What's in the bag?" Pam asked.

"This …" Winifred pulled out her grandmother's satanic bible.

"How'd you get that?" Diana asked.

"I think when Grandmother dropped me off, she accidentally left it behind. Well … I found it."

Pam held the large book, scanning through the pages. "Other than some weird drawings, reminds me of a regular bible."

"Exactly." Winifred pulled out another book.

"A spell book?" Deb asked.

"Let's conjure a demon," Winifred stated. "I mean, we've been initiated, haven't we? We have the right."

Pam tilted her head. "What do we need to do?"

"We need this satanic bible, a real bible, and a candle," Winifred replied.

The girls set everything up inside Pam's bedroom. They pushed the furniture to the side, except for a small table they left in the middle. After setting the satanic bible down first and the Catholic bible next, a flaming candle was placed on top.

The girls held hands as they recited the spell. "Oh, lord Satan, grace us with your blessing through your almighty power. Send us one to temp us not. Send us one to give us power. Send us one to save us from death."

They recited the prayer three times before each took a step back, closed their eyes, and bowed.

Nothing happened.

Pam opened one eye. She glanced around and sighed. "I guess we're not very good witches."

"What?" Deb said, her eyes still closed.

"Nothing's happening," Pam replied, "that's what."

Winifred blew out the candle and shrugged. "Wanna watch a scary movie?"

"Sure." Diana smiled. "Popcorn too?"

"My mom bought us soda," Pam replied.

As the popcorn popped in the skillet, the girls filled their glasses. Pam flipped the channels until she found an old movie, and they settled down for a scary night. Several times they glanced at the closed bedroom door and shrugged.

At about eleven, Pam's mother returned home. "Hard night," she whined. "Bad car accident on the highway. Drunk drivers."

"Anyone dead?" Pam asked.

"Just seven badly hurt. One went through the windshield. What are you four up to?"

"Movie, popcorn, and soda," Winifred replied. "Thanks for the soda."

"Anytime," Pam's mother replied.

The girls settled in for sleep on the living room sofa and floor. Pam's mother was in her bed, snoring.

The clock on the mantel clicked a few minutes closer to three.

Winifred's eyes opened and she glanced around the dark room, something nudged against her soul. With the place quiet, she smiled before pulling the blanket over her shoulder. Taking a deep breath, she sighed slowly.

The clock clicked again and dinged three times, breaking the silence. A deep growl echoed along with a loud bang. Pam's mother was out of bed before the clock clicked again.

"What was that?" she asked with a blanket wrapped around her shoulders.

Another growl wailed along with a crashing and splintering of wood. The girls stood, staring at the closed bedroom door that seemed to be – *breathing*? As another growl and screech blasted through the living room, the doorbell rang along with banging fists.

"Open up at once!" Grandmother's voice sounded stern and serious.

Pam's mother opened the door.

Three people entered. Two warlocks and one witch, all wearing their full attire.

"You four," Grandmother stated, pointing at the girls, "to my car, now! Jennifer, I recommend you remain in your room. You're gonna have a mess to clean up tomorrow. I've already contacted a repair company. One we can trust."

Pam's mother nodded and aimed for her warm bed.

The girls darted outside, jumping into the back of the blue station wagon. They watched as lights brightened and shadows darkened from behind Pam's bedroom curtains. How could Winifred's grandmother know about what they had done?

Grandmother stepped out of the house, clutching the satanic bible close to her heart. She opened the car door and glared at the four sitting on the back seat. As she drove to the farm, no words were spoken. No questions were asked. The two warlocks had remained behind, probably ensuring that the veil had been properly sealed.

That Saturday, the girls spent the day working hard on the farm and not finishing until well after dark. On Sunday, they spent the day on their knees in front of the beautiful lady in the secret garden, reciting the rosary over and over again.

No words were ever mentioned about the event at Pam's house. Aside from the fact that Pam slept on the sofa for a few days, nothing else seemed out of the ordinary. School was still months away and the girls were eager to return. Eager to stop working the field that was just over the hill. The warm air felt more like a baking oven, making sweat evaporate before dripping from the face.

"This is nuts." Diana dropped her shovel. "Why are we digging this up?"

Winifred shook her head.

"I agree." Deb threw her shovel.

"Let's take a break," Pam replied.

The girls looked around and shrugged. With the closest tree over a mile away, taking a break really wouldn't be much of a break.

"Let's sit by the tractor," Winifred suggested. "It's better than nothing."

The large back tire gave only a few feet of shade. Each girl carried a gallon bleach bottle for water. Although hot from the sun, the liquid cooled their thirst.

"Is this punishment?" Diana asked, wiping her mouth. "Are we in trouble for summoning the demon?"

"I think so," Winifred replied.

"Does this old thing run?" Pam asked, slapping the large tire.

"Don't think so," Winifred replied. "It's been here for as long as I can remember."

"Doesn't look like we got very far." Pam stared at the field that was still filled with dry grass.

"Nope," Winifred agreed.

"How long do we have to stay out here?" Deb asked.

Pam shrugged. "Grandmother said until dusk."

"How would she know if we left now?" Diana asked.

Winifred stood and pointed to the hill. "There's still water in the old cist."

"Then what are we waiting for?" Deb stood and grabbed her jug.

The hike to the top of the hill took longer than expected. It was just too hot. Several times, they sat to catch their breaths. From the hillside, the ocean shore in the distance clearly marked the boundary of their small world. The mission's bell tower was visible as was their school. Houses dotted the roads along with shops and banks. The empty fairground seemed barren and cold without the rides and tents.

"I can see forever," Diana stated.

"Look, there's a ship out there," Deb replied.

Winifred shielded her eyes from the sun. "Where?"

"There." Diana pointed.

"Over there?" Winifred asked.

"Come on," Pam whined. "Before the sun is gone."

They trudged the rest of the way up the hill, reaching the edge of the avocado orchard. The branches reached out for miles, creating long rows of dark shadows.

"Creepy," Diana whispered.

"The cist is in the middle," Pam stated. "It's not far."

Several eucalyptus trees providing additional shade rustled in the wind. Winifred took a deep breath enjoying the strong aroma. Most hated these trees, but she loved every one. Their shedding bark always reminded her of the living, of an ever-changing world.

Pausing at the edge of the grove, they glanced one last time at the field below with the old tractor. Each feeling guilty but brave.

"Let's go." Winifred took a step into the shadows created by the ever-growing trees.

As the world darkened around them, the tall cist filled their view. The wooden structure sat atop a cement slab. As large as a house and as tall as the mission, the cist held the cool water that would soothe their sunburned skin.

"Your uncle is okay with us swimming here?" Diana asked.

"He doesn't care," Winifred replied. "We all use it."

They stood at the base of the large round cistern. A strong breeze blew ruffling their hair. A low whistle echoed making them pause.

"Are we alone?" Pam asked.

The girls glanced around.

"No one here but us." Winifred took off her shirt.

The girls stripped and climbed the ladder. Winifred jumped in first, Pam second, and Deb third. Diana sat on the edge, glancing around. The cool water felt wonderful as it calmed their aching skin.

"What's that over there?" Diana asked.

"What's what?" Winifred laughed, splashing Diana. "Get in here."

Diana jumped in, swimming to the edge. She clung to the ladder and smiled. They splashed and yelled and dove. Birds flew overhead as they floated on their backs, clear blue filling their view.

"What did you see?" Winifred asked Diana.

"Don't know," Diana replied. "Reminded me of a cellar."

"Cellar?" Winifred repeated. "Really?"

With the sky darkening, it was time to leave. They stood in the warm wind, allowing their skin to dry.

"Where is that *thing* you found?" Winifred asked, tying her shoes.

"Over here," Diana replied.

The girls followed. It was hard to see much as the sun was about to dip below the ocean.

"We should come back tomorrow," Pam said. "When we can see."

"I agree," Winifred replied.

Inching through the large trees, the darkness grew thicker. That low whistle again rustled through the leaves. Pausing at the edge of the hill, the valley below was nothing more than a deep void. Not even the tractor was visible.

"We better hurry." Winifred skipped down the hillside.

The old tractor remained silent as they approached, but the whistling grew louder.

"What is that noise?" Pam asked.

"Good question," Deb replied. "What is that?"

Winifred took a step into the dead grass, and something touched the back of her legs. Her shorts hitting just above her knees didn't provide much protection. The warmth from the day had left, and the cooler ocean breeze sent chills up their backs.

Pam slapped her legs. "Something is crawling all over me!"

"Me too," Diana yelled. "What is on me?"

Deb screamed and slapped her legs. "It's the grass."

"Gotta be bugs," Winifred yelled.

"No!" Deb slapped her legs again. "It's the grass."

They ran across the field, screaming. The tall grass grabbed at their ankles, pulling them down.

"Help me!" Deb tripped, the grass sucking her into the soil.

Winifred yanked on Deb's arm as the soil covered her friend's legs. "What's this? Help me! Pam? Diana?"

Pam and Diana pulled Deb's other arm. They yanked and screamed as the grass wrapped around their ankles. Deb broke free and stood. Dirt caked her face, burning her eyes.

"We need to run!" Pam screamed.

The girls aimed for the old dirt road, but it seemed to have vanished. Everything looked different. They ran and ran as their feet sunk deeper and deeper into the soil. As the moon crest the distant mountain, the road finally slapped under their feet.

"What the hell was that?" Pam asked, panting.

"Something was pulling me under," Deb stated. "It was as if a million arms had grabbed me."

Winifred wiped the dirt from Deb's face. "We need to leave."

"I agree," Deb stated.

That low whistle echoed through their ears, vibrating across their feet and up their legs. From the field, a pair of red eyes glowed. Hovering just about the grass, the eyes blinked several times.

"What the hell is that?" Pam pointed.

The girls screamed and ran down the dirt road.

The mysterious whistling filled their ears. Deb tripped again, hitting the ground hard. She gasped as the air rushed from her lungs.

Crying, Winifred tried to help her friend to her feet. "We need to go."

Pam grabbed Deb's other arm.

"My ankle," Deb cried out. "I can't walk."

Pam screamed and pointed at the field. "Those eyes are following us."

The trees that surrounded the old farmhouse swayed as if moving to a beat the girls could not hear. They hurried toward the safety of the old house. Tractors and trailers lined the road. The cow barn was just a few more steps. The chicken coop that sat between the two oak trees seemed quiet as the birds were no longer outside. Deep shadows followed everything.

"Listen," Pam whispered.

The ominous whistle was not a sound but a voice, low and deep, that echoed through the night. Several pairs of red eyes now glowed in the distance. With the back door to the house in sight, they ran. Deb hopped.

Winifred grabbed the nob and twisted. She froze. "It's locked!"

"What?" Pam yelled.

"Shh." Deb placed her finger to her mouth. "We're locked out for the night."

Winifred sighed. "We can sleep in the barn."

The girls aimed for the old barn now filled with moaning cows. Darkness was only broken by the dim moonlight that struggled against the thickening clouds.

Pam reached for the old door and sighed. "Locked."

"Now where do we go?" Deb asked.

The glowing red eyes were hovering between the trees. With no place to hide, the girls stood with their backs against the barn. The wind blew stronger. The air grew hotter.

Pam took a step and removed her shirt.

"What are you doing?" Deb asked.

Pam ignored her as Diana took a step and removed her shirt. Winifred and Deb hugged each other.

Several naked men stepped out from the shadows. Their eyes glowing red. Pam and Diana removed the rest of their clothes. Deb wiped her eyes. The men inched closer. No one looked familiar. At only fourteen, Winifred didn't understand what was happening, because the men had no faces.

Pam and Diana followed the men into the darkness.

Deb and Winifred stared at each other as hands reached for them. With no place to go, Winifred closed her eyes and prayed. She prayed she would sleep and never wake up again. She prayed her grandmother would die. She prayed that her little brother would know what had happened to her.

Four

"GET UP!" GRANDMOTHER stood at the door and yelled. "Let's go, girls."

Winifred sat up, wiping her eyes. The room, still slightly dark, was quiet. "Pam?" she whispered.

"I'm here."

"What happened?" Winifred asked.

"Don't know," Pam replied.

"What the hell is going on around here?" Deb asked. "One minute we were swimming, the next we were attacked by grass, and those men?"

"There were no men." Pam pulled on her jeans.

"I saw them." Winifred took off her nightgown.

"No men," Pam whispered.

"Then who were they?" Diana asked.

"Demons," Pam replied.

"De … what?" Winifred asked.

"You're grandmother's demons," Pam said. "We were being punished. Punished for swimming and being late."

"Girls!" Grandmother yelled again.

They hurried and dressed. Sitting at the kitchen table, the eggs and bacon smelled wonderful.

"After you eat, back to the field," Grandmother stated. "This time no horse playing."

The girls ate in silence.

Placing her plate in the sink, Winifred glanced at her grandmother who sighed. Although in her early sixties, the woman was still a beauty to behold. Slender in build, her graying hair made her look wise and powerful. As her grandmother kneaded the almost white dough, a loathing for the woman filled Winifred's heart.

"Don't be so late tonight," Grandmother stated. "They did enjoy themselves, but you have chores to do. I'd rather you not be out all night, doing God knows what." The woman laughed.

Winifred cringed as the cackles filled her ears.

With the sun just barely peeking over the distant mountain ridge, they walked slowly down the road, their bodies aching from the prior night's activities. Farmhands busily worked the fields, ignoring them. The cows inched their way across the dry grass. The chickens plucked at the ground. A crow screeched.

"I want to see what that thing is near the cist," Diana said. "I don't care anymore if we work or not."

"Me too," Deb whispered.

"How's your ankle?" Winifred asked.

"Hurts, but I'm okay."

By the time they reached the backfield, the sun was high in the sky. Carrying their lunch and water, trudging up the hillside seemed to take forever. The trees were not as threatening during the day. The large cist was right where they had left it in the middle of the orchard.

"Now, where is that *thing* you found?" Winifred asked.

"Over here," Diana replied.

Not far from the wooden cistern, a slab of concrete sat ominously between several ancient eucalyptus trees.

"I never knew this was here," Winifred whispered.

"Unless you walk all through the orchard, how would you?" Pam replied.

Winifred bent over, running her hands across the top. "What is this *thing*?"

The slab was not overly large, just enough for a tractor to sit on. A wooden-looking crate rested on top. The roots of the tall trees seemed to hug the concrete as if they were here before time was born.

"Is this some kind of a patio?" Deb asked, kneeling to have a closer look.

"I think it's a door?" Pam stated, reaching for the old wood. "There are hinges. Help me lift it."

The girls grabbed hold and pulled. A loud creak echoed through the trees.

Diana gasped as she tried to count the rungs that led down into the darkness. "Should we?"

"Yes." Winifred stared into the shadows.

The ladder was steep. Several times, Winifred had to reach for the wall to steady herself. After many rungs, a flat surface greeted her.

"I can't see a thing," Pam yelled, her voice echoing.

Winifred hollered back. "There's another door down here."

"Is it locked?" Pam asked.

Winifred pulled on the door and it opened. She stepped inside. "It's a large room," Winifred yelled. "But I can't see much either."

"Without a flashlight, we can't go any farther." Pam stepped off the ladder.

Diana turned and tripped over something. A loud clattering echoed through the room.

Something clipped against Winifred's foot. She reached down, picking it up. "You're not gonna believe this." She flipped on a light. "Tah-dah …"

"A flashlight?" Pam asked.

"There's a couple more," Diana replied, switching on hers.

Diana had tipped over a table that held three flashlights. Heavy-duty ones. Winifred shown her light around the large room. In the middle, more stairs led down.

"What is this place?" Pam asked.

"Have no idea," Winifred replied.

Slowly, they descended the stairs. At the bottom, their lights hit water.

"Pillars?" Pam ran her hand down the side of the one next to her. "Marble?"

The room was large and filled with water that almost hit their waists. Large pillars were everywhere and only several feet apart. Carved arches held the pillars together.

"Is this an underground swimming pool?" Deb asked.

"Water's too cold." Winifred shook her head.

"Can't be a pool." Pam studied the area.

Diana shrugged. "I don't see any walls."

"How big is this place?" Pam asked.

"What if we split up?" Diana shrugged. "We each go in a different direction."

"I don't have a light," Deb stated.

"Deb," Pam replied, "you come with me."

The water swirled as the girls left in different directions. Pam and Deb walked straight in front of the stairs. Diana to the left and Winifred to the right. No walls for Diana or Winifred.

"Over here!" Pam yelled. "A hallway."

Diana and Winifred couldn't run. The water was too high. Although it looked clear, the smell reminded Winifred of rotting eggs.

"What did you find?" Winifred asked.

"A hallway," Pam replied.

A set of stairs leading up greeted the girls. At the top, a corridor ran into the darkness.

"Should we?" Deb asked.

"Yes," Pam replied, "we should."

They walked together, two girls, side by side. Their lights flickered with each step when an odor, stronger than the devil himself, hit. The girls gagged. At the end of the hallway, a dark and heavy door dared them to enter. The sulfur smelled suddenly stronger, more pungent. Pam pushed the door open and screamed. Deb fell to her knees. Diana took a step back, losing her breakfast.

Winifred, however, took several bold strides directly into the room. She flashed her light along the walls, holding her breath. Ancient-looking chains held people. Some still had their skin. Others were nothing more than bones. She couldn't tell if they were men or women, but they were naked. None had hair – that was piled high on a far table.

"My god!" Pam whispered. "What is this place?"

"Another white building?" Winifred replied.

"White building?" Deb repeated.

"Yes," Winifred explained. "Another building like the one in town. A place to sacrifice the living."

"Oh, I get it." Deb shrugged. "I agree. Let's leave. This place is full of evil."

When reality finally hits, the feeling was never meant to be pleasant. It was the end of June, and July was quickly approaching. Once again, the valley was filled with tents. A time for the demons to enjoy a night of sexual pleasure.

Winifred sat at one of the long tables, nibbling on a freshly grilled hotdog. With her bun dripping of catchup and mustard, she took a bite, allowing her eyes to search the crowd. The man who always wore the bull's head sat only a few tables away. A beautiful blonde was next to him. They were laughing and talking freely.

"Ready for tonight girls?" a man the girls did not recognize asked. "I think I'll choose one of you." He laughed as he aimed for the grilled food.

"This sucks," Pam whispered. "We need to escape."

"I agree, but to where?" Deb asked. "Were only fourteen. Well … you two are fifteen."

As the girls whispered, the chief of police, Diana's aunt, and the sheriff walked past, both wearing their uniforms and carrying guns.

"As I said," Deb whispered, "where would we go?"

"Ladies!" Grandmother stood proud, staring down at them. "Time to dress."

They followed the woman to the tent. Four purple dresses were on the cots. Again, a slip of paper was attached to each with their names.

"We know," Pam stated, "nothing underneath."

The girls changed in silence. Neither wanted to state the obvious. With the sun setting, the moon was rising high into the sky.

"A full moon tonight," Grandmother stated from outside the tent.

A low whistle echoed, and the girls froze.

"That's the same noise," Deb whispered.

"Come," Grandmother stated, "I will work your hair."

The girls exited the tent, and the woman ran the brush through their hair, decorating them with tiny, white flowers.

"July first," Grandmother whispered, handing each a yellow pill. "Demons revel! A great evening. Now pop this in your mouth."

The girls eyed each other but followed the order.

"You look beautiful." The woman waved her hand through the air. "Now to the fire with you."

The bonfire was huge, taller than a house, the heat felt from their tent. Other girls stood quietly between the trees, all dressed in their priestess' colors. Men and women drank, feeling the golden brew warm their spirits. No young children from what the girls could see, other than a few close to their age.

The man with the bull's head nodded at the girls. His fake cheeks shining bright against the blaring flames.

Grandmother arrived and all eyes landed on her. She raised her hands and yelled, "Let the festivities begin!"

The flames glowed in the darkening shades, slowly taking form. First a shallow face, then bloody red eyes, a hand, an arm. The wind blew. A voice yelled. The air thickened.

Winifred felt dizzy. She glanced around for a place to sit, but a hand grabbed hold, pulling her into the trees. A strong sticky-sweetness of something malevolent filled her senses. A glass touched her lips and she drank, feeling her stomach warm. The world tilted and she closed her eyes.

Opening them, dark red pupils penetrated deeply into her soul. Something shiny pulled her attention to the side. A blade sliced down her chest, but not deep enough to kill, just enough to draw blood. Something long and hard entered her, slipping deep between her legs.

Winifred screamed.

Darkness thickened, but those glowing red eyes grew larger. Something warm dripped across her face. She tried to scream but something was shoved into her mouth.

"You're training, child," echoed through her mind.

Winifred obeyed, and as she had practiced on the banana, she sucked and licked and sucked.

Moaning and screams echoed. Again something warm filled her stomach. She felt unsettled, chilled, and bland, but no fear. No longing for home. Just a deep cold that radiated from her toes to her head. Her mind remained blank, empty. Her body moved in a motion that seemed familiar but then again foreign. She coughed as something warm filled her cheeks. Gagging and coughing for fresh air, a strong hand slapped across her face. She tried to scream, but again the hand slapped. Again, and again, and again, until all fell dark and a silent scream raked across her soul.

A morning light broke along the horizon, dotting the landscape with an array of colors. Winifred sat up. She was naked and caked with blood. A thin cut running from her collarbone to her waist stung. Glancing around, she froze. Human bodies were everywhere. Many were snoring. A few stared blankly into the morning sky. None wore clothing. The fire had long since died. Only a few logs smoldered with a dull shade of gray, reminding her of her grandmother's hair.

"Pam?" Winifred whispered, loudly.

No reply.

A man's shirt, not far from the firepit, grabbed her attention. Pulling it over her head, she winched as it pinched against her raw chest.

"Deb?"

Again, no answer.

The ground spun, moving the Earth in odd ways. She sat, her stomach emptying onto a man who was no longer breathing. With a deep sigh, she stood, steadying herself against a tree. A few of the tents were no longer standing, crushed with fallen bodies.

"How many are dead?" she whispered.

Stumbling, Winifred made her way through the macabre landscape of human blood mixing with the mountain soil. The world tipped and she fell, her fingers squeezing into cold flesh. Slowly, she raised her head only to lock eyes onto a naked, old man resting against a large tree.

He nodded. "Hell is a chilling place," he whispered. "Is it not?"

Winifred nodded.

The man's chest, wrinkled from age, raised and lowered. "The demons have proven themselves again. We cast and they cast back. How many did they take with them this time?"

"I don't know ..." Winifred couldn't move. Too shocked to do anything, she stared at the old man.

"Read the symbols, my child." He pointed to where the food tent had been. "See and understand."

Winifred stood. Thirst pulled at her throat. She needed water.

"Child," a voice stated from behind.

Winifred turned and stared at her grandmother's eyes.

Still wearing the robe with the purple lining, the woman smiled. "Come with me."

Winifred followed. Her grandmother led her to the running stream. Several were already there, cleaning themselves. None were talking. Grandmother gently washed Winifred with a sponge. Helping her into a nightgown, she led her back to the tent. Handing her a small glass with a silver liquid, she ordered Winifred to drink. Pushing her onto the cot, she covered Winifred with a warm blanket. As Winifred closed her eyes, she noticed that the other cots were full.

An aroma of spring flowers woke Winifred. She sat up. Her eyes burned as did her chest. Pam was leaning against a wall. Deb and Diana were asleep.

"Where are we?" Winifred whispered.

"The attic," Pam replied.

"I don't feel so good."

"They drugged us," Pam stated. "Enough is enough, Winni."

Tears filled Winifred's eyes. "But what do we do?"

"I don't know," Pam replied. "But we *have* to escape."

Winifred nodded.

School started the last week of August. A welcomed release from the farm. From the stench. From the pain. Wearing new uniforms, the girls stepped off the bus and glanced around.

"Hi, Winni." Clarisse ran to Winifred, wrapping her in a large bear hug. "I missed you. How was your summer? Mine was great. I visited my grandmother in Colorado –"

Winifred held her hand over her mouth and ran to the bathroom. Her stomach tightened with each heave. Pam stood behind her holding her hair.

"You okay, Winni?" Deb asked.

"Should I get the nurse?" Diana sighed.

Pam shook her head. "This is not good."

Winifred stood and wiped her mouth. She held her stomach and sighed. "No this is not."

Winifred sat in the chair, staring out the window. Muffled voices echoed from the next room. Her breasts hurt and she felt sick. What was wrong with her?

"Give her this," a man's voice stated. "Make sure she drinks it all. It'll take a day or two. Keep her home. It will solve the problem."

"Understood, doctor," her mother stated.

Winifred followed her mother through the lobby and past several very pregnant women. Sitting in the car, her mother refused to look at her.

"Here," her mother stated. "Drink it all. I'm dropping you off at your grandmother's. She started this shit, she can finish it!" Her mother lit a cigarette and puffed on it madly. "I don't know how much more of this crap I can take." Her mother banged on the steering wheel as tears filled her eyes. "Fucking bullshit!"

Winifred's heart pounded. She was in deep trouble but had no idea what for. Drinking the tart liquid, her stomach growled. Not being able to eat for a few days, she felt weak and vulnerable.

The drive to the farm seemed to take forever. As the trees and houses passed her window, she thought about Billy Stanton, a boy she despised, and actually wished she was on the bus with him staring at her.

Grandmother met them in the driveway. She pulled Winifred by the arm, shoving her into the room with the twin beds. A large white pan was in the middle. Many towels were stacked neatly next to it.

"You stay here," her grandmother ordered. "You do not leave!"

Winifred nodded.

The door closed and Winifred was alone.

The evening passed and all remained calm. It was twilight, the morning sun just cresting the distant ridge. The rooster crowed, and the pain hit.

Winifred doubled over, clasping her stomach. The pain hit again, vibrating from her stomach to her back. A ripple of waves burst through her little body as if Satan himself was ripping her apart.

She screamed.

"Quiet, child," her grandmother stated. "You will live."

As the sun moved across the sky, Winifred held her breath each time a wave hit. Several times, nausea sent her to the pan. The large white pan. Blood oozed from between her legs. Winifred curled into a ball and crawled under the bed. She shivered as more pain hit. Something warm and hard, something foreign, was trying to escape her body.

Winifred screamed.

"I'm here, child," her grandmother stated.

Winifred's grandfather gently pulled her from under the bed. They stripped off her nightgown and her dignity. She struggled to escape their probing hands. The stench of rubbing alcohol was strong. Her grandmother blew something into Winifred's face, and the pain disappeared. The deeper her breaths, the more comfort Winifred felt. The room darkened and she closed her eyes, no longer caring what they were doing to her or why.

"I want to die," Winifred whispered as sleep slowly stole away her reality.

"I brought you some broth." Her grandmother sat a tray beside the bed.

Winifred sat up and glanced around. Feeling between her legs, she understood she was wearing a pad. The white pan was gone as were the towels.

"Nothing to be concerned about," her grandmother whispered. "Happens all the time. Now sip on this broth."

Winifred brought the spoon to her lips. The nausea was gone as was the pain. She glanced up at her grandmother.

The woman smiled.

"What happened to me?" Winifred asked.

"Womanhood," her grandmother replied, "an ancient curse from God."

Five

THE GIRLS SEEMED to stay a few feet away from Winifred after that fitful week. And with her fifteenth birthday only a few months away, Winifred felt she needed her friends' support more than ever.

"Can we talk?" she asked Pam, during lunch. "In private?" Winifred's eyes lowered.

Pam nodded.

They stepped outside and sat in a small, secluded garden.

"What's up?" Pam asked.

"Are you ignoring me? Are you angry?"

Pam sighed. "No, it's not you."

"Then what is it?"

"We need to escape …"

"From my grandmother …" Winifred added.

Pam nodded. "It's not right. You know what happened to you, don't you?"

Winifred nodded. "I agree we must leave, but what do we do? Where do we go?"

Pam glanced into the bushes and sighed. "What uncle of yours owns the orchards? Is he from your mom's side?"

Winifred shook her head. "My dads."

"Why are you not allowed to visit him?"

"Not sure," Winifred replied.

"We need to make a plan. Now that we're back in school and not constantly at the farm, maybe we can talk to him."

Winifred glanced around. Her heart pounded. The thought of visiting her forbidden uncle sent chills all through her. "We can't be seen."

"Understood," Pam replied. "Okay … this is what we'll do. We'll hop off the bus one stop early. We can walk the trail on the other side of the hill, away from your mom. We can then visit your uncle."

"How will you get home?"

"I'll worry about that later. Talking to your uncle is more important."

The afternoon dragged by. When the buses finally hissed to a stop, the girls felt drained.

"What are you two up to?" Billy asked.

"Nothing much." Winifred found a seat. "And you?"

"Spying on you two." He laughed.

"Wonderful …" Pam slapped her hand on her head. "Duh, now turn around and mind your own."

The driver glanced in the rearview mirror a couple of times before taking off. No words were spoken as they watched cars and houses and trees pass. When the bus hissed to a stop, the girls hopped off. Not waiting for the bus to leave, they aimed for the lemon orchard.

"I do hope it's not muddy," Pam said.

"Don't think so."

The orchard was dry. Lemons as large as baseballs filled the trees.

"They should pick these soon." Winifred pulled off a ripe one. "Do you think Grandmother may spot us?"

"I think we're safe," Pam replied.

As they walked, Winifred peeled a lemon. Splitting the fruit with Pam, they sucked, enjoying the tartness.

The path around the hill was anything but short. Not wanting to be seen, they darted between the trees whenever a car passed.

"This way might be too close to your grandmother's farm," Pam stated. "She'll see us."

"We can hike up higher." Winifred glanced at the top of the hill.

"No, let's just hurry."

They ran and their bags banged against their backs. At the edge of her uncle's yard, they paused. The place seemed empty and quiet.

"Do you have cousins living here?" Pam asked.

"No," Winifred replied, "all grown."

"Okay, let's go."

They crossed the small, grassy field, stepping onto the dirt road that led to the front door. The house, not small but not large, resembled an aging ranch, one often found in old movies. The porch creaked as they climbed the stairs.

"What you girls want?" An old man wearing overalls and holding a shovel glared at them. "You causing trouble, selling something?"

Winifred smiled. She had only met the man once and that was to be told to stay away and never come back.

"No, sir." Pam stepped off the porch. "We need to talk to you."

"Who are you and what do you want?" he asked.

"I'm Winni, your niece."

"Why in the *hell* are *you* here?" His eyes narrowed as his frown grew. "You're not to be here. You and your devil-worshiping family."

"Please," Winifred stated. "We need your help."

The man glanced around. "You're asking for a lot."

"What do you mean?" Pam asked.

"You're nothing but trouble, child." He sighed. "You need to leave."

"Please, Uncle, I really need your help. Can you help us?"

Pam slapped her hands on her hips. "What kind of an uncle are you?"

"The kind that doesn't want to end up floating in the river with my eyes glued shut." He held up his shovel, shaking it in the air. "Leave now and never return."

Winifred wiped her eyes, stepping off the porch and shaking her head. "I told you he'd be of no help."

The girls left, leaving the man alone in his yard. No real answers were given, no explanation. Just a deep hatred in her uncle's eyes, telling her to never return.

It was nearing the end of October and a holiday the girls dreaded, *All Hallows Eve*. Again they were in the valley surrounded by tents and a large bonfire. The hooded robes were starting to agitate, black now, the girls' least favorite color – aside from purple.

Wearing their black dresses with orange flowers in their hair, Grandmother handed each a small pill. "Take it just before everything starts. Understood? Now, go."

As they walked, Deb held out her hand. "What if we don't?"

Diana chuckled. "What *if* we don't?"

As the fire blared only a few feet away, Pam pulled the girls between the dense brush. She dropped her pill and crushed it with her foot. The others did the same.

"Follow me," Pam whispered.

The girls aimed for the mountain ridge. When the jagged cliffs soared high over their heads, they stopped.

"We'll follow this ridge deeper into the valley," Pam whispered. "Let's see where it goes."

Darkness fell and the girls continued to walk. Branches slapped at their arms and faces. Without dinner, their stomachs growled. Loud voices and strange music blared in the distance, fading as they walked.

The moon rose higher and an owl hooted. When large boulders blocked their path, they sat.

"Now what?" Diana asked.

"We wait until morning," Pam replied. "If they can't find us, we'll be safe."

"Let's pray," Winifred whispered.

"Pray?" Pam repeated. "To who?"

"To God," Winifred replied.

"Since when did God ever listen to us?" Pam asked.

"It couldn't hurt," Diana whispered.

"Deb?" Pam asked.

Deb nodded.

"Fine, then we pray," Pam whispered. "But we have to be as quiet as possible. Our voices will carry."

The girls recited The Lord's Prayer over and over again. As they whispered the words, a low whistle echoed through the trees.

"Oh, shit." Pam held up her hand. "Hear that?"

The girls strained to see through the darkness. The moon gave little light since it was only a quarter full. An owl hooted and a coyote howled. Again, the whistle echoed.

"What is that?" Deb asked.

Winifred shook her head.

"Hello, girls," a man's voice stated.

Startled, the girls stared into the trees. A dim light flashed and a low whistle blew. The bull's head sat quietly on a man's shoulders. He was kneeling, his arms resting on his knees, his fingers just under his chin.

The girls froze.

"Hello, girls," the man said again.

Winifred scooted closer to Diana. Deb grabbed Pam's arms.

The bull's head raised a little higher, but the man remained in the same position. His feet left the soft soil as he too rose higher and into the trees. The ground vibrated under their feet. Heat surrounded them as if they were standing next to the bonfire. But there was no fire, there was no pit. The air thickened and grew quiet. Suddenly, the man disappeared, vanished, as if never there. But the ground was still growing hot. Pam stood first as the boulder behind her turned red. Flames flickered around it.

"Is the place on fire?" Deb asked.

"We have to run," Diana replied.

"Run where?" Pam asked.

"Hello, girls," the voice said from the top of the boulder.

The girls ran. Not able to see a thing, they stumbled and fell and rolled. Branches tore at their skin. Rocks bruised their bones. They screamed as they ran. Unfortunately, each ran in a different direction.

Winifred stumbled and rolled, her head hitting dead tree stumps and large rocks. Fallen leaves slid her down the hillside, moving ever faster. The water splashed as she hit. The coolness awakened her to a reality she didn't want. She stood knee-deep in the rushing water.

"Hello, girl …" A whispering voice echoed through her mind. "Hello, girl …"

"Stop!" Winifred yelled, covering her ears. "Please stop!"

Some *one* or some *thing* grabbed her from behind. She kicked and screamed, but whoever it was held firm. Blackness covered her eyes and a rag covered her mouth. Struggling was useless as a thick coldness filled her with dread.

Her dress was ripped from her body. She now lay naked against a cold, stone slab. No voices, no sound. She shivered. The cloth still covered her head. She couldn't scream. With her hands tied behind her back, she couldn't move.

Raising her head, she silently recited The Lord's Prayer. Her voice loud and clear from inside her mind.

The bag was jerked off, her head slapping hard against the rock. She rolled, and again, her head hit against the stone. The place was dark and cold and quiet. She still could not see a thing.

Something sharp slid down her thigh, the pain ricocheting up her spine. She screamed, but no sound. Someone grabbed her hair, pulling her head down. The gag was removed and a warm, thick liquid was poured into her mouth. She could either swallow or choke. The choice was hers. She swallowed.

As her world darkened, something sharp slid down the inside of her other leg.

The morning light awoke along with the singing birds. Winifred slowly opened her eyes. Her hands were no longer bound. But she felt heavy, fuzzy. Large boulders were everywhere. She stood and screamed. Her legs, covered in dried blood, ached.

A dress, resting on one of the boulders looked torn. It wasn't one she had worn before. It was a light blue but would fit. Slipping it over her head, the odor of rotting eggs made her gag. Dried blood caked the dress but was better than nothing.

Climbing over the boulders, she tried to determine her surroundings. Nothing looked familiar. The mountainside seemed to run on forever. Her head spun and her world flipped. Tumbling off the boulder, she smacked her hand, snapping her wrist. She cried out, favoring her arm.

As she stumbled through the thorny brush, the sun rose higher into the sky. Winifred had a choice. She could hold her broken wrist or she could shield her eyes. With a dry throat and an achy body, she chose to favor her arm.

A dirt path finally greeted her bare and bloody feet. The dirt was warm, the rocks sharp. She walked and stumbled, wishing and praying that death would arrive quickly.

A small and living tree was just ahead. At the base of the trunk, something sat at an odd angle. Winifred stopped and stared.

"What is that?"

She stepped closer.

It was a human. It was a girl. A naked, young girl.

Winifred screamed. She hobbled as fast as she could. With throbbing feet and bleeding legs, she fell at the base of the tree. Pulling the girl into her lap, Winifred screamed again.

"Deb!" Winifred's body shook with each wave that hit. "Deb! Wake up, Deb!"

Winifred shook the girl, begging for her to wake up. But the girl remained still, eyes staring blankly into the unknown. Winifred rocked her friend back and forth. Tears filled her eyes, breaths coming in shallow spurts. Laying her head on her friend's chest, she sobbed.

The day's sun slowly moved across the sky. From one side of the valley, it rose as it slowly lowered on the other. Birds flew. Clouds drifted. A wild dog paused for only a moment, tilting its head from side to side, before darting into the dense brush.

As darkness thickened, something that sounded like broken shells filled her ears. A low whistle blew softly from somewhere in the distance. Winifred held her breath and again stared into the sky, begging for help.

"Lord have mercy," a man's voice stated as a horse snorted several times. "What in the name of God do we have here?"

Winifred couldn't move. She clung to Deb as if her life depended on it.

"I told you something evil was going on back here," a different voice yelled.

"Go get help," the first voice ordered. "Find the sheriff."

"No!" Winifred yelled. "No! No! No!" Winifred rocked her friend in her arms.

A man knelt next to Winifred, pulling her hair from her eyes. "You okay, child?"

"No … no … no sheriff." Winifred cried.

The man rested his fingers on Deb's neck and sighed. "Lord have mercy."

"Can you help her?" Winifred asked.

"Child, only the good lord can help this girl now," he replied.

"No!" Winifred screamed. "No!"

"You are hurt," he said, lifting Winifred's broken arm. "Let me take her from you."

"No!" Winifred screamed. "No!"

Screeching tires slid to a stop. Footsteps pounded and flashlights lit the ground.

As a hand caressed Winifred's shoulder, a voice whispered into her ears, "Hello, girl!"

The hospital lights were bright. People darted back and forth, cleaning her skin, wrapping her legs, casting her arm. Not much could be seen from where she lay, except for an officer who remained at the edge of her bed.

"Can I talk to her yet?" a man asked.

"Don't see why not," a woman replied.

A curtain screeched as it was jerked aside.

Wearing a suit and tie, a man stepped closer. He smiled. "How are you?"

Winifred remained quiet.

"Can I ask you a few questions?"

Winifred looked at the officer at the end of the bed.

"What's your name?" the suited man asked.

Winifred remained quiet.

"Why were you out there alone?" the man asked.

"Steven," a man's voice echoed through the room. A voice that demanded attention.

The man wearing the suit paused. "Here."

"Out now!" the demanding voice ordered.

"But, sir –"

"No buts," the voice stated. "I said, out now."

The man glanced at Winifred before taking a step back. He nodded at her but frowned.

Winifred stared at the police officer, her eyes pleading for help.

He didn't move.

The sheriff stepped closer and tapped on Winifred's shoulder. He bent lower and whispered, "Keep your mouth shut. Your grandmother is on her way."

Winifred took a deep breath as tears filled her eyes. She glared at the officer who kept his gaze to the center of the room.

Nothing would ever change. Her friend was dead. Where Pam and Diana were was anyone's guess. But Winifred understood that her life would never change.

Winifred sat on her grandmother's yellow couch, staring at her broken arm. The cast now covered in signatures. She ran her finger across the words, *love Pam*, and smiled.

At least Pam and Diana were still alive. *'Fell down the mountain,'* everyone said about Deb. She died cuz she was careless. A tragic accident.

An accident that would happen to Winifred if she wasn't careful. But then again, maybe God had blessed Deb by taking her away. It was Winifred and the others who were still being punished.

Grandmother sighed as she sat in the velvet chair. "We need to talk."

"About?" Winifred asked.

"You turn fifteen in a few days."

Winifred nodded. "That happens to most."

Grandmother chuckled. "Yes, it does."

"And?"

"It is my responsibility to properly train you."

"You already did." Winifred rolled her eyes. "The bananas?"

Grandmother chuckled again. "Not that. You will be the next High Priestess of our coven. You are destined to take my place."

"Your place?"

Grandmother took a deep breath and let it out slowly. "I kept my mouth shut over every trouble you've brought into this family. Tonight, you will spend it with our true father."

"Excuse me?"

"Broken arm or no broken arm, you will spend the night with him." Grandmother stood and shook her head.

A few minutes before midnight, Winifred waited at the attic stairs holding a blanket around her shivering body.

Grandmother pushed gently, urging her to climb.

Winifred stepped up with Grandmother close behind.

"Strip," Grandmother stated.

Winifred obeyed and pulled her gown over her head. She handed it to the woman.

"Go," Grandmother said, "he is waiting for you."

Winifred stepped into the darkness, and the door closed behind her. As the lock clicked, she sighed. Expecting hands to grab and pull her to the floor, she waited. But nothing happened. Not much was in the attic other than cobwebs and an old picture frame.

She wrapped the blanket tighter around her and took a step, but something yanked it away.

Winifred froze, understanding what was next. Instead, all remained quiet.

"Who's there?"

A low whistle sounded. Along with a soft rustle of a damp wind.

"Hello?" Winifred said. "Just get this over with."

Nothing, absolute silence.

Winifred took a step, and at the far end of the room, a dim light lit. It wasn't a flashlight or a candle. Winifred couldn't tell from where the light was coming from. She took another step, and the man with a bull's head appeared. Only this time, no paper mâché, the face was real. He was squatting, resting his arms on his knees. And just like the man in the valley that night, his fingers rested under his chin.

"Who are you?" she asked.

No answer.

Winifred took a step closer and the light dimmed. The man rose a few inches in the air, remaining in the same position. The bull's head was not fake, it moved as the creature smiled.

"What are you?" Winifred asked, taking a step back.

A warm breeze caressed her naked body. She shivered and wrapped her arms around her breast.

"Why won't you talk?"

The creature stood, allowing his feet to hover just inches above the floor. He reached out his hand.

Winifred stared at the thick fingers with sharp, yellow claws. She stepped closer and the bull's head smiled.

His yellow-red eyes glowed in the semi-darkness. Horns curled from his forehead, resting behind his ears. He chuckled. "Hello, girl."

"I'm not afraid of you," Winifred stated.

"You are as you were when you arrived in this world," the bull said. "You are mine."

"I belong to no one," Winifred replied.

The bull kept his hand out, almost as if in a gesture of friendship.

Winifred stared at the hand, studying it.

The man was tall, at least six feet. His skin had a slight reddish glow but it also seeped with dull yellow fur. The face was not human. Fierce eyes that flickered between red and yellow with slits like a snake emanated a sense of hatred and an eerie longing for pain. The creature stepped closer, still holding out its hand.

"It will be easier on you if you submit freely," the creature said.

Winifred did not move or reply.

"If I must take, you will suffer," he added.

Winifred raised her head and eyes to the heavens, reciting The Lord's Prayer.

The creature grabbed her arms, pulling her in close. His breath reeked of rotten eggs and moldy leaves. His oily hot skin felt like dried leather. His prickly hair pinched and moved as if alive.

Winifred held her breath and the creature licked the inside of her mouth with a rope-like tongue. She recited The Lord's Prayer over and over again from inside her head. The more she said the words, the more the bull violated her. The room rocked, her body jerked, his tail and manly parts entered before exiting. The bull's breaths were harsh and deep. The creature moaned and laughed and howled. As suddenly as everything started, it ended.

The room darkened and silence engulfed her reality. Winifred sat up, clinging to the blanket. No bull stood in front of her. No light lit the room.

A rooster crowed, and the attic door opened.

"You are *his* now, forever," Grandmother said, holding out a bathrobe.

Six

A COUPLE OF years had passed and many times, Winifred wondered if her life would ever change. Although she only knew pain and fear, she still questioned her reality.

Billy sat backward on the seat, glaring at her. He smiled and tilted his head. Winifred rolled her eyes, trying desperately to ignore him.

"You look different," he said.

"Oh? How?"

"Not sure," he replied.

The bus hissed to a stop and Winifred stood. Stepping onto the street, she sighed. Billy was standing next to her. "This is *not* your stop," she said.

"I know," he replied.

"Then why are you here?"

"I need you to come with me," he said.

"Come where?"

"I want you to meet someone."

"Someone who?"

Winifred crossed the street.

Billy followed. "Please, no strings attached."

Winifred glanced around and shrugged. "Why not? Nothing more to lose."

They followed the smokey trail of the yellow bus. After passing several homes and a liquor store, they stopped at a small, white house.

"Come in," he whispered, "you're safe."

The front door led into a very small living room with only a couch, a chair, and a TV. A door led to another room with a bed. The place was neat and tidy.

"Billy?" an aging voice asked. "That you?"

"Nanny," Billy stated, "I brought someone to meet you."

"Billy … how –" the old woman stood in the doorway. Her eyes widened as they landed on Winifred. "Lord have mercy …"

"Nanny, this is Winifred, the girl I told you about."

"I know who you are, child," the woman stated.

"I guess you can't talk to me either?" Winifred asked.

"One second." The old woman darted into the bedroom. She reappeared with something smoldering in her hands. "Sovereign Lord," she whispered, "focus your protection …"

"What's she doing?" Winifred whispered.

"Cleansing," Billy replied.

"… Cross of Cavalry … in the name of Jesus. Amen." The woman placed the smoldering bundle onto a plate and smiled. "Well, now we can talk. Please, let us sit."

"How do you know who I am?" Winifred asked, finding a spot on the couch.

As soon as her hands touched the sofa, something familiar hit. She looked around, feeling as if she had finally returned home.

"You feel it, my dear?" the woman asked.

"Have I been here before?" Winifred frowned.

"Perhaps," the woman replied. "What do you remember?"

Winifred stared at the window. The curtains with little red strawberries reminded her of something. Something important.

"Do you know who I am?" the woman asked.

Winifred shook her head.

The woman smiled. "My poor child," she whispered.

"Who are you?" Winifred asked.

"Grab my picture book, Billy," the woman ordered.

Billy darted into the bedroom, returning with a large, leather-bound book. He handed it to his grandmother.

"Hand it to Winifred." Nanny nodded.

Winifred held the book and stared at it. It didn't look familiar. She opened the cover and studied the black-and-white photos of people she didn't recognize. She flipped the page. Again, more people she never met. She flipped again and stopped.

"Is that my … mother?" Winifred asked.

"And your father," the woman replied. "My son."

"You're my grandmother?" Winifred asked.

The woman nodded. "I've been waiting for you."

"Where's my dad?" Winifred asked.

"He died a long time ago," the woman replied.

"How?" Winifred asked, resenting the answer before it was spoken.

"During one of your grandmother's grand events," the woman replied.

"Sacrificed?"

"More than likely," the woman said. "We could never prove anything. Your uncle still resents your mother to this very day."

"That's why he'll have nothing to do with me?"

The woman nodded.

"Billy's my cousin?" Winifred asked.

The woman nodded again.

"We can help you and your friends," Billy stated. "We've got it all worked out."

"But we must move cautiously," the woman added. "Very cautiously. If you want to escape."

"We do." Winifred leaned a little closer to the old woman.

"Very well." The woman rubbed her hands and smiled. "Have you been anointed with *his* presence? You *are* almost seventeen. In about a week?"

Winifred nodded.

"Unfortunately, he will follow you always," the woman replied. "Today is Wednesday. I will make the plans. Billy will let you know. As I said, we must move cautiously. Ears are everywhere. Say nothing. I will make contact with your friends. Say nothing to your mother. Nothing to Pam or Diana. Not a word."

Winifred nodded.

"Billy, guide her home through the backyards."

He paused and held out his hand. Winifred stared, remembering the red hand with the yellow claws. Taking a deep breath, slowly she allowed her fingers to touch his. A warmth more tender than love exploded in her heart. She smiled. Billy smiled.

Winifred opened the back door and stepped inside. The aroma of stale cigarettes filled the air. Glancing into the living room, she smiled. Her mother was asleep on the couch. After tossing her bag on her bed, she stepped to the window and glanced out. The day was still young, the sun not yet ready to sleep.

The rosary swinging from a nail grabbed her attention. She picked it up and gently ran her finger over the cross.

"Oh, Lord," she whispered, "please ..."

A low whisper echoed through her mind as she heard the words, "Hello, girl."

The truck's tires squealed, jerking the old machine to a sudden stop. From the back, all remained dark. Mumbled voices echoed as heavy footfalls pounded. The doors opened and light flooded Winifred's vision. She covered her eyes.

"Okay, darling," the man said, "this is your stop."

Winifred stood and grabbed her small bag. "Thank you."

"No problem … was headn' this way anyway."

Winifred sat, allowing her legs to swing free. She jumped and her feet hit solid ground. "Where am I?"

"Oakland," he replied.

"Time?"

"Time for you to get a move on," he said. "Here."

Winifred accepted the small envelope.

"Ticket and a few dollars." He smiled, tipping his ballcap. "Good luck to yah."

"Thank you."

"Just remember, it is not the religion that is bad. It is the people. Real Catholics provide sanctuary to those in need."

The man drove away, and the huge building revealed itself. Three arches decorated the entrance to the train station. Many were busy knowing their destination, but as for Winifred, she held no clue. Tossing her bag over her shoulder, she climbed the stairs. Voices echoed as she walked through the grand entrance. A loud voice announced an incoming train.

Winifred's heart pounded. Not understanding why she was there, her mind twirled. Would someone meet her? Would someone come for her? Was she safe?

"Winifred?" Pam's voice yelled out loud and clear.

Winifred cried as she wrapped her arms around her friend.

"Diana's in the bathroom," Pam said. "We have a few minutes before we board."

"Where are we going?" Winifred asked.

"Who cares?" Pam replied, still hugging her friend. "We have tickets and money. We're outta here."

The rhythm of the train, or was it the darkness, finally lured Winifred to sleep. No one would ever know where she was. Thoughts of her mother waiting for her to return from school, however, gave her the chills. But then again, her mother could have done something. Together, they could have run away. Maybe in a few years, she would call. See how she was doing. But one person she would never want to see again was her grandmother. The grandmother who was a witch. A real witch that cast spells, sacrificed babies, and handed out bananas. Someone with power and connections, and to Winifred, those connections flew around the world.

Pam nudged Winifred waking her. The train was slowing. It was time to go.

"Where are we?" Winifred asked.

"Somewhere in Texas," Pam replied. "We switch."

The girls stood and stretched their tired legs. Wanting and needing a long shower, they stepped onto the darkening platform. Their stomachs growled. With nothing readily available, they chose chips and a drink. Again, they boarded a long silver tube and found their seats. As they traveled to the East Coast, the rhythm lured them into a reality they never knew existed.

In Florida, a woman met them. A woman who had experienced the same life. A Catholic woman who understood. A woman who would hold their hands, listen to their fears, and a woman who would guide them.

Not an easy road to travel with that low whistle continuously echoing through their minds, and the man with the bull's head who'd suddenly appear in their dreams. An image that would simply recite two words, "Hello, girls!"

Seven

WINIFRED WATCHED SILENTLY as her friend walked somberly down the red carpet, her white veil trailing behind. Diana stood silent but with a large smile.

"You're next." Diana gently touched her swelling belly.

"Don't think so," Winifred replied. "I think I'll be a nun."

Diana laughed. "Right."

Pam's wedding was beautiful as was the reception. The girls laughed, enjoying the evening. It would be the last time the three would be together for a very long time. Tomorrow, Winifred was to report for duty. Her first tour would be in Germany. Far away from her friends and the family she once loved. But as the godmother to Diana's little one, she would definitely have to return.

As the evening ended, Diana and Winifred hugged, watching their best friend leave in a limousine. The woman who had cared for and protected them hugged from behind. The love and devotion the girls felt was sometimes overwhelming.

Church in California held a different meaning than the one in Florida. In Florida, they were free to worship and ask for release. Release from the evil that continued to stalk them, away from the torture they had endured for years. The young girls understood they had been liberated which graced their hearts with hope and not regret.

Winifred boarded the plane with an empty soul, free from remorse. Life was just starting and she was ready. Tomorrow would bring a day worth living. Every once in a while, she would reflect on the men she knew. The man with the fake bull's head. The sheriff who ruled the town. And her grandmother – a woman with power but no soul.

As the engines purred, Winifred allowed her eyes to surrender to the tiredness that always followed. The vision of Diana and her swollen belly filled her mind. What her mother and grandmother made her endure when she was only fourteen was something she would never forget. Forgive, yes, but forget – never.

Winifred had graduated at the top of her class. She was now a radiology specialist. From today on, she would help others who were hurt. Touching her wrist, she smiled. Her sympathy would run deep, she knew what broken felt like.

"Winifred," Caroline yelled. "Ready?"

"Yep." Winifred jerked on her pack, hiking it over her shoulder.

The weekend was a time for the mountains. For Winifred, the rolling hills filled with various shades of green brought joy, regret, and hope. A mixture of emotions no one would ever understand.

"I have a surprise for you …" Caroline said, tugging on her arm. Long blonde hair, pulled behind her ears, fell past her waist. She was in her mid twenties with sparkling, blue eyes that twinkled as she smiled.

"What?"

"You're gonna meet someone."

"Great." Winifred rolled her eyes.

They climbed aboard the train and settled in. The ride was short, only a couple of hours, and now they stood at the foot of one of the most beautiful mountains in Germany.

"I love it here." Caroline waved her hands. "Reminds me of home."

"Thank god it doesn't remind me of anything but fresh air," Winifred replied.

"Caroline?" a male voice yelled.

Caroline ran and practically jumped into the man's arms. A man with the same-colored hair, blonde, but somewhat lightened at the temples. He towered above her friend as they kissed and he swung her around. Her long hair waved in the wind like a blanket rolling across a bed. Caroline was a physician, a surgeon actually, and a friend so close that Winifred considered her a sister.

"Winifred," Caroline yelled. "Come here."

Winifred cautiously approached, her gaze focused on the mountain.

Caroline grabbed her friend's arm, pulling her closer. "This is Winifred. Winifred, this is Grant. Grant ... what's your last name?"

"Taggart," the man replied.

Winifred smiled.

He was tall, almost six feet or so. Dark red hair and freckles, lots of freckles. Green eyes that sparkled like fresh spring grass. His smile lit his face while something kind and caring radiated from his inner essence.

"Nice to meet you, Winifred." He held her hand.

His touch felt – good – comforting. "Taggart?"

"Scottish," he replied. "My parents are from Scotland. I'm first generation American."

She could hear a slight accent. "Nice to meet you too, Grant. And ... I have no idea where my parents were from. Hell from all I know."

Caroline laughed a nervous chuckle, rolling her eyes. "Okay, well, let's get this trek on its way."

After filling their packs with water and food, they set off on foot to the skyway. Enjoying the amazing view, they talked as the little car rose higher and higher into the beautiful green mountains.

"I've never seen so much green," Caroline stated.

"California is probably brown now," Winifred replied. "But it's beautiful here."

"Where are you from?" Grant asked. "I was raised in Connecticut."

"California," Winifred replied. "But I call Florida home."

"She doesn't talk much about her past," Caroline added. "So we don't ask."

Grant nodded.

The ride ended and they grabbed their packs. Hiking through the tall, beautiful pines filled Winifred with renewed hope. Every so often, a bull's head would peek out between the branches, but she'd simply shrug it off, relating it to her inner child's guilt. At least that was what her therapist said. As for her pastor, it was her inner spirit cleansing itself. As for Winifred, it was the demon that would always be connected to her soul.

They found the perfect camping spot, giving them a full view of the valley. Three tents were set, one for Winifred, one for Grant, and one for the lovebirds.

With a fire blazing, Winifred sat on a log, concentrating on the flames.

"Penny for your thoughts." Grant handed her a hot cup of tea.

"Thanks." Winifred took a sip. "I try not to have thoughts."

"Okay, then tell me, what do you do for the Army?"

"You first," she replied.

"I'm a bone specialist." He smiled.

"Bones?" Winifred laughed. "Me too, I take x-rays. Lots of x-rays."

He nodded. "Guess we have something in common."

"I guess so." She smiled.

"What about your parents?" he asked.

"My father died when I was young."

"I'm sorry." He took a sip. "My parents are …"

"Doctors?"

He nodded.

They laughed.

"Things do tend to run in families."

"Yes, they do." He smiled.

The moon rose over the valley as the fire slowly died. The two watched as the evening stars popped out one at a time.

"That's the big dipper," he said, trailing his hand through the air.

"Beautiful," Winifred whispered.

"Yes, she is," he replied.

Winifred smiled. "I'm gonna turn in."

"Me too."

"It's great meeting you." She zipped up her tent.

Winifred pulled the sleeping bag around her shoulder. She sighed and closed her eyes. As sleep tapped on her soul, she said a quick evening prayer.

"Thank you, Lord," she whispered. "Love you, night."

The cool air chilled her naked skin. She strained to understand. Glancing down, her legs floated miles above the valley floor. Shaking her head, she screamed.

A bull's head floated inches away with glowing yellow-red eyes. Drool oozed from the crooked smile. He growled, allowing his tail to enter her, stabbing, inching ever deeper, deeper.

"No!" Winifred screamed and lashed out. "This is not real!"

The bull arched and growled again. With arms stronger than any man, he threw her to the campsite.

Grant stepped out of his tent just as her limp body hit the smoldering embers. He was on her within seconds. Grabbing the water, he gently poured it over the bubbling blisters. "It's okay, I got yah," he soothed. "Tom … Tom, get out here!"

Tom and Caroline peeked out of their tent.

"Oh my god!" Caroline yelled, aiming for her friend. "What the hell? Why is she naked? What happened?"

"Demonic attack," Grant whispered. "Can you grab my small bag, it's just inside my tent?"

"Demonic fuck what?" Tom asked.

"Grab a blanket," Grant ordered.

Caroline returned with a small, red velvet bag. "Here."

"Thanks." Grant pulled out a vial and recited a few words before dripping water over Winifred's burns.

Winifred screamed and moaned.

Tom covered her with a blanket. "What the fuck's happening?"

Grant hugged Winifred. "It's okay, I gotcha, I gotcha."

Winifred tried to open her eyes but they refused to move. The pain was too great.

Grant dropped a few more drops onto her burns still reciting the prayer in Latin. The pain stopped and the bright pink bumps settled, her skin back to normal.

"What the hell?" Caroline asked.

"It's okay, now," he soothed. "You're back, you're safe."

"Tell me what the fuck just happened," Tom ordered.

Caroline helped to dress Winifred in her bedclothes. Grant sprinkled a few drops around the campsite, reciting the same words. He nodded at Winifred who was sipping on water.

"You okay?" he asked.

Winifred nodded.

"What the hell is going on?" Tom asked again.

Grant sat next to Winifred and sighed. "It's called an incubus or spirit lover."

"A what?" Tom replied.

"I've heard of that," Caroline whispered. "Is she possessed?"

Grant laughed. "No, but there is a demon attached to her. Probably since childhood."

"How the hell do you know this stuff?" Tom asked. "You some kind of a priest or something?"

Grant shook his head. "Not quite. My mother's a witch. A white witch. A psychic."

"Mine wasn't good." Winifred wiped her eyes with the back of her hand. "My grandmother."

"What will come next, a scarecrow and tinman? Glinda the good witch of the north?" Tom rubbed his head and sighed. "Jesus fuck man!"

"How often does this happen?" Grant asked Winifred.

Winifred smiled and replied, "Whenever I'm happy. And you made me happy."

"I think I can help. My mother would be able to help more. But I have a few tricks. Such as my holy water. I didn't bring sage, probably should have. I do have my rosary."

"I'd rather not play with the beads," Winifred replied.

"Oh … you're one of those?" Grant nodded.

"What does that mean?" Caroline asked.

Grant shook his head. "It's when you worship one god on a Saturday and another on a Sunday."

"Is that common?" Caroline asked.

Grant shrugged.

A low whistle echoed through the trees and a strong aroma of sulfur filled the air.

"Who farted?" Tom asked.

"No one," Grant replied, "that *thing* is pissed."

Grant set the tray with the hot drinks on the table. He smiled as he pulled his chair closer. Winifred glanced around the small shop. Not many were visiting this time of day.

"Thanks." Caroline took a sip. "Mmm, what is this?"

"Glühwein," he replied, "hot wine, I guess you could say."

"Delicious." Winifred nodded.

"Okay, talk." Caroline stared at her friend. "We're all professionals here. I'm a doctor, he's a doctor. You two are radiologists. None of us are stupid people. We have brains. Therefore, what happened last night just doesn't ..." – Caroline swiped her hand through the air – "... happen."

"Happens more than you may think," Grant replied. "Tom, ever woke up feeling excited?"

Tom glanced at the cashier and frowned.

"Caroline, ever experienced a sensual dream?" Grant asked. "Woke up with an urge?"

"Nothing ever dangled me over a damn valley thousands of feet in the air," she replied. "Does this happen to you all the time?"

"Only since I was fifteen and more often once I left home," Winifred replied.

"Fifteen?" Caroline repeated. "Shit."

"Demons," Grant stated, "have sexually attacked women for centuries. The name incubus actually means *a nightmare induced by a demon.*"

"This is just bull," Tom replied.

"You could say that," Winifred whispered, taking another sip.

"Is your demon a bull?" Grant asked.

Winifred nodded. "A man with a bull's head and a very long and sharp tail."

"Wasn't Merlin conceived by a human and demon?" Caroline asked, rubbing her hands together.

"I believe it's recorded that way," Grant replied.

"Does this *thing* actually talk to you?" Caroline asked.

"Sometimes." Winifred took another sip.

"What does it feel like?" Caroline asked.

"Not good, tingling, vibrations, sharp pain between my …"

"Scientists call it sleep paralysis," Grant added. "If you discuss it with my mother, she'll talk for hours on the subject. According to her, there is a veil between our world and the demons' world. A thin veil, and if that veil is torn, those creatures can and will slip through."

"Is there a way to stop it?" Tom asked. "Repair the veil?"

"Yes, but it's never easy," Grant replied. "Pretty long, drawn-out process. We'd first have to lure the demon in. Be someplace safe. But someplace where we could bind and capture it. It would have to be the right time of year. Demons are afraid of Mars, the god of war. Supposedly, Mars conquered many a demon. Therefore, March is a no-go."

"What about salt?" Tom asked. "I remember something about salt."

"Salt is a purifying stone," Grant replied. "The old saying of tossing salt over your shoulder for good luck? Supposed to chase away bad spirits. Ancient sayings are important. We should pay attention to them."

"You mentioned sage," Caroline whispered, "when you sprinkled the holy water."

"Sage is most common, but actually, just about any plant with a strong aroma when burned will work. Mother Gaia, our planet's heart, is here to protect us. She births many mystical things including plants.

Demons are not of our world. Therefore, anything that connects the present with Mother Earth helps to push away evil."

"Okay, you said good place," Caroline added. "Explain."

"Once we invoke the demon, his power will be strong," Grant whispered. "Regular walls will not hold it. A weak cave would crumble around us. Bricks could fly. Wood would burn. A strong castle that has fought against time would be best."

"And where would we find a castle?" Caroline asked.

"Wait …" Tom smiled. "I may have an idea."

"An idea?" Caroline replied.

"I have a friend who's related to someone who owns a castle," he explained. "He claims that the place is haunted. And … it's not far from here."

Winifred closed her eyes and sighed.

"Let me make some calls," Tom stated. "See if he'd approve."

Grant nodded.

Caroline grinned at Winifred and shrugged.

The days passed as they normally did. Winifred helped her patients on and off the table. She cleaned her apartment or shopped for fresh vegetables. A few times, Grant stopped by for a quick meal, or she would visit Caroline and Tom. Nothing of any importance happened. No one mentioned her demon or visiting a castle.

It was Thursday evening when a knock gave her a moment of pause. When she opened the door, Grant entered, holding a huge bouquet.

"For my beautiful lady." He gave her a hug. "I brought you a surprise."

Grant stepped into the hallway before escorting an older woman into the apartment. She was half Grant's height and sweet-looking, reminding Winifred of a typical American mother. Her graying red hair accentuated a beauty that was more of a feeling than an appearance. A strong aura of warmth surrounded the woman.

"Nice to meet you," the woman said, "I'm Heleina Taggart."

Winifred didn't know what to say. Obviously, Grant had sent for his mother and she responded. But to fly all this way just for her? "Grant?"

"I think your problem is a little outside my expertise," he replied, closing the door. "I'd like for you two to talk."

Sipping on freshly brewed coffee, they sat on the balcony that overlooked the large lake. Winifred kept glancing at Heleina. She wasn't an overly beautiful woman, more aged and weathered-looking. Although in her early seventies, one would still have a task at guessing her age. Her hair was a vibrant red, graying in the front and falling just past her shoulders. Slightly overweight and standing at about five feet, she obviously pushed past life, demanding respect.

"It is a beautiful view," Heleina whispered. "I can see why you chose to live here."

"Peaceful," Winifred replied, "and a long way from home."

"How old were you when initiated?" she asked.

"About ten."

"Ten, that is the normal age," Heleina replied. "I was nine."

"Was your coven large or small?" Winifred asked.

"Large, one of the largest in New York." Heleina took a sip. "Nice, thank you."

Winifred nodded. "Abigor? The color yellow?"

Heleina laughed. "Hate that color to this very day. How about you?"

"Purple." Winifred giggled, a little, taking a sip.

"Ira Levin was inspired to write *Rosemary's Baby* from rumors about the local covens," Grant said. "Old ghost stories from New York's satanic past. Unfortunately, they were not just stories to frighten children."

"No, they were not," Heleina added. "Unfortunately, the stories were real. I'm sure he changed the names and locations, but the overall jest of the novel was based on reality."

"Never read the novel," Winifred replied, "but I enjoyed the movie. Held a lot of realism."

"Indeed," Heleina stated. "Real witches never advertise they are witches. They heavily guard their secrets."

"My grandmother never advertised," Winifred replied. "But she did bring many under her control."

Heleina laughed. "Actually, quite easy to do. Seduce a man, tarnish his reputation, and boom … you have a pawn at your service."

Winifred nodded.

"How many men did you lure?" Heleina asked.

"Lost count, but I do have a keepsake." Winifred stood. After placing her cup on the table, she entered the living room, selecting a decorative box from a nearby shelf. Sitting back down, she gently caressed the top, handing it to old woman.

Heleina cautiously removed the top and sighed, performing the sign of the cross. "May god bless this poor, innocent child."

"What is it?" Grant asked.

Heleina frowned. "You witnessed this?"

Winifred nodded. "Many times."

Grant peeked into the box and sighed. A blue pacifier, almost new looking, sat cuddled between several cotton balls.

"I carry it always," Winifred whispered. "To remind me."

"I don't believe you will ever need reminding, child," Heleina replied. "These are memories you will carry to your grave and beyond. What did you do with the other ones."

Winifred sighed, understanding the implication. "Buried them."

Grant gently picked up the box, entered the apartment, and placed it back on the shelf. With his back to the women, he whispered, "We're gonna help you, Winifred. But we must be cautious."

"Demons have power." Heleina finished her coffee. "But their power is limited. You say he visits when you are most happy?"

Winifred nodded.

"Tells me you carry guilt," Heleina replied. "Perhaps you believe you were at fault. But a child is never at fault."

"I allowed it to happen." Winifred wiped her eyes. "I allowed my friend to die. I should have listened to Pam and we should have left."

"Who died?" Heleina asked.

"Deb."

"How many girls were there?" Heleina asked.

"Four," Winifred replied. "Me, Pam, Diana, and Deb."

"How odd," Heleina whispered.

"Why is it odd?" Grant asked.

"Witches find power in the holy number of three ... the three phases of the moon, the Holy Trinity, the Triple Goddess. The number four is associated with the holy spirit of stabilization, hard work, godly harmony. Why would your grandmother train four at the same time? Unless ..."

"Unless what?" Grant asked.

"Unless Winifred was to take her grandmother's place as High Priestess. Did you grandmother run the coven?"

Winifred nodded.

Heleina shook her head and sighed. "My god."

"What?" Grant asked.

"At what age did *he* take you?" Heleina asked.

"Fifteen ... in my grandmother's attic."

"Take what?" Grant asked.

Heleina stood and touched the railing. "How many times were you pregnant?"

"Once," Winifred replied.

"Well, thank the lord for that. Was *he* the father?"

"Not sure, happened after one of the festivals," Winifred replied.

"Oh … those glorious festivals. I can still feel the cool air on my naked skin," Heleina stated. "Wild men and crazy women. All bouncing on top of each other. Mad with desire, wicked desire. Drugs, alcohol … did she constantly drug you?"

Winifred chuckled. "Kinda sounds like you were there."

"It's the same everywhere," Heleina replied. "It's the same."

"We found the perfect place," Grant said, "for the exorcism."

Heleina nodded.

Eight

THE COOL AIR seemed to chill their souls. Leaves rustled as the breeze struggled against the branches. An owl hooted and a wolf howled. For some odd reason, the night felt darker than normal.

Grant sighed, holding a bible close to his chest. "You okay Winifred?"

Winifred nodded.

"Now what?" Caroline asked, clinging to Tom's arm.

"We enter," Heleina replied. "But allow me to go first."

The old brick structure stood solemn and tall as if challenging a person to enter. Dark shadows embraced the sharp edges as vines fought to cling tight. Something moved within the leaves making the castle come alive.

Tom pulled out a large key, dangling it on the hoop for just a second before unlocking the large, thick door. He pushed and the squeak echoed throughout the trees.

Heleina shined her light into the vacant room. She entered and her footfalls vibrated with each step. The entryway was not small by any means. Double stairs leading up before splitting into different directions greeted them. Baren floors and walls gave the place an eerie feel as if the devil, himself, would step up at any moment and personally welcome them to his humble abode.

"This place is creepy," Caroline whispered.

"Hello?" Grant yelled, his words repeating before fading. "No one home."

"Please stay down here," Heleina whispered. "And remain quiet."

Pulling something from her pocket, she lit the end, blowing out the flames. The smoke trailed up to the silent ceiling many feet above, fading into nothing. She waved her hand through the air, chanting a prayer, and the thin cloud followed. Taking the steps one at a time, she recited a few words.

"What's she doing?" Caroline asked.

"Cleansing the place," Grant replied. "We only want one spirit here tonight."

Winifred nodded.

"What do you mean by just one spirit?" Tom asked.

"If we're invoking Winifred's stalker to join us, we do not need him to bring any friends."

"Friends?" Caroline asked.

"We're ready to begin." Heleina said, returning through a side door. "This castle is not as big as you'd think."

"Big enough for me," Tom replied.

"There's a large room in the back that's perfect," Heleina stated. "Follow me."

The cloud trailed behind the woman as her light flickered down the hallway. Winifred shivered, allowing the memories to flood. Taking a step, she paused.

"What's wrong?" Grant asked.

"She's here," Heleina yelled from the other room.

"Who's here?" Caroline asked, clinging tighter to Tom's arm.

"My grandmother," Winifred whispered.

"How can *your* grandmother be here?" Caroline asked. "The woman has to be almost a hundred by now."

"She is here in spirit," Heleina replied from the doorway. "Very powerful woman." She pointed down the hall.

"Not a hundred, more like seventy-something." Winifred inched into the darkness in front of the others. At the end of the hall, she froze, staring at the dark shadows standing in the middle of the room. One was a woman. A woman wearing a cloak.

"You can face this," Heleina whispered. "You're more powerful than her."

"They will take me," Winifred replied. "And … I must go with them."

"Them?" Heleina asked. "I only see one."

"I see two." Winifred took a step.

"Wait." Grant reach for Winifred, but as his fingers brushed her arm, the bible burst into flames. "What the – !"

Winifred unzipped her jacket, dropping it to the floor. "He wants me."

"No!" Caroline screamed. "Oh my god, I can't move."

"I can't either," Tom stated. "My feet are glued to the floor."

"This is not supposed to happen," Heleina said.

The small group watched, feeling helpless, as Winifred stepped into the shadows, disappearing.

Winifred waited, allowing her mind to trail to more pleasant thoughts as the man with the bull's head violated her in ways she never believed possible. Gagging and coughing, she spit as he exploded inside her mouth. Binding her ankles with ropes, he suspended her from nothing, slapping her with something warm and wet. No part of her body was left untouched. No part of her soul was left untainted.

The dark place felt humid, reeking of rotting eggs, a dying ember of a life that once was. No sound other than the deep breaths of her tormentor filled her ears. Life was no longer in this place. The heart no longer pumped, encouraging the soul to walk. The mind no longer searched for answers. This was a reality that only evil could accept or understand.

A wicked cry echoed through the room. That was when Winifred understood, it was her cry for salvation that she had heard. "Please … may God … have mercy on my soul." Winifred's words escaped through short breaths as a large gash ripped down the side of her breast. She screamed and her world fell silent.

"Here she is," Carolina yelled. "Where's her damn clothes?"

"Over here," Tom hollered from the next room.

Flashlights flickered, creating bright silhouettes along the walls. Everyone was running, panicking.

"How in the hell?" Grant knelt next to Winifred, pulling her hair from her eyes.

Heleina recited The Lord's Prayer as the others attempted to cover Winifred with their jackets.

"She's bleeding," Caroline stated. "I brought no bandages."

"She needs a doctor," Tom replied.

Heleina knelt, holding a small vial of a glowing liquid in her hand. "Please, stand back." She opened the tiny bottle and gently dropped the elixir onto the open wound.

Winifred screamed and moaned.

Heleina recited a prayer but kept the drops flowing. "Pater noster, qui es in caelis, sanctificetur nomen tuum."

"What's she saying?" Caroline asked.

"It's Latin," Grant replied, "The Lord's Prayer."

Winifred moaned and lashed out. "Stop it. It burns."

"Yes, my dear." Heleina dropped more liquid. "It always hurts when we pull the evil out. When we pull *him* out." She continued to recite the words ending with, "Amen."

Winifred sat up, covering her naked chest with her arms. "What happened to me?"

"Here." Caroline handed her friend her clothes.

"It was your grandmother and her demon, the bull," Heleina replied. "How's your side."

"My side?" Winifred glanced under her arms, shaking her head. "My sides are fine."

"What?" Caroline lifted Winifred's arms, examining her flawless skin. "You're ... healed?"

"Wonderous stuff." Heleina placed the vial in her pocket.

"What is that stuff?" Tom asked, blinking.

"It's a plant from a place very far away," Heleina whispered. "Bafflesia root."

"Baff what?" Tom shook his head.

Heleina laughed.

Winifred stood, zipping up her jeans. "Why was I naked?"

"You don't remember?" Caroline asked.

"Not sure if I want to," Winifred replied.

"Are we ready to get started?" Heleina asked.

Winifred pulled her jacket around her neck and shivered. "Ready."

The floor vibrated. An old chandelier high above their heads shook. Dust fell, sprinkling around them.

"Earthquake?" Caroline asked.

Dark shadows stepped from the walls. The demon with the bull's head stood near the door. His arms cradling something, something small.

"What the hell is this?" Tom asked.

The bull stepped closer, a baby screamed from his arms.

"This cannot be real," Caroline whispered.

"Oh, it's real," Grant replied. "But we need to leave, now."

"I agree," Heleina stated, "I must regroup and think about this."

The shadows shimmered before forming into people wearing hooded cloaks. As the man sacrificed the crying baby, Winifred and her friends darted down the stairs and out the front door.

Tom stared at the castle, holding his breath as the chanting grew louder. "We need to run."

"That was some strange shit." Tom took another sip of his bourbon and frowned. "You honestly have *no* memory of what happened."

Winifred shook her head, glancing around the café. Holding her wine delicately between shaking fingers, she stared at the red swirls. "Honestly, no memory."

"It is probably better that you don't," Heleina replied.

"How did you get upstairs?" Caroline asked.

"She was left upstairs," Grant replied.

"Left?" Caroline repeated.

"She shifted between our world and his," Heleina stated. "It is not typical. That demon must be very powerful if he's able to slip between worlds so easily."

"And … how did your grandmother get here?" Caroline asked.

"She can do that," Winifred replied. "She can move objects without touching them too. When I was little, she would suddenly appear in the house when I had just left her in the barn."

"She can manipulate reality," Heleina added. "Only a witch that has walked with demons can do that."

"If Winifred's grandmother is going to interrupt each time we try to banish that … *thing* …" Caroline took a sip of her wine and frowned.

"This may be more than I can handle," Heleina replied. "We may need an exorcist."

"A priest?" Tom asked.

"A priest would be best." Heleina sipped on her coffee.

"Catholics," Winifred whispered.

"You have something against Catholics?" Heleina asked.

"My grandmother and those in her coven were Catholics. We had priests and nuns who attended Saturday's services."

"You'll need a *real* priest," Heleina replied. "Not like the ones you grew up with."

"And where do we find a *real* priest?" Tom asked.

"There's a church not far from where you live," Heleina stated. "I'll have to visit and ask a few questions."

Winifred stood and screamed. Holding out her hands, blood dripped on the table.

"Grant," Heleina yelled. "They are here."

Winifred's back cracked as she stood up straighter, eyes wide, mouth taught. "You shall not succeed," a deep voice stated. "I shall keep her in my maze … for all eternity."

"Who are you?" Heleina asked.

"I am Malus," the voice replied.

"From the Endless Maze?" Heleina asked.

"I am who I am," the voice said as blood oozed from Winifred's eyes.

Several customers stood, backing away. The waiter dropped his tray, shattering empty glasses.

"What do we do?" Caroline asked, taking a step toward the door.

"I will take her now," the voice demanded.

Heleina held up the small bottle with the glowing liquid. After yanking out the cork, she splashed the remaining drops on Winifred's face and yelled, "The Soul of Christ. Water from his side. Passion of God strengthens us and banishes you. Deliver this woman, oh lord."

Winifred screamed, falling to her knees. The room vibrated, the floor rolled as if nothing more than an ocean wave. The lights flickered, and a woman near the back of the café screamed, before dropping to the floor. A man jerked back and forth as if being pulled by an invisible hand. Raising several feet into the air, the man yelped as his body smashed into the wall. Several chairs flew across the room, crashing on top of tables. Patrons screamed, many ran into the street.

Heleina held up her necklace, a cross, yelling out the words of banishment.

Grant helped Winifred to her feet. "You okay?"

"I'm fine," she replied. "What's happening?"

"I think your demon is here," he whispered.

"This is very wrong," she stated. "He's following me, and we're risking everyone's safety. I need to leave."

The room settled, but a few bottles continued to rattle on the shelves. The waiter picked up the chairs, pushing them back in place as if this was a normal occurrence. Caroline tugged on Tom's sleeve as Heleina gathered her things.

"I believe it is time for me to take Winifred home," Grant stated.

"No," Heleina replied. "We must go directly to the church."

The church was not a church but a mini cathedral with many small turrets reaching high and into the sky, mimicking praying hands. Birds sang as they rested on colorful windowsills. With an empty parking lot and no outside lights, the place seemed abandoned.

"Do you think someone is here?" Caroline asked.

"There's always someone here." Heleina aimed for the double doors.

A large statue of Mother Mary decorated the entrance. As Winifred passed, Mary's head tilted, eyes following.

"You're being watched," Caroline whispered.

"What?" Heleina asked.

"That statue." Caroline pointed. "It is watching us."

Heleina stopped and turned. As her eyes swept across the lovely garden, the hands of the mother dropped to her side. "Ignore it."

"That thing just moved!" Tom stated, backing away.

"Ignore it," Heleina repeated. "You will only give him strength. Nothing moved. It's only in our minds. Do not permit him entry."

"I never did." Caroline gave the sign of the cross and closed her eyes.

"Neither did I," Grant stated.

Winifred opened one of the large doors and stepped inside. As she entered, Mother Mary raised her hands in prayer.

"See," Heleina whispered. "Ignore him."

A red carpet guided the visitor to the front of the church. Many empty rows filled the nave.

"This place is huge," Tom stated.

"You've never been in a Catholic church before?" Grant asked.

Tom shook his head.

"Older Catholic churches are made in the shape of a cross," Grant added. "Some of the newer ones are not. The apse or altar is up front. We're standing in the nave. To our right is called the Epistle Side and to the left is the Gospel Side."

Winifred paused near the back to light a candle and say a small prayer.

Heleina continued to the altar. She gave the sign of the cross and knelt. Pulling out her rosary, she kissed it before saying a short prayer.

A man wearing all black, but with a small white collar, entered from a side room. He paused, glancing at each before speaking. "I know why you have come."

"How can he know why we're here?" Tom whispered.

Grant shook his head.

Heleina stood and faced the man in black. "Father, we need help."

The man glanced at the double doors and then at Winifred. "He cannot enter. You are safe here. But I cannot guarantee anything when you leave."

"It must be excised," Heleina said.

The priest nodded. "Understood, however, we cannot, not without permission from the diocese. It must be validated."

"Like the people in the café?" Tom asked. "What do you mean by validated? How much proof must we have? Your damn statue out front moved."

"The devil takes many forms," the priest replied. "You must not be deceived."

"What must we do?" Heleina asked. "She cannot return home."

"You cannot remain here," the Father replied. "We lock up after ten."

"Do demons go home after ten?" Tom asked. "Bullshit!"

The priest's eyes studied Tom as if dissecting him. "I am not an exorcist."

"Is there one close?" Tom asked. "How do we order one? Do you have a catalog we can look through?"

"Tom …" Grant pulled on his arm.

Tom pushed his friend away. "I still say this is all bullshit and fake. You're afraid."

"I am not afraid of a demon," the priest replied. "But I am not trained in the art of banishing them."

"Then who is?" Tom's voice raised as did his hands.

"I am," a woman's voice echoed through the building.

"Who said that?" Tom asked, swirling around.

A nun, darker than a midnight sky with no moon and wearing a traditional black habit, stepped out from the shadows. Where she came from was a mystery. "I am Mother Hildegard. It is nice to meet you."

"Where did you come from?" Tom asked, glancing behind her.

"Where did I come from?" Mother Hildegard laughed. "From my mother of course. Where did you come from?"

Tom smiled, shaking his head.

"Father …" Mother Hildegard nodded at the priest.

The Father remained quiet.

"I am trained and authorized to banish demons," the nun said, glancing at Winifred. "My, my, you are favored by him, and he *will* take you."

Winifred wiped her eyes.

"When did he first violate you, my child," the mother asked.

"Fifteen …"

"A ripe young age for a woman," Mother Hildegard whispered. "Fifteen, the trinity of our essence." The woman held up her hand. "We have five fingers on each hand. We have five toes on each foot. The spirituality of five represents the human condition."

"Condition?" Tom repeated.

"Yes …" Mother Hildegard nodded. "Humans must be free, balanced, acceptable to change, understand versatility, and have a deep curiosity for life. If he took you at fifteen, he has stolen your freedom, offset the scales that will no longer balance, hidden your ability to mature … change from child to adult, and created an unstructured path for you to walk, not the path destined by God. He also curbed your curiosity of the world, making you afraid to seek the truth. Seek God and all his glory."

"The energy of five is adaptable," Heleina replied. "Our life changes that balance on the horizon of existence and can be altered. The path well taken can be lit."

"That is true," the mother whispered, "although dangerous. The veil between realities is discriminate. A violation of the most vulgar. The sexual sensations and wage for gratification will be most difficult to ignore."

"What is she talking about?" Caroline asked. "Sex? Gratification?"

"Demons use sexual pleasures to hold a woman hostage," Grant replied. "The satisfaction from a demon encounter is very intense. No man will ever please Winifred as the demon has for years."

"What the fuck are you talking about?" Tom asked, waving his hands. "There is no way Winifred takes pleasure from what happened in that castle."

"The journey will be hard, especially when seeing the destination." Heleina sighed. "Life doesn't rush, but humans push. Winifred must be willing to confront her future, no matter what her past holds."

"As I said ..." – Winifred held up her hands – "... it's too dangerous for me to be around any of you. I should leave."

"No!" Caroline yelled. "We have to stop this."

"Five is associated with grace," the priest said. His words were not expected, which made everyone jump.

Mother Hildegard took a deep breath and frowned. "Yes, it is associated with grace, but what grace did her demon show? Do you know his name, my child?"

"Malus of the Endless Maze," Heleina replied.

The mother massaged her hands as her eyes raised to the ceiling. After a few moments of silence, she chuckled. "The Endless Maze."

"What's so important about this maze?" Tom asked.

"Will Winifred have to travel this maze?" Caroline asked.

"Winifred." Mother Hildegard stepped closer. "How many of you were there?"

"How many of what?" Caroline asked.

Winifred wiped her eyes with the back of her hands. "There were four of us, but Deb died."

"How did she die?" the woman asked.

"It was during a ceremony," Winifred replied. "One of the overnight ones. The next morning, I found her by a tree. She was slumped over. Blood everywhere. I held her until they came for her.

I don't know what happened to her body or if there was a funeral. No one ever talked about it after that night. It was as if Deb never existed."

Mother Hildegard nodded. "You will need to walk that path along with the other three."

"Deb is dead," Caroline yelled. "Didn't you hear what she just said? Tree? Slumped?"

"I heard her." Mother Hildegard smiled. "But Deb is only non-existent in our realm. Not his. Who are the other girls?"

"Pam and Diana," Winifred replied.

"I will need their full names," the mother said. "In the meantime, you may sleep in our parlor. He cannot enter the house of God."

"Where is this path?" Tom asked.

"Hell," Grant replied, sighing.

"I will go with her," Heleina added.

"As will I," Mother Hildegard stated.

"As will the rest of us." Caroline crossed her arms.

"We'll what?" Tom's eyes widened.

Nine

"WHAT DOES A person need in order to enter Hell?" Caroline asked, opening drawers and searching through the odd contents. "How do we prepare for such a thing?"

Winifred shook her head.

Tom shrugged.

"This room is small." Grant glanced out a window. "Will you be able to sleep tonight?"

"Knowing I won't have a visitor?" Winifred replied. "Like a baby."

Grant smiled, hugging her.

"Okay team …" Heleina entered with her arms full. "I have a few things for everyone."

"Gifts?" Caroline asked.

"No," Heleina replied, "necessities." Holding out her hand, several beaded strands dangled from her arm. "Rosary for each."

"I had one of these as a child," Caroline stated, being the first to accept one.

"I can't use mine?" Grant asked.

"Rather you didn't," Heleina replied. "Don't want you to lose yours. It was your great-grandfather's."

Grant nodded, accepting a pure black strand.

Tom stepped closer and stared at the beads. "I'm not Catholic."

"Doesn't matter," Heleina replied. "These are for protection, not beliefs."

"Beads?" Tom sighed.

"Beads," Heleina replied, shaking her arm. A pure white strand remained alone, and Heleina again shook her arm. "Winifred, this one is for you."

Winifred reached out and gently touched the small oblong beads. "This thing does not hold fond memories."

"I understand," Heleina replied, "but our journey is not about memories but safety. These will protect you."

Winifred nodded, accepting the strand.

"Do we wear them?" Tom asked, placing his over his head.

"You can," Heleina replied, "or drop them in your pocket. As long as they are with you at all times."

Tom shrugged, pulling his back over his head.

"Next, a small vial for each," Heleina stated, "holy water. Just blessed."

"Thank you." Caroline smiled, accepting hers.

"And this." Heleina held up several sheets of paper. "Prayers. The best protection of all. I recommend you select your favorites and memorize them."

"This is it?" Tom asked.

"Were you expecting swords or guns or armor?" Heleina asked. "We will be in the spiritual world. Cardinal weapons will be mostly useless."

Tom twirled his beads around his fingers and laughed.

"And how do we enter this realm?" Caroline asked, squinting at Tom.

"Very carefully," Heleina replied. "As for now, Winifred needs to sleep. You all need to sleep. Go home, eat, and rest. Tomorrow will be a full day … a spiritual lifetime."

Winifred woke to the twirping of birds and bright rays filling the room. The pink walls and fluffy comforter, full and warm, created a feeling of home. Taking a whiff, she sighed.

Bacon and pancakes?

She stood and stretched. Her school jumper resting over a chair gave her reason to pause.

My school uniform?

Sliding off her gown, she dressed, as if only twelve again. Picking up her large, brown bear, she hugged it close.

"Brownie, I've missed you."

"Winni?"

"Mom?"

"We don't want to be late, come eat."

Winifred tied her shoes before darting down the hall. She stopped as her eyes fell on her brothers. John David glanced up briefly from the table before shoving a bite into his mouth. Alexander picked up his water, taking a sip. And her little brother, William, waved at her.

"Mom?" Winifred whispered. "What's going on?"

"Um, breakfast?" her mother replied. "Sit and eat. We leave in ten."

Winifred's chair next to William was empty. She slid in as her mother sat a plate in front of her.

"Sleepyhead," John David stated.

"Couldn't wake up?" Alexander asked. "Probably stayed up too late talking on the phone."

The boys darted from the table, grabbing their packs. Winifred gulped down her juice before following them out the door. Her mother's old Ford sat in the driveway, looking new. She pulled open the back door and slid onto the seat. The tuck-n-roll reminded Winifred of a time long past.

"Winni?" her mother stated, slipping behind the wheel. "You okay? You're acting funny. Are you coming down with something?"

"Maybe," Winifred whispered. "But I'm okay."

As the car wound through the small neighborhood, Winifred studied the houses. They were just as she remembered. There was the red one. No one understood why the owner painted it red, but there it was. And over there was the old tree.

"I'm dropping you off at school today cuz I have to stop by the church." Her mother pulled the car into an empty spot.

The boys jumped out, running to the open doors. A nun wearing a black habit nodded as they entered.

"You sure you're okay?" her mother asked.

"Fine." Winifred slammed the door.

The nun nodded at Winifred as she entered. The long hallway seemed longer today. As the bell dinged, she slid onto her seat. English was her first class.

"Hey." Deb touched her arm.

"Winifred jumped, holding back a scream.

"You okay?" Deb asked. "You're acting like you just saw a ghost or something."

Winifred nodded.

"Class …" a young nun wearing blue spoke from up front. "We're reading …"

Classes progressed as usual. At lunch, Winifred stared at her friends.

"I feel funny," Diana whispered.

"I do too," Pam replied. "It's like I'm missing something or forgetting something important."

"Not me." Deb took a bite of her sandwich. "I feel fine."

"What about you, Winni?" Pam asked.

"Somethings not right," she replied. "I don't think we're supposed to be here."

"What do you mean?" Deb asked.

"I think you're right," Diana whispered. "It's as if I woke up in a dream. I mean … my room, my aunt … all was normal, but then again not normal."

Deb reached for her juice, shaking her head. "You're all nuts."

The bell rang. The girls stood and a low, deep rumble echoed through their ears.

"What's that?" Pam asked.

The school's sirens blared. Students ran to the windows.

"Get under the tables," a nun yelled.

"Hurry," another screamed.

A bright light filled the room, silence deafening their senses. The floor wobbled as the windows exploded. Dirt and heat filled the air.

Winifred screamed as a wave of bricks slammed her against a wall.

"What the fuck was that?" Tom asked, wiping his eyes.

Heleina straightened out her hair, gasping.

Grant reached for Winifred.

"Who are you?" Caroline asked.

Winifred stared at her friends from her previous life, tears filling their eyes. The girls hugged as Deb nestled between them.

"Must be Winifred's old friends," Tom stated.

Winifred nodded.

"Winni?" Deb yelled. "It's been so long."

"Yes, it has," Winifred replied.

"What is this place?" Diana asked. "Where are we?"

Tall green hedges with a slight purple hue surrounded them. The grass, not short but not tall, felt smooth as if they were sitting on a velvet cushion. Dark yellowish clouds rolled slowly overhead, creating vague shadows.

Tom stood and glanced around. "I'm Tom by the way."

Caroline reached out her hand. "I'm Caroline."

"Hi, Grant here, and this is my mother, Heleina." He nodded to the woman.

"I'm Pam, and this is Diana and Deb. I guess you know Winni already?"

"It's nice to meet you," Tom replied.

"I'm not sure if anyone has noticed," Heleina said, "but the girls all look to be about twelve or thirteen years old."

"I'm fourteen," Deb stated.

"Deb," Diana replied, "you died."

"Very funny." Deb frowned.

Everyone stared at her, their eyes darkening with creases.

"You're serious?" Deb asked.

Winifred nodded. "You died at the ceremony."

"It was October, *All Hallows Eve,*" Pam added. "Winni was the one to find you."

"Then how am I here?" Deb stood, brushing off her pants.

"We're not sure where *here* is," Heleina replied. "Tom, do you see a way out?"

"Not yet." Tom followed the hedge that was the shape of a large rectangle. "Hello?"

No answer. All remained quiet.

"So what do we do now?" Caroline asked.

"You have children," Deb stated to Diana. "You were pregnant at Pam's wedding."

"How could you possibly know that?" Diana asked.

Deb shook her head. "Have no idea, but I remember your dress, the colors, you hugging each other and crying. And you ..." – Deb pointed at Winifred – "... you were leaving. They were sad."

"I joined the Army," Winifred replied. "Was shipped off to Germany."

"It's where she met us," Caroline added.

"How can I know all of this if I'm only fourteen?" Deb asked.

"Because you are not fourteen," Heleina replied. "Your spirit lives in a different dimension than ours."

"But ... how did I get here?" Deb asked.

"I'm not sure yet," Heleina replied. "But I have my suspicions."

"There's a gate over here," Tom yelled from across the empty glade.

The small group stood, brushing off their clothes. The grass seemed to want to cling as if full of static electricity. Winifred took a step and the ground moaned.

"What was that?" Winifred asked.

"Come again?" Carolina stated.

Winifred took another step and again the ground moaned.

"This is just odd," Pam said.

Taking a few more steps, the ground raised and lowered as if they were standing on a person's chest.

"I don't know about this," Diana whispered. "Something is very wrong."

"What's the last thing you remember?" Heleina asked. "Anyone, what is the last thing you remember? Before waking up here."

"I was in school," Winifred replied.

"Me too," Deb added.

"Yes, we were in school," Diana stated. "And something happened."

"Yes," Winifred replied, "an explosion."

"No, a bomb." Pam shook her head. "An atomic bomb. A bright light and the windows shattered."

"Lots of heat," Deb added.

"I thought it was a dream," Caroline said.

"What school were you at, Caroline?" Heleina asked.

"My old grammar school," she replied. "We were just finishing lunch when the light hit."

"I think we all had the same dream," Grant said.

"It wasn't a dream," Heleina replied. "Just different realities."

The small group stared at the iron gate. A gate with carved angels and demons on the top. Beyond, a thick mist blocked their view.

"Do we dare walk into that mist?" Tom asked.

"I don't believe we're to stay here." Heleina shoved on the gate.

The sound of metal scraping against metal filled the air. Tom took a step, and their world fell dark.

Winifred stood at the end of the bed, listening as the machine beeped. Her eyes trailed along the slender hoses that seemed to penetrate her mother in all the wrong places. Shadows creased the blue blanket that covered the woman. A woman who looked old and frail.

"It won't be much longer." A nurse adjusted a few things. "Her breathing is quite irregular."

A young girl of about twelve stepped closer. "Grandma?" she whispered.

"She won't answer you," a man replied. He stood behind the girl, gently touching her shoulder as if to comfort.

A tear formed in Winifred's eye. She wiped as another followed.

"It'll be okay," the man stated. "It's just her time."

"Mom?" Winifred whispered. "Mom, I'm so sorry."

Winifred leaned closer, gently caressing the woman's foot.

Without opening her eyes, the woman slightly raised her hand.

"Ma'am," the nurse whispered, "are you in pain?"

A slight moan escaped the woman's lips.

"She's hurting," the young girl stated. "Dad, can you make it stop?"

The urge to run to her mother tugged deep at Winifred's soul, but her feet refused to move. She reached out to touch the young girl, but her hand fell through her image.

"I wonder if Mom is here with us now?" the girl asked.

"I'm sure she is," the man replied.

"Should I say a prayer?" the girl asked.

"If it would make you feel better," he replied.

Two men entered, both priests and carrying a bible. They stood next to the dying woman, gently touching her forehead and hands, leaving a slight oily smudge.

"In the name of the Father, Son, and ..." the priests continued their prayers.

The little girl knelt, repeating the words.

The woman sat up. No longer looking aged and worn, she was now youthful and strong.

Winifred took a step back. "Mom?"

"Winni?" her mother stated, her spirit flowing easily through the priest. "What in the name of Hell are you doing here?"

"I don't know," Winifred replied.

"You always were a fool," her mother stated. "Nothing but a damn burden. Always trouble. If you had been a boy, life would have been perfect."

"Mom?"

The woman stepped closer, ignoring the child and man. Her face darkened with each stride. "I should have left you to die when you were born."

"What are you talking about?" Winifred whispered.

"You were spawned from the most evil, always plaguing, always taunting."

"I was what?"

"Your father … he came from the deepest pits."

"My father was a demon?"

Her mother laughed. The bed shook as she cackled and screamed. Taking another step, her face ignited, flames bursting, engulfing. The heat overwhelming.

Winifred took another step back. "This is not real."

"Oh, it's real," her mother yelled. "So very real."

Several hands rose up from the bed, grabbing her mother's arms and legs. As her mother screamed, the hands pulled her down as if the woman was melting into the abyss. A crevasse opened. With rivers of red and orange and yellow, her mother slowly fell. As she floated into the endless sea of dread, her eyes fixed on Winifred.

A loud swooshing filled the room as the priests completed their prayers. They left, and the little girl stood, kissing her grandmother's hand before slowly walking out of the room.

The man bent down and kissed the woman on the forehead. "Love you, Mom," he whispered.

"Mom?" Winifred repeated. *But that was my mother.*

The man left and the nurse pulled the sheet over the woman's head. "Winifred June Taggart, your husband died in this room only a year ago."

Winifred screamed. "That is not me!" she yelled. "That is not me."

Music blared through Winifred's ears as her fingers drummed to the beat. The man sitting next to her kept adjusting from one hip to the other. She smiled at the woman sitting on her other side who offered her a mint. Winifred adjusted the earphones, feeling the plane lower a little.

"Not much farther," the woman stated.

Winifred pulled out her earbuds and smiled. "Pardon?"

"I said not much farther," the woman replied. "We're almost there."

The stewardess paused, holding out a trash bag.

The woman smiled as she dropped her cup and paper into the dark hole.

Winifred crossed her legs and sighed.

The stewardess stood straighter and the plane jerked slightly higher. Bright sun reflecting on the windows blocked Winifred's view. Again the plane jerked, and the *fasten seatbelt* light blinked.

"Sorry, folks," the captain stated, "seems we're hitting a little headwind. Please stay seated, the ride may be a little bumpy."

Winifred tightened her belt. Shoving the earbuds into a pocket, she sat back and sighed.

Another jilt only this time the plane rose several feet before dropping. The air, although nothing more than a breeze, felt harder than the ground. The engines roared before toning back. Again another jerk and air rushed into Winifred's face. She covered her eyes as the bright sun blinded her. The back of the seat that once pressed against her knees now felt empty and vacant. Slowly, she opened her eyes.

Nothing was in front of her but clouds.

The woman next to her remained silent. Winifred studied her a little closer and screamed. The woman was missing half her head. The man who kept shifting from hip to hip was gone.

Winifred took a deep breath and stared into the bright sun. Her last thought was how dangerous it was to stare directly into the afternoon rays.

Winifred stared into Grant's eyes as tears formed in hers.

"Holy sit!" Tom yelled. "Another one?"

"Damn," Pam stated. "How many times are we gonna die around here?"

"Perhaps until it is final," Heleina replied.

"Final?" Caroline repeated. "Oh, no … we're leaving." Caroline pushed on the gate and took a step.

Nothing happened.

"Let's go," Caroline yelled. "We have to leave now."

Slowly, they traversed the path where the heavy mist grew thicker, syrupy, and a sweet aroma and taste of sugar filled their senses. The ground softened, sucking in their feet.

Winifred screamed, flapping her wings.

The clicking sound grew louder.

White strands clung to her feet, her arms, her body. It was hard to breathe. Hard to move. Hard to see.

As the dark shadow grew deeper, the sweetness turned tart and foul. Hairy legs stepped closer followed by several more. Eyes, too many to count, glared at her.

Pam screamed as the arms held firm, wrapping her with a sticky white string. Grant remained still, covered in a blanket of silk. Winifred couldn't tell where her other friends were hiding. Struggling to escape, the arms pulled her into a strong embrace, wrapping her in a white silk blanket. Taking a slow and steady breath, something long and sharp hit, sinking deep into her abdomen. One more stab, and her world fell dark.

Gasping and choking, Tom rolled as if urging the air to fill his lungs. Winifred knelt at his side, begging him to breathe. Grant and Heleina prayed.

"Shit, shit, shit," Tom whispered between breaths. "Holy shit. Get me the fuck outta here."

Heleina stood and held her rosary over her head. She prayed, almost whispering to herself. Taking a deep breath, she nodded to the others. "Hold your beads in front of you."

"I don't have any beads," Deb stated.

"Neither do I," Pam added.

Heleina yanked on her rosary several times, breaking off a few for each. "Here, no law says you have to have a whole chain."

The girls held the beads close to their hearts.

Pam cried as she slowly recited the prayer. "I believe in God, the Father almighty ..."

"Hail Mary, full of grace ..." Diana whispered.

"Let me think," Heleina stated. "Give me a moment."

The group huddled, some praying, some listening.

"I've got it," Heleina yelled. "A single line behind me."

They lined up, Grant at the end, Deb behind Heleina.

"I have the holy water," Heleina said. "I will cleanse our path."

Before she took a step, Heleina allowed a single drop of the purified water to hit the dry soil. As they slowly progressed along the path that dissolved into the growing mist, their consciousness, their inner essence, remained solid and firm.

"Might be slow moving," Tom stated, "but at least we're still here."

"Amen to that," Winifred whispered, not wanting to jinx anything.

The cool mist felt all-encompassing as if being caressed by a watchful parent. Obviously, the demon was close. However, he could not touch. Not as long as the path was cleansed.

"The weather is rather odd around here," a voice said from within the shadows. "Wouldn't you prefer to join me here, where it's warm and sunny?"

"Ignore him," Heleina stated. "Do not fall for his antics."

"If I'm already dead," Deb added, "why can't I go? I'm tired and hungry."

"You four created the pack when young. Witches are taught in groups, sometimes mimicking the four corners of the Earth. Four is stable and secure. A table with four legs or a shed with four walls. Earth, air, water, and fire. You four are powerful when together. Separate, you lose what strength you have."

"Wait a minute," Winifred whispered.

Heleina held the small vial, pausing. "What are you thinking?"

"Fire," Winifred stated. "We were blown up with fire."

"Yes, at the school," Pam replied.

"Next," Caroline added, "the plane crash … air."

"But the spider and old age," Grant stated, "those don't fit."

"Ashes to ashes, dust to dust," Tom replied. "It does fit. Death of a body can represent the Earth. We turn back to dirt when we die."

"The spider, how could that possibly represent water?" Deb asked. A spider's web is silk. More of a material substance than water."

"True," Heleina replied. "Perhaps water has not happened yet."

"Bullshit!" Tom yelled from the back. "You, Heleina, are dropping water now."

"Let's think about this," Grant stated. "The universe was supposedly created from the primordial waters of chaos, and our world formed from the four essential elements. What could that mean? Earth, air, fire, and water, all four elements are embodied by God. What are we not seeing?"

"This is a maze," Heleina stated. "A maze can also be a puzzle."

"Are we walking on that maze now?" Diana asked.

"Each of the challenges can be considered an answer to a riddle," Winifred replied.

"A riddle?" Tom repeated. "We were blown up, died of old age, suffered a plane crash, and had our insides sucked out from a spider. What kind of a sick riddle is that?"

"I studied dreams in college," Pam stated. "I remember a few. But these concepts do seem to fit. Dreaming of an explosion or seeing a bomb means we need to follow our emotions. Dying is symbolic of the end of a cycle and a fresh start. A crash ... the plane ... could mean one needs to re-examine their life. Perhaps make a change. Re-examine one's goals."

"The last one?" Grant asked.

"Spiders symbolize what is happening during our waking lives, our anxieties, our stresses."

"Okay," Grant replied, "we have emotions, a cycle, goals, and anxieties. What would these have to do with Malus?"

"The angels of Heaven have ranks," Winifred stated.

"What's your point?" Deb asked.

"Maybe Hell has ranks for their demons," Winifred replied.

"Now that is an interesting concept." Heleina tapped her chin. "What if we were not in Hell but inside Malus' thoughts?"

"If true, we could ..." Winifred paused, glancing around.

"What is it?" Heleina asked.

"Where's Mother Hildegard?" Winifred whispered.

Ten

BIRDS CHIRPED AS early shadows danced across the floor. Winifred sat up and glanced around. The room with just a couch and small table remained quiet and calm. She was still in her clothes from the previous night. Her shoes were by the door. Pulling off the blanket, she stood. With her mind twirling through the possibilities, a slight knock gave her a moment of pause. The knock came again.

"Winifred?" a soft voice asked. "You awake?"

Winifred cracked the door and peeked out.

Mother Hildegard's large smile greeted her. "I thought you could join us for breakfast."

Winifred nodded. "Give me a moment." Slipping on her shoes felt normal and comforting. Something she could relate to.

"You okay?" Mother Hildegard asked.

"I think so." Winifred glanced out the window. "Had a really odd dream, that's all."

"Oh?"

"Four nightmares all in one night," Winifred replied. "I'm quite happy to be awake."

"Perhaps a full tummy will help," Mother Hildegard added.

"It felt so real."

"I'm sure it did."

Winifred followed the nun through the various halls, stopping where the Father stood, smiling.

"You have a call and can take it in my office," he said.

"May I?" she glanced at the nun.

"Of course," the mother stated. "Join us when you're ready. The kitchen is just through that door."

Winifred followed the Father to a small room. "Thank you."

He smiled.

"Hello?" Winifred asked.

"Winifred? It's Caroline. I'm sorry to bother you and all, but did you have a weird dream last night?"

"More of a nightmare. Why?"

"Tom woke up screaming. I called Grant and we all had the same dream."

"And what was your dream?"

"More like several," Caroline replied. "First an atomic explosion, then we watched ourselves die and become … oh, I don't know … a ghost? And a plane crash and a spider web."

"Yep, had the same ones."

"Then maybe it wasn't a dream," Mother Hildegard said from the hallway.

Winifred glanced up, meeting the mother's odd grin.

"I didn't mean to listen to your private conversation," the mother stated, "and I'm not. Something just told me you five were taken on a little journey last night."

"A journey?" Winifred whispered.

"Perhaps your friends could join us and we could talk?" Mother Hildegard replied.

"Tell her, yes," Caroline yelled through the phone.

The small office was a little crowded. Tom and Grant stood behind three chairs, each with a woman, and each facing a small desk. Behind the desk sat Mother Hildegard. The room seemed quiet and almost challenging as if the small group was in trouble and being sequestered by the head nun.

Mother Hildegard sighed deeply, entwining her fingers. "Good evening."

"Evening, Mother," Winifred replied.

"I'm not Catholic," Tom stated. "Does that matter?"

"I'm not either, not really," Caroline replied, "just when a kid."

"Doesn't matter what denomination you may or may not be." The mother smiled. "What matters is what is in here … – she tapped her heart – "… or what is in here …" – she pointed to her head. The Lord works in mysterious ways, my friends. Very mysterious."

"As do demons," Winifred replied.

"Unfortunately, my child, your birth was probably preordained. Ordered from the depths. Perhaps, your true father was from the pits." The mother frowned. "It happens when the women are deep in witchcraft."

Heleina nodded. "I am very spiritual." She glanced at the ceiling and closed her eyes. "I believe in a higher power. I also believe in the dark side. What it is exactly or where it comes from, now that is a different question."

"Some will say that demons are aliens from another dimension." Tom crossed his arms.

"I've heard that before," the mother replied. "It could hold merit. Demons are definitely from a separate realm. A boundary the living should never cross."

"It isn't a pleasant experience," Caroline replied. "Now that I've tasted it."

"The actual happenings of your dream last night –" the mother started to say.

"Nightmares …" Tom added the word so harshly that everyone jumped a little.

Mother Hildegard chuckled. "Nightmare … but it may hold a few clues."

"Clues?" Heleina replied.

The mother nodded. "What do you know about the Endless Maze?"

"It's a path through Hell that is monitored by Malus," Heleina stated. "Although, I understand that Baphomet may also be involved."

"Baphomet is about twelve feet tall and was a human once, except for his head … he has a bull's head now." The mother paused for just a moment, glaring at Winifred. "Does that sound familiar?"

Winifred's eyes widened.

"In many covens, the witches will appoint someone to represent Baphomet. However, that evil demon will always mate with the young girls that are introduced to the coven from birth. At what age did he take you, Winifred?"

"Fifteen," she whispered.

The mother shrugged. "Another name for the Endless Maze is the abyss," Mother Hildegard whispered, loudly.

"You mean, Satan?" Tom asked.

"No," Grant replied, "Satan was once an angel for God who was eventually cast into Hell as punishment. Baphomet is a demon lord. Very powerful in all realms."

"Correct," the mother replied. "And why it's so easy for him to cross into our plane of existence."

"So, Baphomet is in charge and rules over Malus?" Caroline asked.

"Correct again. Therefore we are banishing two demons not just one." The mother laughed.

"Two?!" Tom repeated more as a statement than a question. "What the fuck."

"You can say that again," the mother replied.

"Then what do we do?" Tom asked. "Winifred cannot live with a demon raping her whenever he … it feels like it."

"No, she cannot," Mother Hildegard whispered. "But we'll ask for the help of Yeenoghu, a lord demon."

"You, a nun, a Catholic nun will ask a demon for help?" Heleina asked.

The mother chuckled again. "Whether we try to exorcise the demon ourselves or ask another demon for help, what is the difference? Either way, we are interacting with the satanic realm. Yeenoghu and Baphomet are mortal enemies. Yeenoghu would do anything to take a strike and make points."

"Points?" Tom asked.

"There is a war raging within the pits of the abyss. With the veil thinning between our realms, the demons are fighting to be in control."

"You want us to invite Yeenoghu here?" Tom asked. "To our world?"

"No," the mother replied. "I want us to go to him."

"Holy shit," Caroline whispered.

The sound of keys jingling against an aged ring echoed through the arches. Pedestals that held up the decorative ceiling embraced the thin glass windows that had withstood the lashes of time. Red brick, worn from many footsteps, rolled across the floor and up the walls. The halls themselves were a maze inside this church.

Mother Hildegard stood solemnly next to a large wooden door with thick black hinges. Sliding in the key, the old door screeched in protest as she pushed.

"This door has been sealed for centuries," the mother whispered. "No one has entered, no one dared."

"Well …" – Tom snickered – "… are we not the lucky ones."

"Shh …" Caroline raised her finger to her lips. "Have a little respect."

The mother held up an old, oil lamp, allowing the light to show the way. "Please shut the door."

Grant leaned against the heavy wood and sighed. "Closed, Mother."

The narrow passage ended at a flight of stairs that led down. A circular path edging them into the darkness. The mother handed Grant the lamp and nodded for him to lead.

Grant smiled, taking the first step. "Careful," he coached, "narrow stairs."

Winifred followed Grant with Caroline close behind.

Heleina paused as the girls disappeared around the first bend. "I guess we're next."

"Yep," Tom replied, taking up the rear.

The path continued to wind down, deeper into the unknown. At the bottom, Grant took a few steps to allow the others to have room. Water dripped from somewhere as the aroma of staleness stiffened their senses.

"We are close." The mother took the lamp back from Grant. "Follow me."

The lower room was large with water dripping from the walls. Granite bricks, larger than a car, supported the base of the old church.

Winifred tried to see what was off in the distance, but only darkness filled her view.

"What is this place?" Tom asked.

"It was once the narthex," the mother replied. "The original entrance to the church, many years ago."

"People entered from down here?" Tom asked.

"The unbaptized but faithful would be restricted," the mother replied.

"Not a very nice thing to do," Tom stated.

"The church is famous for having a lot of not-very-nice practices," the mother replied.

Tom shrugged and Grant chuckled.

"Here we are." The mother stopped at another ancient-looking door.

"Where does this door go?" Tom asked.

"That is for you to discover." She inserted an old key that was larger than her hand.

The door resisted opening.

Grant stepped closer and pushed.

The door remained closed.

Grant motioned at Tom and they both pushed.

The door moved only slightly as a rush of hot wind escaped, slapping against their faces.

"Damn." Tom took a step back. "Is the place on fire?"

"Hell is always on fire," Mother Hildegard replied. Pulling out a small vial, she clamped her teeth over the cork and pulled. A slight *pop* echoed. "May the lord have mercy on our souls." She sprinkled a few drops on the door.

"I hope you brought more than just that tiny bottle of holy water with you," Tom stated. "I think we're gonna need a lot."

"Does everyone have their rosaries?" Heleina asked. "And … water?"

Hands raised and the beads swayed in the warm breeze.

"Good," the mother replied. "Mine are around my waist … and my neck … and in my pockets …"

"Nervous, are we?" Tom asked.

"Apprehensive," Mother Hildegard replied.

A strong whiff of sulfur seemed to be seeping from the walls. The path, uneven and rough, held a thin coating of something shiny, slippery, but then again, solid.

"Oh, no." Tom reached down, allowing his fingers to gently touch the liquid.

"What?" Caroline asked.

"This is mercury," he replied. "We must walk cautiously. We can't allow the fumes to enter our lungs."

"It's all over the place," Grant replied.

"Will it explode?" the mother asked, holding the lamp a little higher.

"No, but if it's disturbed, the fumes become deadly," Tom replied.

"Okay then," the mother stated, "we walk *very* slowly."

The small group inched their way down the narrow path, entering a larger chamber. They froze and stared. Only a few feet in front was a sea of mercury.

"We cannot swim in this stuff," Tom stated.

"I think there's a ledge of some kind," Grant replied, "over here."

"There must be a way through this," the mother stated. "I believe we are at the start of the Endless Maze."

"We cannot see through mercury," Tom added. "Not like water. We'll have to feel with our feet as we walk."

With each step, they slowly scooted along the wall. Not wanting to breathe in the poisonous fumes, they took small breaths as each step seemed like an eternity.

"We'll never get to the end at this rate," Caroline whispered.

"You'll never leave," a deep voice replied.

The mercury shimmered from inside the darkness, creating a hologram of colors.

The mother raised the lamp higher. "I can't see a thing. Who said that?"

"Winifred?" the deep voice whispered, ominously. "You have come to visit me? Have you been longing for my touch?"

"No," Winifred yelled. "Stay away."

A sinister laugh and the mercury rolled as if a blanket was spread across a bed.

"Just keep moving," the mother whispered.

An arched doorway that seemed to lead back the way they had just walked was a challenge to ignore. The path, clear and fresh and clean, was most enticing, inviting.

"This is not the way forward." Mother Hildegard shivered. "We must keep moving."

The mercury shimmered as if something was glowing from below. Waves rippled and the shiny liquid hummed. From somewhere deep inside, colorful lights lit the pool as if each hum had vibrated a different hue.

Winifred closed her eyes, feeling with her feet, ensuring that each step landed on a solid brick. Several times, her foot slipped, giving her a reason to move even slower. She could close her eyes, but she could not close her ears.

The humming grew louder as they approached another archway. Only this one was on the other side of the mercury pool. The entrance felt warm which was an obvious sign that perhaps they were on the right path. The mother raised the lamp higher, but the darkness was now as thick as the mercury.

"This sucks," Caroline stated. "What is that smell?"

"Steps …" Mother Hildegard inched her way out of the mercury and onto a clear path. "Thank, the lord."

"We are still under the church," Tom stated. "I don't think we're in Hell yet."

"Oh, we're in Hell," the mother replied. "We entered it as soon as we stepped down those stairs."

"Bullshit," Tom whispered. "Just under the fuck'en church no doubt."

As their feet slipped below the arch, the mercury vanished. But warm air still caressed and teased with each step.

"We're free from that shit," Tom stated, "but it's just as bad. It's as if the air is thick and moldable. Can I hold it?" Tom reached out and grabbed a handful of air. "I can. I can hold air."

"You can what?" Caroline asked.

"I can mold the air," he replied.

"No, you can't." She shrugged. "What is wrong with you?"

"Feel." Tom placed something soft and thick inside Caroline's hand.

"What the ...?" Caroline dropped the gooey substance, wiping her hands against her legs. "Don't do that!"

"It's weird stuff," Tom replied. "This air is thick."

"Stop playing with the air," Caroline yelled. "It's gross."

"It's shit," Grant replied.

"This is bullshit!" Tom yelled.

"No," Mother Hildegard stated, "this is shit. We're walking through a hall of human feces."

"Human what?" Winifred asked.

"We are in Hell," Heleina stated. "We left the room of mercury and are now feeling our way through shit. I can almost taste −"

"Oh my god," Caroline yelled.

"Augh!!!" Tom screamed. "I can taste it too."

"Keep your mouths closed," Heleina replied.

"Hold on to each other," Mother Hildegard stated. "We'll hurry through this section."

"No!" Heleina stated. "Stay on the path. Feel with your feet. None of this is real ... only in our minds."

"It feels and tastes real to me," Caroline stated.

"We would not be able to breathe in a room filled with shit." Tom replied. "It's all in our ..."

The smell and feeling of walking through the thickness vanished.

"... minds?" Tom finished his thought.

"Well ..." – the mother shrugged – "... that was indeed interesting. Shall we continue?"

The small group inched through the hall with only the lamp for guidance. Although the air was warm, the stench was gone and just a vague aroma of mildew lingered.

"I don't feel so good," Winifred stated.

"Me either," Caroline replied.

Winifred dropped to her knees, clutching her head. "It's that buzzing."

"No, it's a vibration." Caroline's eyes widened.

"I feel it too, almost like being electrocuted?" Grant asked.

The vibration started in their toes and fingers, inching its way along their nerves. The smooth transition created a ripple in time and reality as it sparked a rawness against the fibers of their inner essence. It was as if their souls had suddenly caught fire. Their minds begged for water. Their hearts longed for peace. A sharp razor had just scooted backward along their nerves, sending waves that rolled and tightened with each breath.

"I can't take this," Caroline yelled.

"What the hell?" Tom screamed.

Heleina curled into a ball, shoving her face into her knees.

Grant held his breath.

The mother took out the small vial, struggling to pull off the cork. At last, the *pop* echoed through their ears. She sprayed a few drops and whispered a few words.

The sensation ended just as quickly as it had started.

"Shit ..." Tom whispered, leaning against the wall.

Winifred felt weak and nauseated. The world had just rushed through her senses, deepening with each breath. "You okay, Caroline?" she asked.

"Yeah," Caroline replied.

"We have to keep moving," Heleina stated, struggling to stand.

"As I said," Tom stated, "you should have brought a wagon full of that special water."

A bright light dimmed their thoughts as the group tried to accept and understand their surroundings. After walking along the dark path for what seemed like forever, a bright light now challenged their passing.

"What is that?" Tom asked.

"Looks like a light," Heleina replied.

"I know that." Tom sighed, loudly. "But where's it coming from?"

"Could be from anywhere," Caroline added.

"Anywhere?" Tom shook his head. "This is just nuts. We're not succeeding in anything, other than to be tortured by some … *thing*."

"I believe that *is* the point," the mother replied.

Grant stretched and his cracking joints echoed around them.

Winifred giggled.

"Sorry," Grant whispered. "I feel stiff."

"We all feel stiff," Mother Hildegard added. "Let's keep walking."

As they approached the bright light, an ominous wall seemed to grow taller. Each step actually pushed the thing higher with deepening shadows that spread to eternity. A single white, wooden door stood precariously in front, blocking them, challenging them to dare cross the threshold.

"Do we dare?" Tom mused.

Mother Hildegard pulled out her small bottle of holy water and stared at it.

"How much is left?" Tom asked.

"Not much," the mother replied. "Maybe we should have brought a gallon after all."

Tom laughed. "Told, yah. Here, take mine."

Grant reached for the golden knob and turned it slightly. The door creaked as it opened. He glanced inside. "It's dark."

"Of course it's dark," Tom yelled. "This whole damn place is dark."

One at a time, they stepped across the threshold and into the blackening shadows. As the last one entered, the door slammed shut and disappeared.

"No going back," Caroline whispered.

The space beyond was not a hallway. Just a deep, dark void of nothingness.

"I feel funny." Winifred rubbed her arms and shivered.

"It's not really cold in here." Caroline now rubbed her arms. "But I feel it too."

"I feel nothing," Grant whispered.

Heleina paused and glanced around.

"What is it, Mother?" Grant asked.

"This place is not good for the soul," Heleina replied.

"No, it is not." The nun held up the lantern and screamed. Falling to the floor, she grabbed her chest and screamed again.

"What's happening?" Caroline knelt, pulling the hair from the nun's face.

"I don't like it in here," Tom stated. "The room with the shit was better than this place."

Heleina walked a few paces away from the others before lifting her hands to the heavens. "I know what's wrong."

"What?" Caroline asked.

The nun screamed again.

"No god," Heleina replied.

"No god?" Tom repeated. "What do you mean, no god?"

"Just as I said." Heleina pulled out her rosary and kissed the cross of Jesus. "My lord," she yelled.

"No echoes," Grant stated.

"No nothing," Winifred added.

Mother Hildegard moaned.

"That is correct," Heleina whispered. "Nothing. We are in a void. So empty, there's no god."

"I feel it too," Tom stated. "Or lack thereof. There's nothing inside me anymore. I used to feel … I mean, I'm not religious, but I always felt that something was in here …" – he tapped his chest – "… a presence. But that's gone. This is horrible."

"The absence of god," Heleina whispered, "where the damned are held in limbo."

The nun moaned, curling tighter into her fetal position.

Caroline picked up the lamp and held it above her head. "No beam. No nothing."

"We're indeed in a void." Heleina stepped closer and knelt. "Mother? Mother, are you okay?"

"I need my lord," she whispered, eyes wide. "I ca … ca … can't …"

"I understand, Mother," Heleina whispered.

"How can there be no god?" Tom asked. "Where'd he go?"

"It is not *He* who has left," Heleina replied. "It is us that were taken away."

"Taken away?" Tom repeated. "Fucken nuts."

"What do we do?" Winifred asked. "We cannot leave Mother Hildegard here and we can't carry her."

"Give me a moment," Heleina whispered. "Let me share my essence. It may sustain her until we leave this part of the maze."

The others nodded, taking a few steps back. They sat, although it wasn't exactly a floor. Trying to accept the vacancy that was holding their souls hostage, their eyes remained glued on each other. Several times, Winifred waved her hand through the air. Her arm flowing freely as if no floor existed. Then again, what held their weight?

"I don't understand." Winifred swung her arms in all directions. "Where's the floor?"

"I don't believe anything exists in here," Tom stated. "Where ever here is."

"We're between dimensions." Grant tried to rest on his elbows, but whatever he was sitting on refused to hold his weight. "Nothing seems to exist in here."

"We exist." Winifred sighed.

"We do, but we also do not." Grant shrugged. "Space and what creates our living world is made out of atoms. Atoms that cling together to create what we touch or use. In here, with us, I do not believe that atoms exist anymore. No god, no light, no darkness, no … anything."

"If we stay too long …" – Caroline gasped – "… could we cease to exist?"

"I believe so," Grant replied. "Mother? Or should I say, Mothers?"

Caroline chuckled.

"I think she can walk." Heleina helped the nun to her feet.

Mother Hildegard straightened her habit, holding tight to her cross.

"Let's start moving." Heleina held the nun's arm.

Caroline swung the lantern as they walked. Grant hummed and Tom sighed deeply with each breath.

The emptiness that haunted their depths was more than just a void. It was a nonexistence of being. Life, death, time, air, up, down – a soul, a spirit, a god – nothing could or would progress or become real, not here. The sterility of the desolation actually seeped through their skin, suffocating, entwining their souls with a misery so real that their authenticity failed to materialize. Their souls were no longer souls but empty vessels, longing to be filled.

Empty hearts without even the slightest touch from God created a suction that challenged a human mind with every step. Thoughts refused to settle, soaring away before the words or visions could form. A beat from a chest was silenced before it could recoup for the second round. Eyelids refused to close, blinking only halfway before reopening. A swallow flowed in reverse, making them cough. Lungs struggled to fill, almost freezing their bodies in time.

"How much farther?" Caroline asked.

"I'm not sure I can do this." Winifred wiped her eyes.

"Do you have tears?" Tom asked.

Winifred shook her head. "Wiping more from habit."

Grant held Winifred's hand, kissing it gently. "It'll be okay."

Winifred nodded.

The walk seemed to take them past infinity, expanding into something greater. But the vast emptiness that redefined their reality was mixing life with death, love with hate, hot with cold – a foreverness flowing into the finite.

"Something's coming this way," Heleina whispered, holding tightly to the mother's arm.

"Walking?" Tom stepped to the front and stared into the darkness. "Who's there?"

Footsteps echoed.

"How can we hear footsteps?" Tom asked. "This is bullshit."

The room spun, scattering the small group apart. The lamp rolled across the emptiness, slowly stopping near a large, black hoof.

Winifred jumped to her feet. Her eyes scanning the shadows. *But how can there be shadows?*

"How did you get in here?" a deep voice asked. A voice that sizzled at the end of each word, almost as if on fire.

Mother Hildegard stood, straightening out her long, black skirt. Holding up her cross, she whispered, "Yeenoghu?"

"Who dares to enter my lair?" the voice asked.

"We do, my lord," the mother stated. "We beg for your help. We need to banish Baphomet and his minion, Malus."

The voice laughed. A deep, vibrating laugh. As the sound echoed, the face of the voice slowly appeared. The creature was tall, at least twelve feet, if not taller. Its body, gnoll-like, sported a burning-ember of a face that somewhat mimicked a human skull but with a protruding jaw. The thing snapped its sharp teeth several times as drool clung to the fangs. Mangy, dark fur covered the creature that wore a leather band around the waist. A dark green fabric, tied in the front with a large knot, drooped between its legs, hanging loose. Black, short fur ran from the top of its head down to the end of its tail. As the creature walked, it dragged a large hammer that scrapped against the imaginary floor. But his feet! His feet were not feet but hoofs. Horse hoofs decorated the ends of his hairy legs.

"You want *me* to help you, old follower of the bright one?" The creature laughed again. "Now, that *is* funny."

"We're serious." Tom stepped closer. "It's not a joke."

"A joke to me." The creature paused, tilting its head. "But … you are serious."

"Very serious." Heleina now took a step. "Will you help us … Lord Yeenoghu?"

Caroline raised her hand. "We know you are at war with –"

"Silence, human." The creature rubbed his chin. "I live for destruction and slaughter. Normally, I prefer to butcher humans … however … a reason, if legit, would allow me to …"

Winifred stepped up to the creature and lowered her head. "Baphomet will not release me from our bond. He demands a child."

"A child?" Yeenoghu stood a little straighter. A difficult thing to do with such strong, thick muscles. "A human–demon child would give him the power to …" Yeenoghu growled, and the floor vibrated. "I will help you."

"You will?" Caroline asked. "Thank God."

"God has no power here in this maze," Yeenoghu stated. "Follow me, followers of the bright one."

Eleven

THE HAMMER BOUNCED as the creature paced. Several times, sparks glittered in the darkness. With nothing to determine their bearings, the lost souls continued to follow the demon lord, Yeenoghu. Something flickered in the distance, mimicking a rising sun. The slapping of water, such as a moored boat, tickled their ears.

"I smell water," Tom whispered.

"I do too." Caroline shrugged.

"That's because we're near the river Acheron." Yeenoghu laughed.

"Acheron is one of the five Underworld rivers," Tom stated. "It feeds into Acherousian Lake. A swampy lake."

"You know of my home?" Yeenoghu asked.

"I studied Greek mythology." Tom chuckled. "At least I thought it was mythology. This is the river of woe. The principal river of the Underworld. Don't tell me, let me guess, the ferryman Charon will transport us across."

Yeenoghu laughed. "Now you see, you know nothing. Charon ferries lost souls from the upper world to the lower. Pharsight will escort us."

The demon stood at the edge of a huge dock that towered over the dark water. Dead trees lined the cliffs that soared high on each side with darkened clouds caressing their endless heights. Something gloomy and huge slowly materialized. A ship. A ship larger than any ship that had ever sailed the Earth's seas now sat, awaiting their arrival. The plank lowered, and Yeenoghu climbed aboard.

Tom took a step and paused. "This thing is vibrating."

Caroline paused. "It feels like …"

"A body," Tom stated, finishing her sentence.

"Yes, as if it's alive." Caroline touched the railing gently, allowing the ship to sniff and approve her entry.

"Humans!" Yeenoghu yelled. "Have you never seen a ship before?"

"Not one that breathes," Tom stated as the hull of the ship expanded and contracted. "Is this thing alive?"

"Of course." Yeenoghu laughed and the plank's vibrations increased. "Umibōzu, meet the worshipers of the bright one."

The ship snorted as if chuckling. A large, oval window blinked, and a yellow eye glared as if judging.

Tom climbed aboard and waited for the others. "Who are the bright ones?"

"Those who reside in the heavens with our holy one," Pharsight replied. "Nice to meet you and welcome aboard Umibōzu of the Acheron Lake."

"Thank you." Tom nodded. "I'm Tom, and these are my friends … Grant … his mother, Heleina …" – he nodded as each stepped onboard – "… Caroline … Mother Hildegard … and Winifred."

"Welcome aboard." Pharsight clasped his extra-large hands and smiled. Long golden hair that swayed gently in the wind, slapped against his legs. He wore an ancient seaman's outfit of brown trousers that buckled at his knees, and a long puffy, white shirt that was overly stained, obviously yellowed from time. The man's protruding, thin nose almost consumed his otherwise bland face. Blue-slit eyes were almost hidden between the thick blonde 'brows. "We will depart shortly."

Winifred gasped at the size of the ship. No military had anything that would or could compare. Stairs led off in all directions to only God knew where. Doors and windows, boarded and locked, obviously hid only the most darkest of secrets.

"Come." Yeenoghu waved his hand.

A cavern, deeper than an endless pit, filled the horizon – darkened skies with dim clouds. As the ship left the dock, several hawk-looking heads floated across the water. A deep bluish hue lit the thick body that held the seven long necks that resembled snakes.

"We are in the bowels of Hell," Yeenoghu stated. "My home of Tenarus is not far. This lake, Acheron, is one of six that touches my world's shores."

"Who are they?" Winifred asked, pointing to several people wearing black robes. They stood at the edge of a cliff that was only a few feet above the rippling waves.

"Those are the fallen gods," Yeenoghu stated. "They are pledging an unbreakable oath, vowing to partake of the water's non-blessings and from which their hatred and betrayal floats."

"Fallen gods?" Tom asked.

"There are many gods down here," Yeenoghu replied.

"What about our god?" Mother Hildegard asked.

"That is the Supreme Creator of everything good and bad," Yeenoghu replied. "Even we worship the Creator."

"Is he not the one true god?" Mother Hildegard asked.

"He is our Creator," Yeenoghu stated. "Therefore, he is everything and everything is him. The gods are many and have ruled humans throughout eternity."

"Name a few," Caroline stated.

"Over there by the shore is Owuo, the god of death and destruction. And up there, by that dead tree is Nephthys. Yesterday, I met with Osiris, lord of the Underworld. And there's Birtum, Ninazu … too many to list."

"Are they all down here with you?" Tom asked.

Yeenoghu laughed. "Of course not."

A strong breeze soared across the deck along with a huge skeleton of a fish. Hundreds of smaller fish swarmed as if following a mother duck. The aroma of sulfur and burning hair spread, along with the sensation of pending death.

"We are close." Yeenoghu breathed in deeply. "Oh, the wonderfulness of home."

"If your home smells like that flying fish …" Tom rubbed his nose.

The light at the end of the valley grew brighter. The light was not in the sky but along the cliffs.

"Is the water … glowing?" Winifred asked.

"That is the essence of life flowing away from the damned that are now being judged," Yeenoghu replied.

"Being judged?" Heleina repeated.

"We are all judged one day." Yeenoghu nodded.

The ship slowed as another dock came into view. Only this dock was trimmed with large, flowing trees and lanterns and pillars with deep golden trim. The city beyond seemed to flow up and into eternity. Rays with yellow hues of red and blue bounced across the many balconies that framed the large city with floor upon floor of homes. Humans and creatures hurried about as if existing within a private reality of life.

"There are people here?" Grant asked.

"Are there not people where you live?" Yeenoghu chuckled. "Humans are indeed stupid."

They followed Yeenoghu off the ship as Pharsight waved from the bow.

"What a beautiful city," Grant stated.

The pillars, only a few feet apart, held up the trailing gardens decorated with various shades of green and red and yellow. Large flowers bloomed, filling the air with a sweetened touch of affection.

Fish jumped across the glowing waters that flowed along the streets. Various small boats carried passengers to and from, too many to count.

"This …" – Mother Hildegard waved her hand through the air – "… is Hell?"

"You think I should live inside fire and brimstone and be tortured by the stings of dragons or the bites of infected bats?" Yeenoghu raised a 'brow and frowned. "Hmm?"

"I'm just surprised," the mother replied. "This city is absolutely beautiful."

"My palace is at the top." He pointed with his hammer that was longer than Winifred was tall.

"You mean that round building up there?" Caroline asked.

Yeenoghu didn't reply. Instead, he walked down the center of town, nodding at his loyal citizens.

As they reached the large, golden doors, decorated with what resembled cherubs, the small group had to stop to catch their breaths.

"What a hike," Tom stated, breathing heavily.

"How many stairs did we just climb?" Caroline rubbed her legs.

"A million," Winifred replied. "You okay Mother Hildegard and Heleina?"

The women nodded, still doubled over and breathing hard.

Winifred glanced over the railing and sighed. The balconies were just too many to count. Each covered in flowing vines and golden lanterns. Far below, the lake wound through the streets as if a sleeping snake was nestled between desert rocks.

"You like?" Yeenoghu whispered from behind.

Winifred started, glancing briefly over her shoulder. "Oh, yes. It is beautiful here."

"May I be so bold as to ask, how were you given to Baphomet?" Yeenoghu smiled.

The creature's dark eyes beamed with a gentleness she had never know, at least before that day. His strong muscles reflected the lantern's light displaying an imperious allusion of power.

Winifred smiled. "You may ask. My grandmother gave me to him. I was fifteen. I think I became pregnant from one of our encounters. But she made me lose the child."

"How sad," he replied. "However, I could look for that child. See if they are here. If not in my kingdom, maybe another."

"You could find my child?"

Yeenoghu nodded. "All terminated life comes directly here."

"They do not return to Heaven?" Winifred wiped an eye.

Yeenoghu glanced at the darkening skies and frowned. "I'm afraid not. Those souls are lost forever. Some remain as children. Others grow old and feeble."

"Why punish the unborn?" she asked.

"It is not a punishment but an abandonment." Yeenoghu shook his head. "Those with the spirit of life have the power to banish those without. An unborn soul needs nourishment from the mother and encouragement from the father. The only time a soul is returned to the heavens is when that spirit chooses to return on its own. Not when abandoned by the mother."

Winifred allowed the tears to fall.

Yeenoghu reached out a finger larger than her arm and gently wiped one away. "You are able to cry."

Winifred nodded.

"That is a gift from the Creator." He kissed her tear. "A true gift indeed. Come, allow me to be your host. You and your friends should rest and eat. After all, you still exist within your life force."

Yeenoghu held out his finger and Winifred gently clasped her hand around it. They entered the parlor where the others were waiting.

"This is an amazing place," Tom stated. "I'm impressed."

"Thank you," Yeenoghu replied. "Please, allow me to host your visit. We will speak more tomorrow."

"You have a tomorrow down here?" Mother Hildegard asked.

"The universe still spins, does it not?" Yeenoghu shook his head and laughed.

"Wow," Caroline stated as the girls entered.

The golden walls reflected the afternoon light with a heavenly glow. Large pillars held up the vaulted ceiling that was decorated with beautiful murals. The room displayed a large hearth with a blazing fire. A single oval rug seemed to pull in the over-stuffed chairs that faced the grate. On the center table, trays of steaming food, fruits, drinks, and breads, begged to be tasted. On both sides of the fireplace, doors led into separate bedrooms with a shared bath.

"Amazing." Winifred walked through the rooms, studying the colorful walls and furniture. Several times, she glanced out a window and sighed. "Can this all be an illusion?"

"If it is," Caroline replied, "we're having the same one."

"I honestly thought Hell was nothing but demons and witches and ghosts. What did he say, oh yeah, fire and brimstone."

Caroline laughed. "More like a five-star hotel."

After filling a plate with various items, they selected a chair and settled in to fill their empty stomachs.

"Funny," Winifred stated, "we never thought to bring food."

"Who'd think we'd need to bring food to another dimension?"

"I guess you're right." Winifred took a bite of a large bun and hummed. "Delicious."

"What if this is an illusion and we're eating dead stuff?"

"I hope this meat is dead." Winifred laughed.

With full tummies and after hot showers, it was time for sleep. They had thought about each picking a room, but with the echoes of voices and heavy footsteps, they decided to share a bed.

Tucking the covers over her shoulder, Winifred closed her eyes, and for the first time in many years, her sleep was uneventful and long. No demon visited. No nightmare yanked her awake. Just a deep slumber with her last thoughts trailing along those beautiful dark eyes of the lord demon Yeenoghu.

What seemed like sunlight filled the room, giving a moment of thought to Winifred. Remembering where she was and why, she sat up and concentrated on the walls that surrounded her. Nothing had changed. If this was an illusion, something would be different. But everything was exactly as she remembered.

With a towel wrapped around her head, Caroline stepped out of the bathroom. "Sorry, I can't resist the hot water."

Winifred nodded. "We should hurry. We're supposed to meet everyone for breakfast."

"There are clean clothes in the drawers and closet." Caroline pointed at the jeans that now hugged her thighs. "Comfy clothes too."

"Great, I'll dress and we can run downstairs." Winifred picked out sweats and a t-shirt. An oversized sweater and clean tennis shoes finished her off. Tying her hair back with a new scrunchie, she was ready to go.

A man, who resembled an ancient English butler, was waiting patiently just outside the door. They followed and were soon reunited with their friends. A large dining room filled with scrambled eggs and other breakfast items greeted them as did Yeenoghu.

"Good morning, my friends," he stated. "Please, feel free to fill your plates. As you can see, I already have mine at my seat. Winifred and Caroline, would you care to join me at the head of the table."

Winifred nodded.

Caroline glanced at Tom who smiled.

"Tell me of your proposition," Yeenoghu stated between sips of a hot beverage.

Mother Hildegard cleared her throat before speaking. "We have come to ask for your help in breaking the bond between Winifred and the two that stalk her ... Baphomet and Malus. At first we thought it was just Malus. But no. We now believe that Malus is working for Baphomet."

"You are probably correct," Yeenoghu stated. "And what do I receive in return?"

"Hadn't thought about that," the mother replied. "What are your terms?"

"Normally, a soul or a firstborn or ..." – he smiled – "... just joking. I do not need material things. As you can see for yourselves, I have everything a demon lord could ever want." Yeenoghu winked at Winifred. "But what I do ask for in return is a good word to the Creator, our one true god ... is that not how you see our Creator?"

Mother Hildegard nodded.

"Is God a man or woman?" Caroline asked. "Have you met 'im."

Yeenoghu chuckled. "Yes, I met him. But he is neither male nor female. Perhaps, a little of both."

"Both?" Tom repeated.

"If you are the Creator, why would you not create duplicates of yourself? Would you not prefer to watch and enjoy your creations grow and learn and repopulate your worlds? An ever-evolving movie? Is that not what you'd watch on those glassy screens?"

Grant smiled.

"We will tell our God whatever it is you wish us to say," Heleina replied. "You have been most pleasant. I will say, you're the kindest demon I've ever met. Not to mention the most handsome."

"Why, thank you, my lady." Yeenoghu lifted his cup and nodded. "I agree to the terms. I will ready my troops and we will war against Baphomet and Malus. However, you will be required to continue traversing the path of the Endless Maze."

"Why?" Heleina asked.

"Because I cannot suddenly transport you back from where you came." Yeenoghu raised a 'brow. "That is one trick I cannot do."

"Where will you fight Baphomet?" Tom asked.

"Not here in my beautiful city," Yeenoghu replied. "Took too long to build. Can't stand that creature ... and he *is* a creature. A slimy one." Again, Yeenoghu winked at Winifred.

Winifred smiled and her stomach churned. Having a demon's wink meeting her gaze was not expected nor especially welcomed. Although the creature was handsome and indeed powerful and gentle, he was still a creature of Hell. As for now, Winifred preferred the living.

"May I walk with you?" the voice was soft and caring.

Winifred turned and smiled. "Lord Yeenoghu." She shrugged. "Of course, you may walk with me. I wish to see your beautiful city."

"We spent eternity adding a little here or there." He waved his hand through the air.

"How did you become a demon?"

"It is indeed a long story." He chuckled. "Perhaps if I simply say not to argue with the Creator? Would that give you a clue?"

Winifred nodded. "How long have you been down here?"

Again, he chuckled. "How many times has the Earth rotated around the sun?"

"That is a long time."

"Indeed." Yeenoghu nodded. "I was banned from Heaven before the Earth was formed."

"Then how can we be inside?" Winifred tilted her head.

"We are not *in* the Earth," he replied. "We are in another dimension. The only thing in the middle of the Earth is a hot core of pure metal."

"Then why do they say that Hell is in the middle of the Earth?"

"Good question." He nodded. "Middle Earth, Lower Earth … it is rather odd."

They stopped by the fountain. Winifred sat, allowing her fingers to run through the ripples. Several birds landed on a nearby branch and their songs filled her with a longing for home.

"This is amazing." Winifred glanced at the demon and smiled. "You have trees, flowers, light … even birds." She shrugged. "So much like Earth."

"Much of this city mimics my home world," Yeenoghu replied.

"Where was your home?"

"Not in this galaxy," he replied. "My home was in the Abella stars. So far away, no one on Earth even suspects it exists."

"What was your world like?"

"Huge, twice as large as Earth. But just as beautiful. Blue skies, large oceans, wonderful mountains that broke through the clouds. One day, I will return and visit."

"I hope you do," she replied.

"I would like to spend more time with you," he stated. "Will you have dinner with me tonight?"

Winifred nodded. "Certainly, I would enjoy that."

"Wonderful." Yeenoghu laughed. "Then it is a date. I will see you tonight."

Yeenoghu stood and nodded. As he walked away, Winifred followed the rhythm of his stride. He was indeed tall. He was definitely handsome. He was a powerful and respected ruler. But he was also a demon and not human.

A slight knock pulled Winifred from her thoughts.

"I believe that is for you," Caroline stated. "You know what you're doing, right?"

"I'm not doing anything," Winifred replied, opening the door.

A thin, red demon with large ears, an inverted nose, white eyes, and wearing a dark blue uniform stood at attention. "Ms. Cranston?" The demon, that resembled a bat without wings, saluted, clicking his heels together.

"I'm ready." Winifred winked at her friend as she closed the door.

The demon did not escort Winifred to the dining hall. Instead, they walked silently up a long flight of stairs. At the top, a table set for two was on the balcony. With no walls or ceiling, the openness felt light and airy.

"Please, Ms. Cranston …" the demon waved for her to enter.

Winifred stood by the railing. Large mountains with peaks higher than the solar system was wide, reached high and into the darkness. Birds soared past to destinations unknown. Below, a winding river flowed through the city, lit only where the lanterns stood.

"It is indeed beautiful up here."

The voice startled her. "Yes, it is. I make you nervous, Winifred?" Yeenoghu asked.

"A little." She shrugged.

"May I ask why?"

Winifred allowed her eyes to trail from his toes up to his head.

"Because I am a demon?"

"Perhaps," she replied.

"I will not harm you."

"I know you won't."

"Let us eat." Yeenoghu held out his finger which was as long as Winifred's arm.

She smiled, allowing him to escort her to a chair.

Dinner was wonderful – steak, potatoes, and a salad. A normal dinner she would have ordered in any restaurant on Earth. Sipping on wine, she stood and walked to the railing.

"Tell me about your childhood." He tilted his head.

"Now that is where my life ended." Winifred took another sip, allowing the liquid to warm her insides.

"Ended?" He blinked several times. "You mean started?"

Winifred shook her head. "Ended. My grandmother was a witch. A very powerful one. The head of her coven."

"And you were tortured by others?"

"Very much so," Winifred replied. "Lost my virginity at ten."

"Ten?"

Winifred nodded.

Yeenoghu shook his head and sighed. "I often wonder what goes through a human's mind sometimes. My citizens were once bad people. Very bad. Not everyone here is from Earth. My citizens are from various galaxies and planets. A few from different dimensions. But all who sinned against the Creator."

"But your city is so beautiful." Winifred giggled. "I could live here."

"My citizens repented, and the Creator somewhat forgave their sins. But not enough to enter Heaven."

"And you created this beautiful city for them?"

Yeenoghu nodded. "That is why I need a good word on my behalf. My family, mother and father, are in Heaven. I would love to rest my head in my mother's lap one last time."

"I will definitely say a good word on your behalf." Winifred touched the demon's arm. "In fact, several."

"May I take you somewhere?" he asked.

Winifred nodded.

Yeenoghu whistled and stared into the sky. A creature with large wings resembling a bat landed a few feet away. The creature was taller than an average house. Round glowing eyes stared out from under four large and colorful horns. Its tail switched several times, allowing the creature to balance on the two muscular legs.

"May I?" Yeenoghu asked, pointing to the creature.

"May you what?"

Yeenoghu nodded, and the creature flapped. Raising several feet into the air, it reached out with its giant claws, grabbing Yeenoghu and Winifred around the waist. After several more flaps, the three were soaring high above the city.

Winifred glanced at Yeenoghu and smiled. The feeling of a weightless freedom filled her with a sense of power she never knew existed. As the city faded far behind, the creature flapped toward a distant rising star. The more it flapped, the brighter the light. Just before the brilliance filled their view, they were gently placed on a cliff's edge.

Yeenoghu held out his finger again, escorting Winifred to the edge. He pointed at the light. "The Creator," he whispered. "This is as close as I can get."

"That's God?"

The bright light twirled like a rainbow floating across a sea of oil with a warm hum of pleasant voices.

"Angels?" she asked.

Yeenoghu nodded. "I come here to talk with our Creator. I think *he* listens." He sat back, dangling his large, muscular legs over the edge.

Winifred sat on his thigh as if it were a sofa. "Listen, Yeenoghu, the Creator is our god. A god that loves and forgives. Whatever you did or did not do was probably really bad. But the God I know ..." – she glanced at the twirling light – "... will forgive you. One day, you will enter Heaven."

"I pray you are correct." He laughed. "Constantly battling my archenemy can be quite tiring at times."

Winifred nodded.

"There is something about you that amuses me," Yeenoghu whispered. "Your beauty is beyond this city. You could remain here with me. Be my wife."

"Wife to a demon?" Winifred giggled. "Now that would be an interesting wedding."

"I could protect you."

Winifred stood, her face now equal to his. She placed a hand on each side of his head, leaning closer. Their lips met. A warmth spread across her soul with a mysterious longing. But it was a different type of longing. This was a longing for home and safety and –

"Please stay with me," he begged.

"I wish I could," Winifred replied. "But I am alive. You are not. My life force would upset the balance. Perhaps when I die ..."

"When you die, you will be taken to the light." Yeenoghu's gaze returned to the heavens.

"Not if I kill myself," she whispered.

"No!" he stated, his smile flipping to a frown. "Never say that. You do not want your soul tormented forever down here."

"Why would I be tormented?"

"Those that take their life force for granted ... I cannot stress the importance of how much you need to value your soul. Do not rip it from your life. Never rip your soul. You run the risk of becoming a demon. Do you want to be like me?"

Winifred shook her head, leaning in for another taste of freedom.

The morning light greeted Winifred's eyes. She stirred only a little as the blankets tugged on her arms.

"How was your evening?" Caroline asked.

"He was a gentleman," Winifred replied. "We ate and then we flew to a cliff where I was able to see the light of Heaven. It was beautiful."

"Did you see God? Or should I say the Creator?"

"No, just light, but Yeenoghu asked me to stay here and be his wife."

"No shit." Caroline laughed. "I thought he liked you. What about Grant?"

"I said *no*," Winifred replied. "It would be too difficult for me down here. He wants to return to Heaven and then what? I'm left here alone?"

"True." Caroline jumped from the bed, hurrying to the bathroom.

A light rap on the door made Winifred stand. She pulled on her robe. The same red demon in full uniform stood at attention.

"The lord needs to see you downstairs." He again saluted and snapped his heels together.

"Hi Hitler to you too." Winifred sighed. "Give me five?"

The demon nodded.

Winifred slammed the door.

"Who was that?" Caroline asked with the water running.

"Hitler." Winifred pulled on her jeans.

Caroline opened the door. "Hitler?"

"Long story, short joke."

The men greeted the girls as they entered the dining hall. Mother Hildegard nodded, taking her seat. As the servants sat the food on the table, Yeenoghu entered.

"Ms. Winifred," he stated. "We found your child."

Winifred coughed, catching the bacon in her hand. "My child?"

Yeenoghu smiled. "It's a boy."

"A boy?"

"And he is here." Yeenoghu stepped aside as a demon nurse, bluer than a morning sky, entered, carrying a squirming baby in her arms.

Winifred stood, her heart pounding. "Oh my god."

The nurse handed the child to Winifred and nodded.

"Does he have a name?" Winifred asked.

The baby looked at his mother and cooed. His yellow-red eyes glittered in the morning light. A large smile creased his rosy cheeks.

"You never named him?" Yeenoghu asked.

"I never understood what happened to me until I pieced everything together. But that was when I was much older ... much older." Winifred smiled at her son. "So you need a name, little guy?"

Heleina took a seat next to Winifred, gently rubbing the baby's head. "Name him now, Mommy."

"Mommy?" Winifred whispered, keeping her eyes on the child. "You are beautiful, son."

"How about Kiran?" Grant asked. "That means *Ray of Light.*"

"Ray of Light?" Winifred repeated. "Kiran? I like it. I name you, Kiran Yeenoghu Cranston."

"I am honored, Winifred." Yeenoghu rubbed his eye.

"Thank you." Winifred kissed Kiran and smiled. "I want him to stay with me."

"I will have a crib brought to your room," the nurse replied. "Along with a few supplies."

Winifred cradled her son in her arms. "If I had only known," she whispered. "I would have protected you with my life."

Kiran reached up and touched his mother's cheek.

Winifred kissed his chubby little fingers and cried.

The sounds of trumpets and war cries pounded through Winifred's ears. She jumped from the bed, wrapping her baby in her arms.

"Oh my goodness," Caroline yelled from the balcony. "Winifred, get out here."

Winifred peeked around the curtains. Her eyes widened as she stared at the amazing sight. Millions of flying demons, similar to the one that soared her through the clouds, flew in formation, darkening the skies, their cries slicing through the thin air. Their endless rows upon rows seemed to flow out until forever. A never-ending display of pure power.

"Look over there," Caroline yelled, pointing.

Several large, floating ships were next. The decks were filled with demons and humans wearing military uniforms, standing at attention. At the rear, which seemed to take forever to arrive, floated the mighty ship of Yeenoghu. As it passed, the lord demon stood at the bow, raising his hammer high above his head.

"Wow," Caroline stated. "Is that not impressive?"

"I hope he's okay," Winifred whispered.

"With all of that?"

A war cry echoed from behind the massive ship. Along the horizon, yellow and red flames soared, reminding Winifred of the first dream – an atomic bomb. The ground shook. The buildings swayed. Birds screeched, soaring through the sky in the opposite direction. The citizens screamed, running for cover.

"Maybe we should go inside," Caroline stated.

"What should we do?" Winifred asked.

A heavy knock on the door and it flew open.

"Girls!" Tom yelled. "We are leaving now. The war has started."

"Grab only what you can carry," Grant stated. "Hurry."

The girls dressed and filled a small bag for Kiran.

"We will take turns carrying him," Heleina stated as they aimed for the city streets.

Bright flashes and flames danced across the mountains, the ground rolling under their feet. Thunder boomed and lightning filled the sky with rings of fire.

"May God have mercy on their souls." Mother Hildegard kissed her cross.

"I don't think they have souls," Heleina replied.

"I think they do," Winifred stated.

The streets were empty. Only the lanterns shown through the blasting waves of agony.

Kiran struggled in Winifred's embrace.

"I think he wants to see." Caroline pulled him into her arms.

With the baby on her shoulder, Kiran's eyes landed on the fires. He pointed and cooed.

"Yes, baby," Winifred said. "We're going in the other direction. Mommy will protect you."

"We will all protect you," Grant stated.

A trail that led between the mountains and away from the war seemed to be the only retreat. Carrying Kiran was not easy. He was heavy and eager to watch the war raging on the other side of the mountains. The higher they climbed the louder the war cries sounded. Reaching a tall peak, they paused to glance at the explosions.

From a distance, Winifred could have sworn she saw Yeenoghu on his ship, but then again, she wasn't sure. Her heart reached out to him, and from somewhere inside, she heard a faint voice, *Be safe my love.*

"I will." Winifred waved as they descended the far side of the mountain toward the city of Pandæmonium – *Paradise Lost*.

Twelve

WITH THEIR FEET aching and their legs swollen, the dim lights of Pandæmonium flickered in the distance. The domed city looked more like a prison than a place to live. No trees or flowers grew near this monstrosity. Just a large concrete-looking building that was larger than one of Yeenoghu's beautiful mountains.

Their path led straight to the middle. As did many others that surrounded the building.

Tom stopped at a sign and frowned. "Infernal Council. Doesn't sound pleasant."

"Should we go around?" Caroline asked.

"The path goes straight through," Heleina replied. "Perhaps, we should too?"

"I agree," Mother Hildegard said, still clutching her cross.

Cold, stiff air whipped through their legs, grating against their souls. Winifred shivered and she hugged Kiran closer.

"Let me carry him for a while." Grant took the child from her. "Give your arms a rest."

"Thanks," Winifred whispered. "I'm so happy to have him with me. I still can't believe what they did to him."

"I can," Grant replied. "What if we have a million just like Kiran. Just you and me."

Winifred smiled. "Sounds inspiring."

Caroline winked at her.

The dome grew in size the closer they walked, large red doors beckoning them forward. Demon guards, wider across than tall, shielded the entrance. Glowing yellow eyes and shimmering horns that decorated their massive faces gave the group a moment of pause. Large chains held the monsters in place.

"May we enter," Mother Hildegard asked, bowing.

"Old follower of the bright one, what business do you have here?" one of the beasts asked.

"We must pass through this dome to reach the other side," she replied.

"Our Father is presiding today," the other beast said.

"Father?" Heleina asked.

"Satan," the first beast replied.

"We cannot exactly go around this thing," Tom stated. "We have no choice. Will your Father object?"

The second beast laughed and the ground vibrated. "Satan welcomes all fallen angels to his liar."

"Super fantastic," Tom whispered.

The two guards stepped back and their chains grated against the ground, sounding heavy.

"Thank you," Mother Hildegard stated, walking past.

The stadium was as wide as it was tall. Rows upon rows of humans and demons were so vast that those at a distance were no larger than a fingernail. In the middle was a huge mound, and at the top sat a demon that resembled Satan.

"So *this* is the Infernal Council?" Tom asked.

"Shh." Caroline nudged his arm. "Stop it, already."

A lightning bolt and large boom echoed through the arena. Several humans sitting in the back ducked. The demons sat up straighter.

Satan resembled a man, but a large man. He had to be over a hundred feet tall and as wide as a common house. A giant compared to a mortal man. Naked and wearing only a crown, he was obviously demanding nothing except absolute respect. A red cape draped over his right shoulder, trailing across his legs, reminded Winifred of flowing blood.

"Where do we go now?" Caroline whispered.

"I don't know," Grant replied, bouncing Kiran in his arms. "I don't see a path."

"Neither do I," Heleina whispered.

The door had opened onto a huge balcony with over a hundred rows of seats, each with either a human or demon. No aisle was to the right or to the left, and a railing blocked their way.

Kiran squirmed in Grant's arms, obviously tired of being carried. His eyes teared as he reached for his mother. Winifred cuddled him in her arms.

"What are you doing here?" a female voice asked.

Winifred glanced around as the voice sounded familiar.

"Who's there?" Heleina whispered as loud as she could.

From somewhere inside the shadows, a face slowly appeared.

"Deb?" Winifred stepped closer. "Oh my —"

Deb slapped her hand over Winifred mouth, pushing her back outside. The others followed.

"Deb?" Winifred repeated.

"Yes, it's me, and what are you doing here?" Deb hugged Winifred around the neck.

"We're trying to make it through the Endless Maze," Mother Hildegard replied.

"These are my friends." Winifred nodded at the shocked eyes. "That's Tom, Grant, Caroline, Heleina, and Mother Hildegard. This is my son, Kiran."

"I know who he is." Deb smiled at the baby. "But what are *you* doing here?"

"What are you doing here?" Winifred asked.

"I was killed, remember?"

"I know that, but –"

The two beasts grunted, dragging their knuckles along the ground.

"Over here." Deb pushed Winifred near a large boulder. "Listen, you cannot stay here."

"We can't go back," Caroline added.

"What do you mean?" Deb asked.

"Wait …" – Winifred held up her free hand – "… Deb … what *are* you doing here … in Hell?"

"I was a witch," she stated. "Because I participated in the sacrifices, as did you by the way, was destined to come here. But you are not dead yet."

"Does that mean the rest of us will come here when *we* die?" Winifred asked. "Me, Diana, and Pam?"

"Eventually." Deb shook her head. "Unless you do something *really* special to counter the sins we committed while in the coven."

"How can we get around this dome?" Tom asked.

"I don't think you can," she replied. "But you *cannot* go back *in* there. Satan is presiding, and you don't want him to see you. Your life force is strong, and there are so many of you. You glow like a lit candle in a dark room. Very obvious."

"Then what do we do?" Mother Hildegard asked. "There is a war behind us. The devil's in front, and no passage to the sides."

"A war?" Deb asked. "What war?"

"The war between Yeenoghu and Baphomet," Grant replied. "We asked Yeenoghu for help in banishing Baphomet."

"Then you did bind with Baphomet?" Deb asked, her eyes on Winifred.

Winifred smiled at Kiran. "This is *my* child, and the father, I believe, is Baphomet."

"Does *he* know?" Deb asked.

"I don't think so," Winifred replied.

"You better hope he doesn't find out." Deb pushed Winifred farther away from the two beasts.

"It wasn't her fault," Caroline stated. "She was only fifteen."

"Fifteen is old enough to know better," Deb replied. "We were stupid and naive. We should have fought back. Now you are carrying a demon's child. What are you gonna do with him? You can't take him home with you."

"Why not?" Winifred's eyes watered.

"Will you *never* learn?" Deb walked in a circle, tapping her chin. "Now, I understand why Satan is here. Normally, we never see or hear from him. I guess this *war* is bringing too much attention."

"What does that mean?" Caroline asked.

Deb glanced away and sighed. "I'll help you through this dome. But you must promise you'll leave as soon as you can. This world will implode if you remain too long. Six humans with full lives. Damn." She shook her head.

"How will we get through this dome?" Grant asked. "I'd prefer not to run into Satan. It doesn't sound pleasant."

"Believe me ..." – Deb glanced at the two beasts – "... it wouldn't be."

"Will I ever see you again?" Winifred asked.

"One day, I'm sure. But for now, follow me."

They entered the dome, but instead of walking straight, Deb took a sharp right just past the beasts. Many capes of various sizes and colors hung on hooks. Hooks that were too many to count.

"Is this a coat closet?" Tom asked.

"Something like that," Deb replied. "Pick one that will cover you from head to toe. You cannot glow in there."

Each picked out a cloak, draping it over their heads.

"Let me carry the baby," Deb whispered. "He doesn't glow like you. No one will pay him any attention. Walk in a single line and keep that cloak pulled tight. Just following the feet in front of you. Don't show your faces."

Winifred handed her old friend her baby. He cooed briefly before settling in Deb's arms. With Deb in front, the others followed one behind the other.

The railing that had blocked their way was now gone. Instead, they were greeted by a path that led down and to the bottom of the inner dome.

"How …" Winifred started to say, but Deb turned and placed her finger over her mouth.

Kiran laughed and cooed.

Stepping down the first hundred steps or so seemed endless. At the end of the balcony, more steps led even farther down. Every few hundred rows, a beast with a large club stood guard. The stench was almost unbearable. Several times, Diana gagged, urging her stomach not to react.

At the base of the inner dome, Winifred glanced up at the crowd. Thousands upon thousands of rows circled high above. All types of creatures kept their eyes on Satan who was now speaking loudly.

"Better to remain here in Hell than serve *Him* in Heaven," Satan stated and his voice echoed through the stadium. "Farewell to our souls that once graced a presence with an ever-lasting mind casting judgment upon judgment and never once facing the truth."

Deb followed the base of the inner dome. Several demons sat up a little straighter, taking notice. She ignored them with her small entourage following just like baby ducklings.

"What *He* believes can be disposed, and I argue cannot be great. It is only I that rules Hell. No light shall challenge me. No one is equal to *my* raging storm that is just cresting the distant ridge. It is my fire

165

that is everlasting. It is my presence that will vouch for your sins that are continuously dredged across life's grave."

Deb disappeared somewhere under the lower dome.

Winifred paused, glancing into the darkness.

Caroline tapped her shoulder. "What's wrong?"

"I don't like this," Winifred whispered.

"Where'd she go?" Caroline asked.

Heleina tapped on Caroline's back.

Caroline shook her head, raising her hand.

"We can't just stand here," Heleina whispered.

Caroline waved her hand in the air.

Winifred stepped into the darkness, holding her breath. The feeling of nothingness touched her face and she backed out. It felt as if she had walked into a thin veil of water. Wanting her baby in her arms, she held back the urge to scream.

"God doth not need us and we do not need *Him*," Satan yelled. "Trust in *me*, your lord, and stand with *me* as I follow the path to freedom and away from that ever beating heart."

"Deb?" Winifred whispered into the veil. "Deb, bring me my baby."

Silence. No reply.

"I don't think that *was* Deb," Caroline whispered.

"Then who has my baby?" Winifred asked.

"Who's child is this?" Satan's voice boomed from above.

The small group froze. Since the dome raised up several stories in the middle and they were at the bottom, they couldn't see what was happening.

"It is Baphomet's son," a familiar voice stated.

Immediately, Winifred recognized who was speaking. It was the demon, Malus. Malus had masqueraded as Deb to trap them and steal her child.

"Baphomet's, you say?" Satan laughed. "Then ... where is the mother?"

"Below, my lord," Malus replied.

"Below what?" Satan asked.

"Below the dome," Malus stated.

A dreaded silence spread through the stadium just like a rogue wave that had spread across an empty beach. Many fingers pointed to the bottom of the dome as voices raised and screams echoed.

"I believe *we* have our eyes on her now," Malus said.

"Bring her to me," Satan ordered, and the stadium filled with the sounds of shuffling feet.

Some *one* or *thing* grabbed Winifred around the waist, pulling her up the flight of stairs. As the cloak was ripped away, the crowd silenced. The room lit as if a million stars had just broke free of a night's sky, and six bright, life forces now lit the inside of the evil darkness.

Satan's eyes didn't look real. They didn't exactly look fake either. As she studied the dancing pupils, Winifred wondered how the devil could see anything other than shimmering light.

The creature glared through double cat-slit eyes that glowed a perfect emerald green. Satan was taller than about twenty men standing shoulder to shoulder. Her head never reached his knees. The giant sat as rigid as a cedar but as flexible as flowing water. The contrast made her a little dizzy.

Malus held the baby by the nape of his neck.

Kiran screamed, lashing out his arms and legs.

"Give me my child!" Winifred yelled, taking a step.

Something pulled her back by the hair, making her stumble. "Let me go!" Winifred slapped at the large hand that held firm. Twisting and struggling to free herself, she bit a finger.

The beast yelped, releasing her.

Winifred ran for Malus, pulling her baby from his puny grip.

Startled, Malus stumbled and fell.

The crowd cheered and laughter filled the room.

"You bitch!" Malus shrieked, jumping to his feet.

Satan slapped the demon across the face.

Again, the demon shrieked.

"You scream like a woman," Satan yelled.

The crowd roared, laughing and cheering.

Malus stood, waving his arms through the air. "You dare mock me?" he yelled. "I brought that demon half-breed to you. I am lord of the Endless Maze!"

Satan laughed. "And you *dare* challenge *me?*"

Winifred cradled Kiran in her arms, kissing his cheek. "You leave *me* and *my* child alone!"

"I will *do* as I please," Malus yelled.

Satan laughed. "You argue with this female human as if you are nothing."

The crowd chanted. "Burn him ... burn him ... burn him ..." The voices grew louder and louder.

"Burn him in the lake of fire," a voice yelled out.

"Lord, hand him the Retribution Eternal," another voice hollered.

The crowd laughed.

"Everlasting punishment," a woman screamed.

"No!" a demon from above yelled. "Put him through the physical death of leverage."

"Cut off his penis and testicles," a voice hollered. "Make him eat them for breakfast."

The howl and laughter from the stands grew louder and more violent. A beat echoed as feet pounded in unison.

Satan raised his hand and laughed. "Brothers and sisters, I hear you, and although your suggestions have merit, I'm afraid this demon has no balls."

The stadium vibrated stronger as the crowd screamed.

"What shall I do with you, Malus? You have caused quite the turmoil. My kingdom has never felt so unraveled. War, fighting, rumors, and the veil was cut. Indeed, what to do, what to do …"

Malus glared at Winifred, his eyes dripping red tears. Clasping his clawed hands, blood ran down his legs.

"You have no power over me," Winifred yelled. "Not anymore. I'm not afraid of you. I'm not afraid!"

Malus stepped back and his form shriveled.

The crowd hushed.

Satan clapped twice.

Malus rose high above the crowd, struggling to be released. He screamed as his insides suddenly switched with his outsides. Standing back on his feet, he resembled a bubbling heap of bacteria covered in blood and black goo. Raising his arms and widening his eyes, or what was left of his eyes, he screamed, but the sound gushed inward through the gaping hole that was now his mouth. Insects, resembling maggots, nibbled at what was once blood veins and muscles.

Winifred pointed and laughed. "Look at you. You are nothing. Nothing. Just your true colors."

Two guards stepped forward, each hesitant to grab a gooey arm. They both raised a 'brow and sneered. Turning their faces away, they dragged what was left of the demon lord down the stairs.

"What will happen to him?" Tom asked. "Will he burn in Hell forever?"

"I may just plant him with the daisies," Satan mused.

The crowd cheered.

"Fertilizer ... may I ask why *you* are here?" Satan glared at the small group.

"We must traverse the Endless Maze." Mother Hildegard held her cross closer to her chest.

"Mother Hildegard?" Satan stated. "Ha, ha, so nice to see you again, Tlaltecuhtli." He motioned to Winifred and laughed. "Do you not realize who is actually with you?"

Winifred stared at the mother. As her eyes focused on the aging woman, Winifred screamed.

Mother Hildegard faded, her image swaying between the bright rays, morphing into something purely unknown. Her mouth opened wide and long, sharp teeth grew, filling the massive gap. Six slanted eyes ran from her lips, up through her forehead, ending where four horns burst through the skin, bluing the edges. The old woman's back curved, growing thick spikes that folded upon each other. Using a snake-like tail for leverage, the creature stumbled as a slender tongue slithered in and out as if sniffing for a reality that didn't exist anymore.

"Tlaltecuhtli?" Satan chuckled. "I thought that was you."

"What did you do with Mother Hildegard?" Winifred demanded.

"I don't believe there ever was a Mother Hildegard," Heleina whispered. "Maybe we were tricked."

"Tricked by a demon," Grant stated.

"This is bullshit," Tom yelled. "Pure bullshit."

"I agree." Satan nodded. "Would someone *please* put a leash on this dog."

Several beasts darted toward Tlaltecuhtli who dodged their hands.

Satan laughed and the crowd roared.

Tlaltecuhtli galloped on all fours, its claws clicking against the center dome – first to the right, then to the left – a free-for-all within the pits of Hell.

Kiran laughed and clapped.

One of the beasts tripped, rolling several times before diving off the top of the dome. The ground shook when he hit hard against Hell's floor, flames flying high, his head exploding.

Winifred sighed. "Enough!"

The stadium quieted. The flames died.

Satan studied the woman holding the infant. He tilted his head before grinning. "The exit is just down those stairs and through those double doors. You may go. I have a war to attend to."

Winifred glanced at Caroline who nodded at the stairs.

Grant held Heleina's arm, and together the small group left almost as quietly as they had entered.

"That was too easy." Caroline brushed her hair from her eyes.

"Way too easy," Tom added.

"Was there ever a Mother Hildegard?" Winifred asked.

"I don't believe so." Heleina wiped her eyes. "I'm ready for a shower and a warm bed."

"Is this all part of the Endless Maze?" Caroline asked. "I mean, look at everything we've been through. This is crazy."

"If we're even here," Tom whispered, "and that was really Satan."

"What do you mean?" Winifred asked.

"I don't know," Tom replied. "It's just that … well … I don't believe in demons or God or anything spiritual. I like things that are black and white … you know, solid. But everything that's happened over the last … I don't even know what day it is anymore."

"I understand what you are getting at." Heleina nodded. "It's as if reality has ceased to exist. Time isn't real down here."

"Yeenoghu told me that we're not inside Earth." Winifred kissed Kiran. "Said we were in another dimension. Why didn't he tell us that the mother was fake?"

"Maybe that *thing* faked out Yeenoghu too?" Tom stated. "I mean, Satan, or whoever that was, said *he* was the overall lord demon. Maybe only *he* could see through the trickery."

"Trickery," Heleina repeated. "Demons ... masters of trickery and deception. Maybe we'll never know what is or is not real ever again."

"That is not very comforting," Caroline whispered.

"Not supposed to be," Heleina replied. "Never forget ... the devil's between the beads." Heleina held up her rosary and frowned.

Tom stepped up to a sign and read off the words. "City of Dis."

"It's a city that forever burns within the sixth circle of Hell," Grant stated.

"How many circles are in Hell?" Caroline asked.

"Nine." Heleina kissed the cross on the rosary. "That is if you read Dante."

Thirteen

"WE'RE MISSING SOMETHING," Caroline stated. "Something is very wrong."

"As I said earlier ..." – Tom sighed – "... bullshit."

Caroline laughed. "First, I don't believe that Hell has circles."

"Maybe you don't read Dante." Heleina smiled.

"No, I don't." Caroline shook her head. "And second, I think we've been through more circles than just nine."

"Then you *did* read a little Dante once?" Heleina laughed.

"A little." Caroline grinned. "Required reading. But ... we are definitely inside an Endless Maze. I know that now."

"How do you know?"

"Because we are all aware of everything. Even the tricks," she replied. "And ... I do not believe Malus was destroyed back there. Nor that he was cast into a pit. That whole affair was just too easy. Not to mention ... if that *was* indeed Satan, why did he let us go?"

Heleina glanced around, rubbing her hands. She paused before replying, "Something to do with you, Winifred." Heleina smirked. "He looked at you through very odd eyes."

"They were odd eyes." Winifred kissed Kiran. "Double cat-slits. That's four pupils in total. See ... Mommy can count. I will teach you how to count, Kiran."

A large pit grew deeper the closer they walked. Red and orange bricks glowed under large lanterns that stood stark against the blackened sky. Demon bats flew in and out as if on a mission. They were obviously large, for at such a distance, a normal bat would not be visible. Several gnarled trees with what looked like distorted faces guarded the entrance. The knotted bark that twisted and turned in unnatural ways almost seemed alive.

"Those are some nasty-looking trees." Tom stepped closer. "Are they alive? Will they talk?" He poked his finger at one.

"We're not in a storybook." Caroline sighed, rolling her eyes. "We're in Hell."

"Just checking." Tom shook his head and shrugged. "Ugliest damn trees I ever did see."

"Wonder why they're out here like this?" Grant asked, allowing his hand to trail along the bark. "Feels wicked."

"Let's just keep moving." Heleina shivered. "This place gives me the creeps."

"I've been creeped out ever since the mercury pool." Caroline smiled.

The city was nothing more than a large brick circle that fell directly into an endless and flaming pit. People who walked along the millions of edges seemed to have a purpose, only to end back where they had started.

"Endless circles?" Caroline whispered.

"You did say this was the City of Dis," Heleina replied. "And if it is one of Dante's circles, maybe the man actually walked the halls of Hell."

Grant laughed. "Just like us?"

"We can't pass through here," Caroline stated. "We'd just walk in circles like they're doing. We'd be stuck in Hell forever."

"We cannot go around," Grant replied. "We found a path through Satan's dome. Therefore, there must be a way through this city too."

"Another puzzle to solve," Winifred whispered. "I'm starting to hate puzzles." She tickled her baby. "How about you, Kiran? You wanna solve this puzzle for mummy?"

The others stared at Winifred, frowning. Their eyes widened, understanding that something was happening to their friend.

"Winifred?" Caroline gently touched her friend's shoulder. "You okay?"

"Why do you ask?" Winifred's eyes wiggled just slightly before fading to a deep red.

Caroline glanced at Tom and then back at Winifred. "Maybe we should sit for a while."

"Let me carry Kiran." Grant held out his hands.

Winifred jerked the baby away. "No! No one carries my son but me. I don't know if you're a human or a demon."

"Winifred …" Grant caressed her arm.

"Don't touch me!" Winifred yelled. "Stay back. All of you, stay away from me." Winifred hugged Kiran tighter. After a quick glance, she darted between the gnarly trees and past the city's gates.

"Stop her!" Caroline yelled. "She'll be caught in the circles."

Grant and Tom sprinted after Winifred. But she was too quick, her feet fluttering faster than a fly's wings. Floating over the galleries that soared only down, she hovered for a brief moment before falling. Kiran flew from her arms and she screamed.

Winifred's mind soared in all directions at once. The round balconies were becoming smaller the farther she fell. Heat caressed her body, tucking her inside a warm blanket. Strong arms hugged, guiding her, slowing her descent. Tears filled her eyes, and again, she screamed.

"Shh, my love," a voice whispered. "I've got yah, I've got yah."

Winifred stared into Yeenoghu's large, caring eyes. His smile lit his face with an affection that felt protective and safe. "Why are you here?" she whispered.

"I've been keeping an eye on you," he replied. "Humans do not really fit in here." He chuckled, reaching out his hand and catching Kiran.

The large creature that had flown them to the mountaintop where they watched the lights of Heaven grasped Yeenoghu around the waist, and the verandas grew wider the higher they soared. The large bat gently placed them at the city gates, where Yeenoghu released Winifred from his strong embrace.

"Yeenoghu?" Caroline ran to their friend. "Did you win your war?"

"The war is still waging," he replied. "We will fight until eternity ends."

"Why?" Tom asked.

"How do you banish a demon when he is already banished?" Yeenoghu laughed. "But if we war, he will not have time to bother Winifred. Even demons cannot be in two places at the same time."

"Really?" Caroline nodded. "I'd love to know more."

"No you wouldn't," Yeenoghu replied. "Allow me to help you pass through the City of Dis."

"We'd appreciate that." Tom reached out his hand.

Yeenoghu held out his finger and they shook.

"How will we pass the circles?" Heleina asked.

"Where is Mother Hildegard?" Yeenoghu glanced around as if counting the humans.

"It was never the mother but a demon," Caroline replied.

"That would be impossible." Yeenoghu sighed.

"Why?" Caroline's eyes widened.

"Because she had a life force." Yeenoghu's eyes widened. "She is lost somewhere down here."

"Oh my god," Caroline stated. "That's why we escaped so easily."

"What are you talking about?" Yeenoghu asked.

"We had to pass through Pandæmonium," Caroline replied. "Winifred's friend who died said she could help us. But it really wasn't her friend, and Kiran was taken by Malus who gave him to Satan, and Satan —"

"Stop." Yeenoghu raised his hand. "First, you listen to me and you listen good. Satan would never allow a mortal in his presence. Your life force is very painful to the dead. That is why we have the veil that separates our worlds. We must be protected from you and you must be protected from us."

"I never knew …" Caroline shook her head.

"Second, Pandæmonium is sacred. The guards would never have allowed you to enter. It would take you several lifetimes to find it."

"But —" Caroline's word was halted by Yeenoghu's large hand.

"You are in a challenge. You are walking through the Endless Maze. A path not well traveled by humans, but a path that shifts with the tones. A fleeting thought could bring a deluge of changes that would only fold one reality onto another."

"You mean," Tom stated, "we are in an ever evolving situation. And us simply walking this path is a crapshoot? Our thoughts are creating the challenges?"

"Something like that," Yeenoghu replied.

Winifred cooed at Kiran, kissing his cheek.

"I think Winifred is in trouble," Caroline whispered. "She's not doing so good."

"Guilt," Yeenoghu replied. "Guild is one emotion humans have problems dealing with. The pain from our actions and non-actions run deep. Once time passes across a threshold, there is no returning. No way to undo what was done."

"Now, you're talking in riddles," Grant stated.

"I think I understand," Heleina replied. "Humans wear our emotions on our sleeves." She shrugged. "As they say ... and because of that, guilt is an emotion that can destroy us."

"Your souls are vulnerable when in human form," Yeenoghu stated.

"Do you have a soul?" Tom asked.

"Every creature with a beating heart houses a soul. Every soul traverses through a life that was predetermined at the time of creation. Think of it as a school or college of existential thought. A new soul knows of nothing. Therefore, depending on how the Creator formats that particular awareness will determine how a soul will evolve, what they will experience."

"Wait." Tom raised his hand. "Are you telling us that ... wait —"

Yeenoghu laughed. "Yes, some souls are created to experience pain, murder, fear. Others may experience love, pleasure, happiness. Just depends on the Creator and what that soul needs for its life force to ascend."

Heleina stepped closer. "Are you saying that the soul is not our life force?"

"Every creature owns a soul," Yeenoghu replied. "And it is through our souls that our life force experiences the existence of the various dimensions. Think of a soul like a vehicle that transports one through the cycles. Not the other way around."

"Then Hell is just a dimension, a world where ... bad souls are punished?" Heleina asked.

"Somewhat," Yeenoghu replied. "That is why some demons look horrible, they are terrifying to others who have not committed the same type of sin. Our souls interpret their actions in a way that we can relate."

"You mean ... these demons look different than what we're seeing?" Tom asked.

Yeenoghu nodded. "And why my fee to Winifred was nothing more than a request for a good word to be placed on my behalf with the Creator. I wish to return to Heaven. Not until I return and wash away my past aggressions may my life force truly shine again."

"What about Kiran?" Caroline asked.

"Kiran was never assigned a soul," Yeenoghu replied. "He is a damaged life force destined to wander through the spectral planes of existence forever."

"But he's being punished," Tom stated. "And due to no fault of his own."

"He is not being punished," Yeenoghu replied. "He feels no emotions, no pain. He simply wanders without the vehicle of a soul to guide him."

"How can we save Kiran and return him to the Creator where he belongs?" Caroline asked.

"From the mother, a life force is created. From the father, the blueprints of the body is formed. Together, they make a child through their bond. Winifred can merge Kiran's spirit back into hers, and he can be born again and with a soul."

"How does she do that?" Caroline asked.

"What about babies that die before they are born?" Heleina asked. "Do they wander forever?"

"No, the Harvesters collect those life forces, re-emerging them with the mother's."

"Why couldn't they do that for Kiran?" Caroline asked.

"Because Kiran's death was not preordained. His path was interrupted prematurely. The Harvesters were never notified."

"Bureaucracy is in Heaven too?" Tom asked.

"Bureaucracy." Caroline rolled her eyes.

"Winifred would have to take Kiran to the Soul Splitters and ask for their life forces to be reunited … twin flames merged into one."

"How does she do that?" Heleina asked.

"Kiran will have to die in Winifred's arms, and she would then have to accept his force back into hers."

"That doesn't sound too terrible," Tom whispered.

"However …" – Yeenoghu raised his hands – "… a demon could pull both life forces into its own at the same time, which Malus could easily do."

"I didn't think he was destroyed by Satan," Caroline whispered. "I knew it was too easy."

"Indeed." Yeenoghu glanced at Winifred and smiled. "One day she *will* make a wonderful mother."

"Is that why mothers love their children so much?" Caroline asked. "Cuz they're actually a piece of their life force?"

Yeenoghu nodded. "Exactly, and why one should never procreate without fully understanding how their spirit is affected."

Grant sighed, deeply. "Where do we find these Soul Splitters, and how do we protect these two …" – he pointed – "… as they merge?"

"And where is Mother Hildegard?" Heleina asked.

After a lift from several large bats, the small group stood precariously at the edge of a tall cliff overhanging a vast bed of human skin. Thousands of faces, male and female, stared up, almost begging for mercy. Snakes coiled from the rips and tears, before striking out with their fanged jaws, hissing.

"What is this place?" Tom asked.

"The gates of Avernus," Yeenoghu replied.

Several demons flew past, their arms yielding large spears and shields.

"Who are they?" Heleina asked.

"Avernus is an upper city in Hell. Many lost souls begin their journey through here. Some never stay. That is why it has become a battle ground where demons and lost souls continuously fight. Demons love to torture, and humans love to argue. Makes the perfect combination." Yeenoghu laughed.

"That's not funny," Caroline stated.

"Perhaps, but still true." Yeenoghu glanced at Winifred. "The Soul Splitters are here, in this city."

"Must we walk across that?" Tom pointed at a snarling face, and a large snake jumped into the air, snapping at his finger. "Damn." He yanked his hand away.

"Yes," Yeenoghu replied. "This is the entrance."

"Isn't this just wonderful." Tom snarled at the face on the ground.

"Winifred," Yeenoghu whispered, "are you ready?"

Winifred kissed Kiran and smiled. "He will disappear when we merge. Correct?"

"Yes, my love," Yeenoghu replied. "I'm afraid you will have to wait for Kiran to return to you one day."

"You mean, once I return to Earth, I can marry, and he will be one of my children?"

"That is correct," Yeenoghu replied. "I wish it could be me you marry, but alas that is not to be."

Winifred met Grant's eyes and smiled. "I'm sure someone out there will want me as their wife one day."

"I am sure of it," Grant stated.

Yeenoghu took a deep breath and sighed. "Shall we begin?"

Winifred cuddled Kiran tightly, following behind the demon while avoiding his tail.

The path hugged the mountainside, winding in and out of caves, deep crevasses, and tall ravines. No trees or plant life. Just barren rocks and smoldering vibrations. At the bottom, the stretched human skin with faces awaited them.

Heleina reached out her foot and tapped on the patchwork quilt. As if a trampoline, her touch made the skin vibrate even more. Snakes jumped, snapping and hissing.

"Who are these people?" Caroline asked, studying a young woman's face.

"Many different races make up this river," Yeenoghu replied. "It is the Creator's way of punishing those who believe they are better than others … just because of how they look. Many kings and queens are woven within this potpourri of colors."

"Blue and green?" Tom asked, stepping onto the taunt but limber path.

"Not everyone here is from Earth," Yeenoghu replied. "Humans live throughout the universe in different galaxies and worlds."

With each snake that lashed out, Yeenoghu waved his hammer and the creature flew across the many faces, only to regain its composure before diving into a gaping hole.

"Hello, Yeenoghu," a blue face with orange eyes said. "Who are your friends?"

"Well, hello, Merneith." Yeenoghu nodded. "Merneith was one of the first rulers of Egypt."

"She's blue," Tom stated.

"If you're skin was stretched into millennia, you'd be blue too," Merneith snapped. "This isn't comfortable."

"If you're an ancient queen, how can you speak our language?" Tom asked.

"In Hell, all languages are the same," Yeenoghu replied. "You are simply understanding what she is saying."

Caroline smirked at Tom and smiled.

"Where are you going?" Merneith asked.

"To see the Soul Splitters," Yeenoghu replied.

"I don't believe they are here." Merneith frowned. "I believe they were summoned to the war between you and Baphomet. As was every other demon. In fact, Beelzebub and Asmodeus were just here looking for you earlier. Wanted to know if any of us had seen you."

"Who is Asmodeus and Beelzebub?" Tom asked.

"Two very annoying fallen angels," Yeenoghu replied. "This probably isn't good news. Thank you, Merneith, for the information. We will leave you now."

"You're welcome." Merneith smiled.

They hiked back to the top of the cliff and Yeenoghu whistled. The bats returned, grabbing the humans in their huge claws. Landing on the balcony of Yeenoghu's castle, they adjusted their stance before gathering with questions.

"Almost back to where we started," Caroline said. "I feel like we're running around in circles."

"There you are," Mother Hildegard stated. "Where have you been?"

"Mother Hildegard?" Heleina ran to her, wrapping her arms around her neck.

"You'll never believe what happened to us," Caroline stated.

"Please stay here, while I check on my war." Yeenoghu nodded as large claws grabbed him around the waist.

"Why did you leave me here?" Mother Hildegard asked.

"Actually," Heleina replied, "we didn't. We followed you out of this city, but you changed into a demon, and you led us to Satan, and Winifred fell into a pit, but Yeenoghu rescued her –"

"Oh my." The mother shook her head. "I was in the bathroom and when I came out, everyone was gone. I honestly thought you had left me behind."

"We would never do that." Heleina shook her head. "As soon as we realized what happened, we wondered how we would ever find you."

Mother Hildegard watched as Winifred played with the baby, oblivious to the rest of the world. "What's wrong with her?"

"I think she's losing it." Caroline pointed to her head. "She was betrayed by her friend, but she wasn't *really* her friend but a demon, and it's just been horrible." Caroline sighed. "I'll take her to our room."

"Maybe sleep would help," Heleina replied.

The demon butler stood by the door and bowed. "Dinner is served."

"That's all he really does around here," the mother whispered, "is serve dinner."

Fourteen

WINIFRED STOOD ON the balcony, watching the flames dance on the other side of the mountain. Yeenoghu was somewhere over there, battling the demon that had raped and haunted her body and soul. How could Yeenoghu taunt her memories, capture and hold her hostage within her thoughts? Was she falling in love with a lord demon? The city lights sparkled from inside the darkness, giving her a moment of pause. Glancing into the perpetual gloom, she longed for the warm touch of the sun's rays. The cool caress of a summer's breeze.

The memories of her childhood were flooded with a sadness that made her heart ache. What was her little brother doing? Obviously, he wasn't playing with cars anymore. He was too old. What was her mother doing? Was she still alive? The old farm probably no longer grew vegetables, and the pigs were most likely dead by now. After fleeing as a teen, Winifred never returned home. She had called her mother a few times just to hear the woman say, 'hello,' before hanging up.

Deb's face flashed briefly in the darkness. She was once her best friend and for many years. They had trained together. Trained on how to lure innocent men to their painful deaths. How many had Winifred help to kill? How many babies had she stolen from their buggies when their mothers glanced at something in a store's window?

"What part of Hell waits for me?" she whispered.

"Winifred?" Caroline stood at the door. "You okay?"

Winifred sighed. "I'm fine."

"May I join you?"

Winifred nodded. "Of course."

"You've been so absorbed lately that I didn't want to intrude."

"It's fine," Winifred whispered.

"Tell me about your childhood."

Winifred leaned against the railing. A tear fell and her heart pounded. "I was ten when my grandmother indoctrinated me into the coven. That meant I was raped by several men at the same time, one right after the other. Happened every few months. At fifteen, I was handed over to Baphomet who was waiting for me in the attic. I became pregnant after one of the ceremonies, and the coven performed a home abortion. I remember Baphomet hiding between the shadows. I'm sure it was him. But never really understood what had happened to me. Eventually, I put two and two together, but by then it was too late."

"I'm so sorry —"

Winifred raised her hand. "Don't be. Has nothing to do with you. Church on Sundays and the devil on Saturdays." Winifred held up her rosary and smiled. " Guess God is in the beads and the devil is what holds them together."

"The devil's *between* the beads," Caroline whispered. "Kinda makes sense. In an odd sort of way."

"We can't have God, the good, without the devil, the bad." Winifred wiped her eyes with the back of her hand. "Holding Kiran makes me feel whole somehow. I know I can't take him with me, but if I could make him a part of me somehow, I'll be okay."

"You can give him life again one day." Caroline touched her friend's arm. "Have a family. Worry about Christmas presents, school clothes, the price of electric bills."

Winifred laughed.

"Grant would make a wonderful husband." Caroline raised a 'brow.

"Yeenoghu has been so wonderful to us," Winifred stated. "It's as if he represents everything that is real. So much stability."

"He built this city for so many lost souls." Caroline glanced over the railing. "Everyone is happy here."

"I bet they crave the sun," Winifred replied. "But something about life is missing from this place."

Caroline laughed. "Yeah, life."

Kiran stirred and Winifred tensed. "I guess it's almost time?"

"Yeah, it's almost time."

A knock on their door pulled them from their thoughts. It was Yeenoghu who was patiently awaiting their presence.

"Who won?" Caroline asked.

"It was a tie," Yeenoghu replied. "However, with the temporary cease-fire, Baphomet and Malus have been ordered to leave you alone."

"Then it's over?" Winifred asked.

"Yes … and no." Yeenoghu nodded. "Are you ready to reunite with your son?"

"Where must we go?" Caroline asked.

"Downstairs," Yeenoghu replied. "The Soul Splitters are here." He smiled.

Winifred giggled. "I'll get the baby."

"Wait." Caroline held up her hand. "Who gave what order?"

"Order?" Yeenoghu asked.

"The order to leave Winifred alone," she replied.

"Oh …" – Yeenoghu laughed – "… the Creator."

The girls followed Yeenoghu just close enough to avoid the switching tail. Entering the throne room, Winifred nodded at Grant who stood patiently next to the others. Kiran wiggled in her arms as she approached several demons who stood solemnly near the large front pillars.

Yeenoghu paused and frowned. "No one but you can do this."

Tears fell from Winifred's eyes as she nodded.

"How do you want to end his life?" a Soul Splitter asked.

Four Soul Splitters – one violet, one indigo, one blue, and one vermillion – waited patiently, each wearing a matching-colored cloak. With large bald heads sporting thick golden eyes, a thinning nose, and taunt lips, they remained somber as if awaiting the results of something unpleasant.

Remembering the tiny baby struggling inside the bull's arms, Winifred closed her eyes, pushing herself back into years past. The abuse had turned into a strength that split her world into many, but it had also kept her safe. Between broken breaths, she whispered, "A knife, please."

The vermillion Soul Splitter stepped forward, holding a red dagger.

Winifred sniffed, accepting the small item. Closing her eyes, she cuddled Kiran closer to her pounding heart. "I love you, baby boy."

Caroline sniffed, placing her hands over her eyes.

Mother Hildegard recited a prayer of forgiveness.

Grant and Tom stepped closer, clasping their hands.

Yeenoghu stood behind Winifred, allowing his large fingers to caress her stiffened back.

Winifred rested Kiran openly on her arm. Clutching the knife tightly, she held it in the air.

The baby cooed and smiled, eyes wide.

"God forgive me," she yelled.

The dagger hit the baby's chest and blood filled Winifred's arms, dripping down her legs. Holding Kiran in close, she closed her eyes and silently prayed for forgiveness.

A light, brighter than a million suns, lit the room. The Soul Splitters chanted, their song lifting and binding the lost spirit.

Winifred sighed as her life force reached into the netherworld, searching for that one lost ember that always glowed brightly during those lonely nights.

A bomb exploded outside her school window, an old woman died in front of a granddaughter, a plane crashed with no survivors, and a spider's web glistened inside the morning dew.

Staring into the bright light, Winifred took a deeper breath. The air was fresh and clean. The staleness had finally lifted. The burden of guilt was gone. In the distance, a woman stood foreshadowing the future, wearing a long, black robe with a purple lining. As Winifred breathed deeper, pushing away the pain, the woman faded into the light.

Creatures with feathery wings glided down, landing only a few feet away. With no heads and just a center eye, they teared ever so slightly. Fluttering their wings, a soft breeze gently pushed Kiran's life force back into Winifred soul. Winifred opened her arms, allowing his little spark to ignite her ever-evolving ambiance.

As the two souls merged, an explosion rocked the city with a longing of home, of love, of purity, of strength, and of salvation. The citizens howled, understanding that a lost soul had just reunited with its creator. An everlasting bond that was growing stronger, never again to break, sealing two fates into one.

The knife clattered across the floor.

Winifred opened her eyes and her arms were empty. Kiran was gone. Only his diaper remained. She fell into Yeenoghu's large arms and cried. Her slender body absorbed his strength to hold her sanity together, embracing her with love. She snuggled, secured inside his protective veil.

A morning light brushed gently against her awakening eyes. Winifred sat up and stretched. If felt as if she had slept a million years. Jumping from her bed, her feet tangled inside something left on the floor. Picking it up, she sighed. Kiran's baby's blanket.

Winifred glanced around not understanding where she was or how she had arrived. An open suitcase sat on a chair. Her favorite purse on a dresser. She glanced out the window, hugging the blanket to her heart. A large backyard with a swing set greeted her.

Finding her robe on the bed, she sighed as she tied the belt around her waist. Still holding the blanket in her hand, she opened the door.

Two little arms wrapped around her legs and a small voice echoed, "Aunt Winni, you're awake."

"Hi, sis." William took the blanket from her. "Sorry, they still play with these old things." William handed her a toddler that had chocolate smeared across his face.

Her eyes stared into the little boy who smiled, grabbing her hair.

"Hungry?" William asked. "You've been sleeping like a log. Plane ride take it out of yah?"

Winifred sat at the table and cuddled the boy in her arms. She could still feel the warm blood running down her legs. Could still feel where his heat had entered her heart.

"What day is it?" she asked.

"Saturday," William replied. "You've only been sleeping for one night. Army working you that hard?"

"Yeah." She took a sip of orange juice. "Army working me really hard."

"Well, you have a week to recover." He sat in the seat next to her. "Mom'll be over later. I didn't tell you yet, but Grandma's not doing so well. You might want to visit while you're here. Doctors don't hold much promise. But the lady is in her nineties."

"Nineties?" Winifred frowned, the numbers were not adding up. Her brother nodded.

"William, what do you remember of us being kids?" Winifred asked.

"Not much," he replied. "You worked the farm a lot. I was too young. When John David died, I thought I would too. Tragic accident."

John David died?

"How *did* your brother die?" Stella asked. "And how old was he?"

"I think Winni was about twelve?" William replied. "John David was the oldest, eighteen or so. He fell off the tractor on my grandparents' farm. The large tire crushed his chest. He lived long enough to reach the hospital. Mom was totally lost with John David dead. Alex never recovered. When he joined the Army and left, Mom really lost it. Then Winni left and it was just me and Mom. Yah know, sis, we hardly visited Grandma after you left. The farm kinda fell apart and they sold it about a year after you moved to Florida. Boarding school, right?"

Winifred nodded.

"A lot changes throughout the years." William took a bite of scrambled eggs.

Evening shadows had deepened, marking the coming of night. Winifred's heels clicked as she walked through the empty halls, the light from the nurse's station guiding her way. She stood at the door marked 415, and with a deep breath, she entered.

The woman resembled a stranger. Short, silver hair now framed the once vibrant face. Pale and sickly, her breaths were shallow and short.

Winifred stood at the bed, placing her hands on the cold metal railing. Glancing around, no little girl waited, no man stood guard. Winifred was alone.

A small light just above the woman's head was enough to give a peak of the future. It was obvious that the reaper was not far away.

Winifred inched closer, caressing the woman's wrinkled hand. The hand that was once strong and demanding. A hand that had given her a banana for practice. A hand that had slapped and pushed and –

"Oh, Grandmother," Winifred whispered. "You were such a sick woman. But I forgive you. You really were all I had. You gave guidance, but not in the direction that was right."

The old woman opened her eyes. Instead of the powerful spirit, only a wilted essence lingered, her glossy eyes searching through the haze as if expecting something more.

"I'm not sure what's happening to me," Winifred whispered, "but I forgive you. Maybe one day, we can talk. But until then, I'll continue to search for the truth. The truth you hid from me, from my mother."

The woman's breath shortened, shallowed.

Winifred wiped Grandmother's brow with her fingers. Her skin felt damp and thinning. She smiled, caressing her cheek. Leaning over, she whispered, "Grandmother, enjoy Hell like I did."

The woman's eyes widened as she took her last breath. Machines beeped and the nurse rushed in.

Winifred smiled. "My grandmother just died."

The nurse checked the dials and touched the old woman's wrist. "Yes, she's gone." Holding the sheet, she gently raised it over the woman's face.

Winifred pulled the sheet back down. "No … I wish to look at her for a few more minutes."

The nurse nodded, leaving quietly.

"Yeenoghu? Are you here?" Winifred whispered.

No answer came, but she could feel his large fingers against her back. Winifred knelt, pulling out her rosary. "In the name of the Father, and of the Son, and of the Holy Spirit…"

She prayed for her grandmother's lost soul. She prayed for her sanity. She prayed for her deceased son. And – she prayed for the Creator to forgive Yeenoghu. Professing her love for the lord demon, her heart suddenly felt stronger. Life was evolving as was her spirit. Didn't matter what the lessons were as long as she continued to learn. And as long as she understood and accepted that her one true lover was an ancient lord demon. A demon she prayed she would one day meet again. A demon that had reunited her with her child. A child conceived in sin but loved throughout his short life. A life that would one day grace her with his presence.

Standing, her knees creaked. Smiling, Winifred pulled the sheet over the witch's face. Placing the beads in the aging hand, she allowed the cross to fall over the thumb as if her grandmother had already received the lord's forgiveness.

"Bye, Grandmother." Winifred nodded. "Thank you, Yeenoghu. But I wouldn't allow *this* person in *your* city if I were you."

As the door closed behind her, Winifred heard Yeenoghu laugh.

Winifred grabbed her bags and sighed. Spring in Germany had arrived with blooming trees and flowers. The sense of life thick and wonderful. She stepped outside the airport and closed her eyes. The warm rays felt wonderful, but then again, everything felt so wrong.

"Hello, beautiful."

Winifred smiled. "Right on time."

Grant kissed her cheek, taking her bags. "Have a good time?"

Winifred nodded. "We buried her in the family plot. Can a witch be buried? Or should we have burned her at the stake?"

"Funny." Grant opened the car door. Sliding in behind the wheel, he smiled. "Will your family be here for the wedding?"

"Of course." Winifred sighed. "It's great to be home."

"Caroline and Tom will be over for dinner. And before you say anything, I've already ordered food. You need do nothing but relax."

"How's your mom?"

"She's home and happy," he replied.

"My memory is a little fuzzy."

"Oh? Like how?" he asked.

"I don't remember returning from –"

"We promised *not* to talk about that," he stated. "Remember? Talking only gives time power. You've been free for how long now?"

"That's talking about it." Winifred smiled.

"We'll write a book," he stated. "Oh … we received a letter from Diana and Pam while you were away. They will be here for the wedding too. Looks like it'll be a full house."

"Mespelbrunn Castle is large enough for everyone." Winifred watched as the beautiful landscape passed by her window.

Grant reached for her hand.

She gently squeezed, admitting the defeat of life versus death, good versus bad, and the warmth versus the cold.

The large lake reflecting the castle turrets melted everyone's heart. Winifred's wedding gown floated over the grass as if carried by angels. With three bridesmaids wearing bright, yellow gowns, she felt like a royal princess, pampered and spoiled. Grant, wearing a purple tuxedo, was most handsome, reminding her of a prince. All he needed was a white horse to rescue her, if he hadn't already.

The place in northern Germany was once a simple house. Throughout the centuries, it grew into a large castle. Winifred picked the site after reading about the history. If a castle could grow and mature, then maybe she could too. The old buildings once held demons within its walls, but it survived. Therefore, the reflective pool not only mirrored the sturdy foundation but also Winifred's inner fears and hopes.

After the wedding, everyone danced into the wee hours of the morning. For three beautiful days and four wonderful nights, Winifred, along with her family and friends, enjoyed the splendor of their gracious hosts.

It was the last night, and Winifred wanted to sit alone with her old friends. The girls had already matured into wives and mothers, but their souls were still deeply entwined.

"Do you ever think about Deb?" Winifred asked.

The garden was in full bloom as the evening sun dropped slowly behind the colorful mountains. A slight breeze pulled the flowers' aroma across their laps, making the girls yearn for more. Birds chirped, welcoming them to the garden.

"Sometimes," Diana replied, "but mostly it's too painful. I just don't understand. I tried talking to my aunt about it all, but she pretended nothing ever happened. She even refuses to admit there was a farm."

"My mom claimed it was just my imagination," Pam added. "Nothing I said or did could change her mind. I was just a stupid Catholic girl playing a stupid game."

"What about Deb's funeral?" Winifred stated. "I mean, my mom never asked what happened. Kids at fourteen do not just die on a camping trip."

"Well, not much we can do about it now," Pam stated. "What was, was. We just have to learn and move on."

"Are you okay with everything?" Diana asked.

"Yes and no," Winifred replied.

"Does that ghost still follow you?" Pam asked.

"You remember that?" Winifred whispered.

"Yes," Pam replied. "We invited him into our world that night together? Tore up my bedroom."

Winifred had almost forgotten about their little ritual. She laughed, pulling the hair from her eyes. "We were so young and naïve."

"What *were* we thinking?" Diana asked.

"Deb was there too," Pam whispered.

Winifred nodded. "Yep. How old were we? Eleven? Twelve?"

"Young and stupid," Pam replied.

The girls sipped on their wine, welcoming the awakening of the evening stars. The children screamed as the fathers chased them over the freshly mowed lawns.

"I guess life begins again tomorrow." Pam sighed.

"I'll miss you guys,' Diana stated.

"Ditto," Winifred whispered. "Life, huh?"

Winifred stood on her balcony that overlooked the quaint German town. She waved when the old lady from across the street glanced up. Their eyes met and a large smile creased the woman's face.

"Caroline's pregnant," Winifred whispered.

Grant wrapped his arms around her waist. "We could try again."

She squealed.

He tickled.

She playfully slapped.

Making love throughout the night, all Winifred could think about was Kiran and how much she wanted him in her arms.

Winifred stood in front of the aging church, staring at the statue that had once reached for her. Life felt uneventful without a word from the Underworld. It had been five years since she said, "I do." But still, no baby. No Kiran to hold. No little one to kiss and care for.

Caroline and Tom's little boy was almost three now. He would be starting school soon. The promise from Yeenoghu didn't seem real anymore. Maybe the merge didn't work. Maybe Kiran was still down there, alone and afraid.

Pushing on the door, the old church creaked as if in protest of being disturbed.

"Hello?" Winifred's voice echoed across the empty altar.

She quietly entered, her eyes scanning the dark shadows. At almost thirty years, her chances of bearing a child was coming to an end. The front bench beckoned her, making her sit. She stared at the man who clung to the cross.

"Is this my punishment?" she asked.

The church remained quiet.

Winifred stared at the almost naked man. She yearned to be with Yeenoghu if only for a few moments. Standing, the aroma of melting wax filled her with memories.

"Are you okay, child?" A priest stood a few feet away, his hands caressing a bible.

"Can you open the door to Hell for me?" she asked.

The man's eyes widened as a 'brow raised. "I'm afraid I do not understand."

"There's a door down that hallway that leads to Hell," she replied. "Can you unlock it for me?"

"Child, there is no door down that hall."

Winifred's eyes darted around the church. She tilted her head and sighed. "I went through that door and it led me to Hell. Mother Hildegard guided me and my friends."

"Mother Hildegard?" the priest repeated.

"Yes, Mother Hildegard." Winifred wiped her eyes. "A nun. She wore a black habit. Carried holy water with her."

"Follow me," he said.

They walked down the same hallway she had walked years earlier. But no door to Hell was in the wall, instead hung a painting of a nun, a woman as dark as the deepest night.

"You mean her?" he asked, pointing.

"Yes, her." Winifred ran her fingers across the dried and cracked, colored oils.

"My child, that woman died over a hundred years ago," the priest replied. "She would not have been able to guide you anywhere, let alone Hell."

Winifred stood back, slapping her hands over her eyes. "This makes no sense."

"My child," the priest stated, "stay and talk to the mother. Many come here to ask for forgiveness."

As the man walked away, Winifred stared at the portrait. "Yeenoghu, she whispered, why have you forsaken me?"

The portrait fizzled into the mist and the door to Hell visualized. Winifred glanced around only briefly before pushing it open. The same stairs were now before her, leading down into the inviting darkness. At the bottom, she felt her way using the walls as a guide.

When she reached the familiar mercury pool, she sighed with relief. Yeenoghu's city was not far now. Inching around the mercury was more difficult since she didn't have a lantern. But she pushed herself to walk. Entering the far hallway, she hurried her pace.

"Yeenoghu," she yelled. "Yeenoghu, where are you?"

Entering the void of nothingness, she paused as the static pain flowed, her heart failing to beat.

"Yeenoghu? Where are you?"

Ignoring the deafening silence, she ran. She ran through the darkness screaming.

"Yeenoghu?"

Hitting something hard, she bounced, her breath ripping from her chest.

"Winifred?" a deep voice echoed.

"Yes," she cried. "I'm looking for Yeenoghu."

Large hands gently picked her up, caressing her inside strong arms. "I am here, my love."

Taking a deep breath, the familiar aroma of Yeenoghu filled her with the calm she had so yearned for. He carried her back to his beautiful city. They sat on his bed, his gaze soft and caring.

"The Creator never came for you?" she asked.

"No," he replied.

Gently, he removed her clothes. Releasing the belt from around his waist, he stood luring over her. Carefully and with more love than she could ever desire, Yeenoghu finally consumed her fully with the passion they so strongly desired. Their love for each other more powerful than ever.

"I love you, Winifred," he whispered.

"And I love you," she replied.

With those last few words, the world dissolved and faint echoes of angels' trumpets blasted. A warm explosion burst through her body, searching for that deep longing of life. Her heart pounded and her mind swirled.

"Winifred?" Grant's voice was calm. "Winni?"

Winifred opened her eyes. The world slowly focused and she smiled.

"What were you doing in that church?" he asked.

"What church?" Winifred tried to sit up but couldn't. Her hands were strapped to a bed. "Where am I?"

"They said you tried to kill yourself," Grant whispered. "You were found naked behind that old church."

"What?" she shook her head. "No, I talked to the priest and he showed me an old painting of Mother Hildegard. Said that the mother —"

"Sleep, my love," he whispered. "Sleep."

"Mrs. Taggart." The woman's voice always grated through Winifred's ears. "Would you like to tell me now what happened?"

The office was nothing special. A small room with a chair and lounge. The lone lamp was the only light. Winifred allowed her eyes to trail around the room, reading off the certificates that hung on the wall.

"Winifred?" the woman said. "I have all the time in the world. If you do not wish to talk today, we can talk next week."

Winifred smiled. "There's nothing to talk about. As I said, I remember nothing." Winifred smiled as the memory of making love to Yeenoghu filled her with a sexual desire that Grant could never fulfill.

"You didn't try to kill yourself?"

"No."

"How did you break your hip?" the woman asked.

"I don't know."

"Why were you naked behind the church?" the woman asked.

"I don't know."

The woman nodded. "I'll fetch your husband," she whispered. "No more today."

Winifred's hip slowly healed. But her stomach refused to be calm. Every morning she rushed to the bathroom, releasing her evening meal. Sleep seemed to be the only escape these days. As the days turned to nights and nights turned back to days, her world rotated on an hour-by-hour basis.

Sitting in the doctor's office felt foreign and invasive. The poking and prodding was more than she wanted to endure. As the door opened and the doctor entered, she smiled.

"Fine, let me know what I'm dying from." Winifred held out her hands.

"You won't die from this," the doctor replied. "You're with child."

Winifred stared at the doctor. At almost thirty years of age, being pregnant was the farthest thing from her mind. She thought about Grant. "How far along?"

"You're about three months," the doctor replied.

"Three months?" Winifred stated.

Allowing her mind to wander, she counted back on her fingers. That was close to the night she spent with Yeenoghu. She and Grant had been married for over five years and no children. Touching her belly, she smiled. A love child between her and her demon. Was it even possible?

Winifred stood and nodded. "Thank you."

"You're welcome." The doctor wrote in her chart. "Talk with the receptionist about future appointments. I want to see you every six weeks. During the last trimester, we'll drop it down. You good?"

"I'm good."

Winifred rode the train in silence. As the houses and trees flew past, so did her life. A baby cried from somewhere in the back. A child ran up and down the aisle. A couple kissed in the next row over. Life was happening all around her and a new life was growing inside. But who was the father?

"We need to talk." Winifred placed her fork on her napkin and folded her hands. "I'm pregnant, Grant."

"What?" a large grin creased his face. "Baby, that's wonderful –"

Winifred raised her hand, shaking her head. "We need to talk."

"Okay." Grant studied her eyes, probably searching for a clue.

"I want to talk about Hell," she stated.

"We are not –"

"Yes, we will," she said. "Do you remember leaving Hell?"

Grant looked away.

"Stop already," she replied. "Just stop. Do you or do you not remember leaving Hell?"

Grant shook his head.

"Neither do I." She picked up her water and took a sip. "How did we get back? When did we get back? I woke up at my brother's house for Christ's sake. I buried my grandmother. What the fuck. And … we never talk about it."

"My memory is from picking you up at the airport," he replied. "Nothing has made any sense."

"Absolutely, nothing," she repeated. "But I'm pregnant. Remember when I was found at the church?"

Grant nodded.

"I went … I'm not sure why. I think I wanted validation for what happened to us. To know that it was real."

"I can understand that," he replied.

"But the priest said that Mother Hildegard lived over a hundred years ago. He showed me her painting that was hanging on the wall. When I stared at it, it turned into the door to Hell. I entered and found Yeenoghu."

"You think he's the father?"

"I don't know," she yelled. "Nothing is making any sense."

"You still love him, don't you?"

"Love who?" she asked.

"Yeenoghu."

Winifred shook her head. "Look at everything I was going through at that time. That demon saved me from Baphomet and Malus. And … he gave me my son. Of course, I'm gonna have feelings for him, wouldn't you? He saved me."

"We saved you!" Grant yelled. "Caroline … Tom … my mother, Mother Hildegard, *we* saved you. We went to Hell for you. You brought that demon back here to be with you? And now, it's inside you?"

"What do you want me to do?" Winifred asked. "Abort the baby?"

Grant stood, throwing his napkin on his plate. "Yes, that is exactly what I want you to do. Abort that demon baby!"

Winifred froze. She could not believe what she was hearing. "Are you serious? All the guilt and pain I experienced and you want me to go through it again? How do you know it's not yours?"

"We tried for five years and nothing."

"What does that have to do with anything?"

Grant sighed. "I guess everything."

"Then leave …" – she stood – "… or I will."

"There's the door," he said, pointing.

Winifred grabbed her purse. She walked into the street and screamed.

Fifteen

THE MILITARY GAVE Winifred an early out. With no place to go, she turned to her mother. Standing in front of the old house sent chills down her spine. Winifred never expected to return. But here she was, back in California, staring at her old front door or lack thereof.

"Come in," her mother stated. "Don't let the flies in."

Winifred entered her old room. Nothing had changed. The bed was still near the far wall. The dresser still had her old things – a mirror, cologne, hairbrush, and comb. After hanging up her clothes, she sat near the dresser and pulled up the floorboard. Reaching inside, she dug out a couple of old pacifiers.

It was real. Everything that had happened to her had been real. Her life, her torment, her fears, all real.

"Mom?"

"Yes." Her mother smiled.

"May I borrow the car?"

"Of course. Would you like to talk?"

"Not right now." Winifred grabbed the keys and darted outside.

The drive to the mission was shorter than she remembered. As a child, it seemed to take more than half a day. Parking the car took some effort as spaces were at a premium in the small town. Standing by the wall that used to be pink, but now white, it didn't seem as tall or intimidating. She glanced into the garden and frowned. The old statue and fountain were gone, replaced by an oak that towered over the mission. Laughing to herself, she sighed. The place looked so small. Just one room. Several smaller buildings had been built along the back, but nothing as grand as what she remembered. The white building that was owned by the coven was just around the corner. Leaving her car behind, she walked past the park and up the short street.

"This road used to run for miles." Shaking her head, she laughed. "Odd how perspectives change."

The end of the white building stuck out like a slice of stale bread. Her heart pounded as she approached. The windowless building still held a silent control that hung over her like a heavy cloud. How could an empty building feel so threatening?

Slowly, she reached out a hand and tried the door.

It was locked.

She walked to the back and sighed. The small chair and table were still there. Although old and frail, they were a powerful reminder of a life that had long passed.

The back door had been kicked in.

"No need for a key," she whispered.

Peeking inside, the heavy drapes were gone. Nothing remained except for a large empty room. She entered and the darkness felt only somewhat threatening. Using a small flashlight, she glanced around. The stairs were still there, but the balcony had long since fallen. On the floor, the painted pentacle that was once dark and bold was now barely visible.

She kicked a few things with her foot. Something small scurried across the floor. The power that once filled this room was gone. No witch stood hailing a false god. No warlock stood at a table, holding a knife for a sacrifice. Just a huge empty space with a ceiling that was rotting and breaking away.

Winifred laughed. She laughed so hard that her stomach cramped. She touched her belly and smiled. Feeling strong and empowered, she left the way she had entered.

"Push!" a nurse yelled.

"Winni," the doctor stated from between her legs, "one last push, and he'll be here."

Winifred held her breath and pushed. Her hip ached but she pushed harder. A warm gush touched her legs and a baby cried. She rested her head and smiled. "He's here," she whispered.

The doctor placed the baby on her chest.

The nurse wiped his face.

The baby whimpered, gasping a few times.

"Kiran," Winifred whispered.

"What?" the nurse asked, cleaning the baby's eyes.

"Kiran," Winifred repeated. "His name is Kiran."

The nurse screamed and backed away.

"What?" Winifred stared at the woman who was pointing at the baby. "What is it?"

"His eyes!" the nurse yelled. "And his feet!"

Winifred pulled aside the blanket and lifted Kiran's chubby leg. A small hoof was attached to where the foot should have been. Raising the top of her bed, she cuddled the baby in her arms.

Kiran opened his eyes

Winifred held her breath.

Kiran had his father's eyes – dark brown with a slight yellow tint and red slits instead of round, black pupils.

The doctors had no explanation for the feet. His eyes were explained by a genetic disorder. Otherwise, the child was perfectly healthy.

They returned home a few days after Kiran was born. He weighed seven and a half pounds and was almost twenty inches long. Sleeping most of the time, the baby was a breeze. Winifred slept when he slept and piddled around the house when he was awake.

When Kiran was almost six months old, a knock on the front door gave Winifred a moment to think about visitors. She didn't need onlookers being noisy. Visiting the pediatrician was bad enough. But to have strangers come by only to stare?

Her mother signed for something and closed the door.

"What is it?"

"From the probate office," she replied. "Here is one for you."

Winifred opened the envelope and gasped.

"From my mother's estate," her mother said.

"This is a lot of money." Winifred stared at the check. "How wealthy were your parents?"

Her mother shrugged. "I guess heading up a coven and having friends in high places pays off."

"This is enough to live on for the rest of our lives. How much did you get?" Winifred asked.

"Five million," her mother replied. "And you?"

"Ten million?" Winifred rolled her eyes. "What do I do with ten million dollars?"

"Live." Her mother shrugged again.

Winifred and her mother bought a house on several acres that were far from town. Nestled deep inside a hidden valley, they felt safe from the outside world and roaming eyes.

As her phone chirped, Winifred glanced at the name. "Hi, Caroline."

"How's Kiran?"

"Wonderful," Winifred replied. "How are your little ones? How's Tom?"

"The little ones are no longer little and Tom's great. Have you heard from Grant?"

"Divorce was finalized years ago," she replied. "No child support. The lawyer said I was crazy not asking for any. But I don't need it. Don't want his money anyway."

"Did you ever really love him?"

Winifred allowed her heart and mind to wander. "Not sure. Sometimes, I think I did. But honestly, probably not. He was more of a security blanket, a habit."

"Habit? A black habit?"

The women laughed.

"What do you remember of our visit to Hell?" Winifred asked. "We've never talked about it."

"Nothing." Caroline sighed. "I just remember waking up with a newborn in my arms and Tom smiling. It was so odd."

"I hate to ask this ... but could we still be there?"

Caroline didn't respond.

"What if we never left? What if we're still traversing the Endless Maze?"

"Don't say that." Caroline sighed. "My god, Winifred, what if we *are* still there?"

"It's just that life has been so sketchy. So on and off. One minute I'm here and the next I'm over there ..."

"I know, right? When I'm alone and everyone is asleep, I try to piece my life together and there is no continuous line. It's all mixed up. And you know what is really weird?"

"What?" Winifred wasn't sure if she wanted to know the answer.

"Several years ago, I visited that castle where we were going to do an exorcism. Remember? And your grandmother showed up with those shadows."

"I remember."

"I walked through the place," Caroline stated, "and nothing had changed. And … where your grandmother first appeared …"

"Yeah?"

"There's a burn mark on the floor."

"Burn mark?"

"Yes, and something like a vortex floating in the air." Caroline's breathing became heavy.

"Wait … what?"

"When you go to bed tonight, write yourself a note," Caroline stated.

"What do you mean?"

"Just do it. Write a note on the mirror, and on a piece of paper. Tape the paper to the mirror. Call me when you read it next."

"You mean tomorrow?"

"It won't be tomorrow," Caroline replied, ending the call.

Winifred pulled out a marker and scribbled on her dresser mirror. She then printed the same words on a piece of paper, taping it next to the words. Shrugging, she climbed into bed.

The birds chirping woke Winifred from a deep sleep. She moaned as she climbed out of bed. Glancing at the clock, she sighed, almost ten. Time to pull her mother and Kiran out of bed for the day. Although he was almost eighteen and home-schooled, Kiran needed to remain on a schedule.

Using her brush, she pulled the bristles through her thick hair. Leaning a little closer, several words written in black grabbed her attention.

Call Caroline when you read this...

Winifred frowned. "When did I write this?"

A frayed piece of paper, yellowed from aging tape, rested on the dresser. Unfolding the paper, her mind flipped a few times. Grabbing her phone, she tapped on Caroline's number.

"See what I mean?" Caroline didn't even say hello.

"I don't understand," Winifred replied.

"We've lost many years," Caroline stated. "I wrote a date on my mirror. The last time we spoke was over seventeen years ago. Winifred, I think we're still in Hell."

Winifred stared at her reflection. The wrinkles of times had tweaked the corners of her eyes, sagging them slightly above her cheeks. "Oh my god, I think you're right."

"None of this is real."

"We have to find our way through this maze," Winifred replied. "It's another puzzle."

"Mom?" Kiran said from the hallway. "Who are you talking to?"

Winifred turned to her son and smiled. "Malus, you can stop this charade now. Your tricking days are over."

The floor vibrated and the room spun.

Winifred screamed as a bloody knife materialized in front of her.

Yeenoghu whispered softly in her ear. "It's okay Winifred, you're okay."

"No!" she yelled, pushing herself from his strong embrace. "We're not okay."

"What are you talking about?" he asked.

Winifred stood and stared at the Soul Splitters. "You did not protect us. Malus has taken Kiran. That is why he's gone." She flung the diaper across the room. "You didn't protect us."

"What are you talking about?" Yeenoghu asked.

Caroline screamed and her body jerked as it floated across the room.

Tom hovered, yelling, slamming into a wall before crashing to the floor.

Mother Hildegard suddenly aged, her skin flaking as if overbaked.

Heleina dropped to the floor, melting as if wax, sealing the floor with her essence.

Grant stood silent. His eyes darting from friend to friend.

Yeenoghu stood with wide eyes. "Damn you, Baphomet. You have broken our truce."

"Where is my child?" Winifred aimed for the Soul Splitters, grabbing the one with the vermillion robe, hitting and slapping him across the face. "I'm tired of this shit. Where is my child?"

"The spirits merged," he yelled, trying to dodge the assault.

Yeenoghu grabbed the flailing Winifred. "We'll figure this out. Shh, we'll figure this out."

The small group huddled around the dining table, sipping on coffee or tea.

Mother Hildegard kept dropping sugar cubes into her cup, tasting after each swirl.

"I had a life," Caroline stated.

"*We* had a life." Tom circled his hand through the air for emphasis.

"I divorced you?" Grant asked.

"I don't know where I was." Heleina shook her head. "I just remember darkness."

"I was stuck in a damn painting," Mother Hildegard yelled. "Try that for eighteen years. Hard on the back."

Grant shook his head and laughed. "Our wedding was beautiful." He gently touched Winifred's hand.

"Yes, it was beautiful," she replied.

"I don't remember *my* wedding." Caroline glared at Tom. "Probably cuz we never had one."

"This is quite the maze." Tom sipped on his tea. "How do we know what is real and what isn't?"

"When we finally step out of Hell," Mother Hildegard stated, "we'll know."

"I'm not so sure," Winifred replied. "I mean, I buried my grandmother. I visited old places. I raised a child for Christ's sake."

"Hell is not supposed to be pleasant," Heleina added. "It's supposed to be torture."

Caroline stood. "Yeenoghu needs to look into this. For him, our lifetimes never existed. We never left this place."

"But we did," Winifred stated. "I lived a life. Maybe not the best, but I did live."

"I divorced you?" Grant asked again.

"Perhaps life is nothing more than an illusion." Tom poured his tea onto the table, watching as it dripped to the floor. "What if none of this is real? Just a movie playing inside someone's mind?"

"Speculating is not doing us any good!" Caroline snapped.

"We must work together." Mother Hildegard dropped another sugar cube into her cup. "If we don't, we will fail."

"I would never divorce you, Winni," Grant whispered.

"Perhaps," Winifred replied. "But we must stick together."

The breeze felt cool against Winifred's face as she stood where she and Yeenoghu had shared a private dinner. The city lanterns glowed against the darkness, creating a kaleidoscope pattern.

"You and Grant married?" Yeenoghu asked from behind.

"Supposedly," she replied. "But it was you that gave me my son."

Winifred walked up to the sitting demon and climbed into his lap. "How could we make love?" she asked. "You're several times larger than me. But when I was with you, you were so gentle and caring."

"Love is just an illusion."

Winifred leaned in close, allowing their lips to meet. Her heart raced and her mind fluttered. "I think I am in love with you."

"And I you, but we are of different worlds." He frowned. "Our love can never be."

"But I am here now." She pulled off her blouse.

His eyes trailed down her bare chest. Tilting his head, he smiled. "Marry me, Winifred. Be my wife *here* forever."

"Yes," Winifred whispered. "I will marry you."

Bright lights blared as the explosion rocked the city. Screams and shouts filled the street. The Soul Splitters glanced around, understanding that something was very wrong. Yeenoghu stood. Winifred and Caroline screamed. Tom and Grant ran for the balcony.

"What in the hell is going on around here?" Yeenoghu yelled.

Winifred sat, feeling dumbfounded. "We are in a time warp."

"What?" Heleina yelled. "We're in a what?"

"Time warp," Winifred replied. "The same moment is being played out over and over again."

"Is that possible?" Heleina asked.

"It's possible," Yeenoghu replied. "And I think I know who is responsible."

"How can you stop this?" Mother Hildegard asked. "By the time we've figured it out, another life is playing."

Yeenoghu raised his hammer into the air and screamed. "Satan, I hail the most powerful, the most mighty. I call on you to stop this madness."

The vibration stopped. The wind stopped.

Mother Hildegard opened one eye and peeked around the room.

"Did that work?" Caroline whispered.

Thunder roared from a distance. Winifred ran to the balcony. Over the far mountain ridge, fire danced. A war was raging. A war between demons. "Where's Yeenoghu?" Winifred darted into the next room. "It's happened again. We're back at the start of the war!"

"Stand back." Winifred whistled.

They waited.

She whistled again.

The fluttering of wings sounded as several flying demons soared out of the clouds with outreached claws. Winifred pointed at the fiery mountains where the flames seemed to be growing. As the city lanterns faded into the darkness, the sounds of the battle grew louder.

Explosions rocked the mountainside as rows upon rows of demons marched. Yeenoghu stood on the bow of his ship, yelling out orders. She couldn't see Baphomet from where she stood but knew he was down there somewhere.

A bomb blew and rocks rained down from the surrounding cliffs. Demons yelled as they rushed into battle, slinging their swords, raising their shields. Horns sounded and the beasts marched. Large flying creatures dropped boulders from above, splashing the demons' blood across the open field.

"Now that's a war," Tom yelled. "How crazy is this?"

Mother Hildegard held her rosary, making the sign of the cross.

"Can't we do anything?" Caroline asked.

"Like what?" Winifred shrugged. "Grab your sword and pitchfork."

"I guess you're right." Caroline sighed.

"Wait!" Winifred waved for everyone to huddle. "Listen, I know that Satan and these demons are all powerful, but we have something more."

"Something more?" Tom asked.

Winifred glanced at the mother and smiled.

Mother Hildegard nodded.

The group huddled, each clutching their rosary. At the same time, they made the sign of the cross.

Silence.

"Again," Winifred whispered.

Again, the group clutched their rosaries, making the sign of the cross.

Darkness fell, covering them like a warm blanket. As if a bucket had fallen over their heads, nothingness created a deafening silence. Their eyes searched through the blackness, but blindness had already attacked their senses.

"Where are we?" Caroline whispered.

"I'm not sure," Winifred replied.

"Do we dare look around?" Tom asked.

"Not sure," Heleina said.

Grant stood and took a step back. "There is nothing here."

"But where is here?" Winifred asked.

"We wait," Mother Hildegard whispered.

The friends stood in a circle holding hands. As they said The Lord's Prayer, a dim light flickered from the distance. They repeated the words over and over as the light grew brighter and larger.

"Something is coming," Heleina whispered.

"Just let it happen," Mother Hildegard replied.

Holding hands, they prayed, over and over again. As the light drew closer, their beads glowed. Taking a deeper breath, they screamed The Lord's Prayer.

"Our father, who art in heaven ..."

"I hear your prayers," a voice said.

"How do we know if it's not you or another demon tricking us again?" Heleina yelled. "We don't trust you anymore Malus."

They continued to pray. "... thy will be done ... on Earth as ..."

"You are no longer on Earth," the voice stated.

"Enough, Malus!" Heleina yelled. "We do not care about your illusions. We can remain here and pray forever if that is what it takes."

"... our daily bread, as we ..."

The mountains returned along with the raging war. Bombs exploded as large bats soared through the blazing fire. Blood pooled before creating deep rivers in the soil. Both sides yelled as swords cut through the dense smoke, creating white lines of fear.

Winifred closed her eyes and prayed. She prayed for every thought that touched her mind. She forgave everyone for anything that had happened to her. She begged for her own forgiveness. Releasing her soul, she leaned back, falling into the nothingness of the malicious demon's liar.

Sixteen

THE MORNING LIGHT dawned through a misty haze. Winifred opened her eyes, feeling the warmth of the blankets comforting her. Yawning and stretching, she smiled.

Sitting up a little straighter, her apartment in Germany greeted her. She picked up the phone before glancing briefly at the calendar on the wall. It was one day before her friends would try to exercise her demon.

"There has to be a way to stop this madness," she yelled.

Winifred showered and dressed for work. As she rode the train, she studied those sitting around her. They seemed content in their hurried life. Why couldn't she be content?

Walking to the medical center, her mind wandered. Changing into scrubs, she readied for her first patient. A little boy of about three or four.

"He fell," the mother said.

"Where did he fall?" Winifred asked as most children's bones were flexible and hard to break.

"He stumbled on the stairs," the mother replied, refusing to make eye contact.

Winifred helped the little boy onto the table. "I'll need you to leave while I snap the pictures."

The mother paused before walking out the door.

Winifred smiled at the little boy. "Can you lay real still for me? I'm gonna take your picture now."

The little boy nodded.

Winifred walked behind the shield and hit the button.

The machine beeped and hummed.

"Okay, let's move your hand this way," she whispered. "How did you break your arm?"

"Daddy did it," the little boy said.

"Oh? And how did Daddy break your arm?"

The machine hummed and beeped again.

"Like this." The boy grabbed her arm, twisting it.

Winifred helped him off the table. "Sit right here for me, okay?"

The little boy nodded.

Winifred stared at the dials, understanding. It was not a clean break but a twisting of the bone. She sighed, lowering her head. Picking up the phone, she smiled at the little guy who was sitting patiently on the chair.

"Sarge?" Winifred stated. "I have a situation."

"I'll be right down."

Kiran entered her mind and she thought about someone hurting him. She would have to attack them. No one would ever hurt her babies.

"What's up, Winifred?" the sergeant asked.

"It's a twisted bone," she replied. "Not a break. Means abuse."

"Wrap it up, Winifred. This is the Captain's son. Not a fucking thing we can do about it."

Winifred frowned. She opened the door and nodded to the mother. "Not a break, just a slight twist. It happens sometimes."

The little boy glanced once at Winifred before reluctantly following his mother down the hall.

"Nothing we can do, huh?" she whispered.

Winifred closed her eyes and concentrated, allowing her spirit to leave her body and float across space. She had looked up the little boy's address before leaving for the day. All she had to do now was concentrate on the location.

Opening her eyes, she found herself standing in front of a large house. A rather nice-looking house. The mother was in the kitchen washing dishes. The father was in the lounge.

Winifred entered through a large window. She hovered in front of the man who was puffing on a cigar.

His eyes widened as she materialized.

"You twisted that little boy's arm," she whispered, "so I will twist you."

The man screamed as his body morphed into something no longer human.

She left as quietly as she had entered, hovering just outside the window.

The mother ran into the lounge, carrying a hand towel. She paused and screamed. Running to her husband, she gagged before backing away, understanding that he was dead.

The authorities arrived, hesitating before entering the room.

Captain *What's His Name* sat in his chair with his cigar still clinging to his lips. But his head was twisted on backward, and the cigar was burning a small hole in the chair. The arms were bent at odd angles, not broken, just twisted. With his feet dangling behind the chair, the authorities had no idea how his torso and bottom half were opposite each other. A demonic site for a demon of a man.

"Yeenoghu?" Winifred whispered. "Please give this man a personal tour of Hell for me."

Winifred opened her eyes. Rolling over, she pulled the blankets closer around her neck. Taking a deep breath, she allowed the darkness of sleep to consume her.

Standing at the x-ray machine, Winifred's heart pounded. If felt good to take that man's life. After being tormented as a child, the thought of any child being abused was something she would never accept. Then again, was her life just a dream? Was she still in Hell, stumbling through the Endless Maze?

The day ended and it was time to meet Caroline and Tom for dinner. Afterward, they planned on exercising her demon, Baphomet, and his crony, Malus, in the dilapidated old castle.

But nothing was making any sense. How could she know about Yeenoghu if she hadn't entered Hell yet? Why were her memories so jumbled? Was the past mixing with the future? Would the rip in the veil ever be resealed?

"Feels like déjà vu," Tom whispered. "As if I've done this before."

Caroline laughed.

Winifred stared at her friends and frowned as Grant and Heleina entered the restaurant.

"Afternoon." Grant pulled out a chair for his mother.

"How is everyone?" Heleina asked.

"Tom said we've done this before." Winifred took a sip of her wine. "Have we?"

"I've been having the same strange feelings," Heleina replied. "White wine, a Chardonnay will work."

The waiter nodded.

"We have been here before," Caroline replied. "But, shh." Pulling out a notepad, she wrote:

We're in a time warp. Don't say the words or time will trip, and we'll have to start over again. Pretend as if everything is normal. Follow my lead.

The note passed from person to person who nodded.

Caroline took the note and blacked out the words. "Yah know what? There's that new movie in town. Why don't we go see it? I don't feel like tripping through a dark forest tonight. Do you?"

"Nope." Winifred nodded.

"Movie sounds great," Grant replied.

Heleina nodded. "I'm in."

"Okay then, let's go." Tom stood.

The five left the restaurant and hailed a taxi. As the car neared the corner, a nun resembling Mother Hildegard entered the cafe. Glancing around, she frowned, before leaving the same as she had entered.

The four Soul Splitters eyes searched the room as if something wasn't right.

Winifred leaned against Yeenoghu, clutching her chest. "Kiran's in me," she whispered. "I can feel him."

"Something is wrong –" a Soul Splitter started to say.

Yeenoghu raised his hand. "Do not speak the thought."

Caroline nodded.

Tom crossed his arms.

Grant hugged his mother.

Mother Hildegard took several steps but paused. "Wait." She held up her rosary and whispered something no one could hear.

Everyone froze in place, not moving, not blinking. Several times, Grant glanced at his watch. Mother Hildegard tapped her foot as if counting.

Time passed, slowly at first, but speeding up as the seconds ticked. With no sun to set over a horizon, it was difficult to know how long they had waited.

"Sir," the demon in uniform stated, "Baphomet and Malus are here to speak with you."

Winifred glanced at the door, holding her breath.

A huge demon with glowing yellow-red eyes entered. His head barely fit through the large double doors. Behind, the tiny demon that resembled a pig without a skeleton followed.

"Yeenoghu," Baphomet stated. "We have a problem."

Yeenoghu held Winifred in a strong embrace. Not looking at his visitors, he replied, "And what is that?"

"Malus …" – Baphomet pointed to his partner – "… has created a situation where we are repeating our steps. I do not know about you, but as for me, I am tired of this game."

Malus nodded, his hands shaking.

"However, he cannot reverse this plague." Baphomet clasped his hands. "I do not know what to do."

"I do," Mother Hildegard replied.

"Who are you?" Baphomet asked.

"I am a nun," she stated, "representing the bright one."

"The bright one?" Baphomet repeated. "How did you get here?"

"Does that matter if she can help?" Yeenoghu hugged Winifred a little tighter. "We just merged two life forces with the help of the Soul Splitters. She is vulnerable and cannot be moved."

"You must sign a truce," Mother Hildegard stated. "A truce that will be most painful and expensive."

Baphomet sat, and the floor trembled from his weight. "What are the terms? I do not like what I am experiencing. Yeenoghu, are we warring or are we not? Have you won or have I won? We have fought so many battles over the last hour I've lost count."

"You must go where the bright one lingers." Mother Hildegard held up her rosary. "It is there, you must speak your penance."

"Beg for mercy?" Baphomet shook his head. "Never!"

"Then remain in this loop," Mother Hildegard replied.

Baphomet sighed deeply. He closed his eyes, pounding his fist into his hand. "Damn you, Malus, I told you to leave the girl alone!"

Malus glanced away, trying to hide his shaking hands.

Standing on the cliff that overlooked the large river, the demons seemed more like mountaintops to Winifred than entities. Yeenoghu carried his hammer and Baphomet carried his sword. As for Malus, he stood behind them, trying to control his shaking hands.

"Our world is threatened," Yeenoghu stated. "If the bright one enters, our darkness will vanish. How will our souls redeem their virtue without a place to contemplate their sins?"

"My kingdom will merge with yours," Baphomet replied. "What a horrid thought."

Yeenoghu laughed. "Indeed."

"You must raise your hands in prayer," Mother Hildegard stated.

"Do what?" the demons said at the same time.

"Like this ..." The mother raised her hands as the rosary beads waved in the wind.

"What happens then?" Baphomet asked.

Mother Hildegard shrugged. "I have no idea."

"How do you know this?" Yeenoghu asked.

"A voice keeps telling her," Heleina replied. "I can hear it too."

"A voice?" Grant asked.

"A voice," Heleina replied. "A woman's voice."

Winifred touched Yeenoghu's shin with her tiny hand. "Grandmother?"

"Grandmother who?" Baphomet asked.

"I think it's my grandmother talking to us." Winifred shook her head. "Another trick maybe?"

"We do this on three?" Baphomet asked.

Yeenoghu nodded.

"One … two …"

The bright light flashed. Winifred fell into Yeenoghu's arms, screaming. The four Soul Splitters slapped their hands on their heads.

"Again?" Mother Hildegard asked.

Yeenoghu waved as the small group walked the path that led out of town. Malus stared up at Baphomet who held his breath. Winifred allowed her heart to ache as she entered the darkness. Perhaps, a futile attempt, but they had to try.

As before, the large domed filled the landscape. Only this time, no demon sat in the seats. No humans screamed. No beasts guarded the entrance.

Following the path that the fake Deb had shown them, they soon exited the dome, heading for the endless pit that was the City of Dis. Souls were still walking in circles, and the ugly trees were still ugly. As they approached, a yellow demoness, somewhat resembling a cow, stepped forward.

"I am Azazzel," a soft voice said. "You're my last mission."

"Last mission?" Winifred repeated.

"Yes," Azazzel replied. "I've finished my time here and will soon be with the bright one. I'm to escort you through the City of Dis."

The friends eyed each other before beathing a sigh of relief.

"Thank goodness," Heleina whispered. "We were wondering how to pass without being caught in the endless circles."

"It's easy." Azazzel shrugged. "You take the bridge."

"What bridge?" Winifred asked.

"That bridge." Azazzel grabbed a handful of dirt, tossing it in the air. The dust settled and a footpath materialized. "You just need to understand the tricks."

"Tricks?" Winifred repeated.

"Tricks." Azazzel laughed and her face lit. "Every city has a trick in order to pass. You just have to figure it out. That's all."

"What about this Endless Maze?" Heleina asked. "Is there a trick to it?"

"Of course." Azazzel sighed, grabbing another handful of dirt. As the dust settled, an arch materialized. "You must go that way. When you come to a decision, toss dirt into the air. The dust will show you the way."

Winifred nodded. "Thank you." She stepped under the arch and smiled. After a forever of traversing the barren landscape, the mercury pool was finally just in front of her with bright colors flashing from below. They navigated along the pool's rim with their backs against the bricks. The long hall was a most welcomed relief. Taking the stairs two or three at a time, they yelped as they pulled the old door shut behind them.

Mother Hildegard yanked out her ring, shoving the huge, old key into the lock. With a loud click, she recited a short prayer.

"Throw some of the water on that door!" Tom ordered.

The mother laughed, releasing the last few drops.

They entered the sanctuary, feeling dirty and tired.

"Could you not find what you were looking for?" the priest asked.

"Father," Winifred stated, "how long were we gone."

The priest frowned, shaking his head. "Maybe five minutes? Have you changed your minds?"

"Not at all." Winifred darted for the large, entry doors.

They stepped into the warm sun, allowing the rays to penetrate their souls. As they passed the statue of Mother Mary, each raised their hands, performing the sign of the cross. Mother Hildegard kissed her beads and waved.

"How do you feel?" Grant asked Winifred.

"Like I need a shower." Winifred shrugged.

"I feel dirty, but cleansed at the same time," Heleina stated.

"Me too," Tom replied.

Walking down the street to their cars, they greeted everything they met – people, trees, cars, dogs, and cats. Life felt different somehow. Life felt clean.

Standing in her apartment, the phone rang. "Hello?"

William was crying. "Grandmother is dead."

"I'll leave right away, love you." Winifred hung up the phone and frowned.

Grant nodded.

"My grandmother just died. I have to fly home."

Seventeen

WINIFRED STOOD IN front of the old mission, allowing her eyes to trail along the ancient brick wall. It wasn't white but still pink. The statue was still in the garden, although the fountain was now filled with flowers. Glancing down the street, the old white building was gone, replaced with a diner. Large windows facing the street felt welcoming as if the secrets were gone.

Diana and Pam stood at the mission doors with their little ones clinging to their hands. Off to the side stood her mother and brothers. After a few hugs and kisses, they entered.

Winifred walked up to her grandmother who lay sleeping between the silk sheets. For the first time, the woman looked at peace with the world. Winifred reached for the old woman's hand but paused. Would she be whisked away through another time warp? As their fingers touched, nothing happened. The hand didn't feel real. It was cold to the touch.

A cool breeze caressed Winifred as she leaned over, kissing her grandmother on the forehead.

"I forgive you."

Winifred glanced at Father Hurley and smiled. The man looked ancient. When Winifred was little, it was Father Hurley who would chase her through the church, demanding respect. Now, she was sure the man could hardly stand without help.

"Father?" Winifred nodded.

"Miss Winnie?" he stated.

"It's me, Father."

"And me, Pam." Pam stepped closer.

"And me, Diana." Diana touched Winifred's shoulder.

"All but one," Father Hurley stated. "Deb is with our maker." He gave the sign of the cross. "Girls, I am sorry for your loss … and for your youth."

"Thank you," Winifred replied. "But it is no true loss to me."

"Nor me," Pam whispered.

"Nor me," Diana said.

"We forgive you, Father," Winifred stated, before walking away.

Not stopping to console her mother, Winifred stepped outside, taking a deep breath. The ocean breeze felt salty against her skin. The sun warm. Stepping down the stairs, she stood by the old wall, running her hand across the top. "We were so little," Winifred stated. "Just babies."

"Just babies," Pam replied.

"Deb was just a baby," Diana whispered.

"Did we ever find out what happened that night?" Winifred asked. The women shook their heads.

"Maybe we should?" Winifred shrugged.

"What for?" Pam replied. "Grandmother is gone. As are most of the others. If not, they're older than dirt. What would come of it?"

"Perhaps, nothing," Winifred said. "You know that I had an abortion?"

"We know," Diana whispered.

"Sometimes it feels as if everything happened only yesterday." Winifred ran her other hand over the wall.

Diana pushed the small gate open and stood in front of the statue of Mother Mary. "She was so tall once."

"Very tall," Winifred replied.

"What happened? Can statues shrink?" Diana laughed.

"Grass." Winifred wiped her foot over the soft green growth.

"The bricks are gone," Diana replied.

"I still have scars on my knees." Pam chuckled.

"It's as if God has washed the evil away," Winifred added. "Maybe a good thing."

"Sometimes," Pam replied. "But sometimes it's better to remember. To make sure it doesn't happen again."

"Oh, it'll happen again," Diana stated. "Just because our past was cleansed doesn't mean evil won't lurk around every corner."

Pam laughed.

"What?" Diana asked.

"I arrived several days ago." Pam shrugged. "I had Doug drive us into the mountains. To the old valley."

"Anything still there?" Diana asked.

"There's a cross carved into the tree where they found Deb, and the stream is still there, although dry now. Everything else is gone. Here, I took a picture of the tree." Pam pulled a photo from her purse. "Picked these up this morning from the drugstore."

Winifred stared at the photo, tears filling her eyes. She glanced at the lady statue and sighed. "We miss you, Deb."

"We love you," Pam whispered.

"See you one day," Diana added.

Winifred pulled out her rosary. "The devil is between the beads."

"What?" Pam asked.

"The devil ..." Winifred whispered, "... is between the beads." Winifred pulled on the rosary, breaking the chain, and the beads bounced across the grass.

Pam and Diana pulled out their beads, yanking them apart.

"For Deb." Winifred made the sign of the cross. "Pray with me?"

"Of course," Pam replied. "Just because we were surrounded by evil doesn't mean we do not love our god. Jesus walks beside us now. Maybe even this pretty lady."

"Mother Mary, full of grace ..." the girls recited together.

After a short visit, Winifred returned home. Planning a wedding seemed to consume most of her time, as well as snapping pictures of broken and twisted bones.

Sitting on a bench near the lake, she engulfed herself in the rhythm of the ducks swimming or the flapping of a bird. Twirling her engagement ring around her finger, she wondered if she truly loved Grant. He was handsome. He did love her. Why would she question such a thing?

"May I sit?" A tall man with dark hair smiled at her.

Winifred nodded.

The man sat and placed his extra-large hands in his lap. His dark eyes and 'brows reminded her of someone she once knew and admired.

"This is a lovely spot," he stated.

"Yes, it is."

"Strange how life changes us." He glanced at her and his warmth tickled her heart. "What once was sometimes repeats itself. Other times, we simply walk in circles. Pretending that everything is perfect."

Winifred raised a 'brow and smiled. "Circles?"

"Do not allow your regrets to darken your path," he whispered. "Always carry a light."

Winifred nodded.

"I must travel a long distance soon." He stood and nodded. "Have a safe and exciting life, Winifred."

Winifred glanced at her watch and sighed. Jumping from the bench, she searched for the stranger. But he was gone.

"How could he ...?"

Darting up the path, her eyes trailed across the parking lot.

No one.

She ran back to the lake, following the little ducks' trail.

No one.

Sitting on the bench, she sighed. Glancing into the clouds, her heart warmed. Yeenoghu had just come to say goodbye. She could smell his essence. He was taking a long trip, obviously leaving his city behind. Would he now walk with the bright one?"

The leaves turned and her children grew. Kiran was away at college, as were, Katara and Kennedy. Two girls and a boy. A beautiful boy. Since she had her children late in life, she was in her sixties by the time Kennedy left home. With just her and Grant, life was simple. After buying a house in Montana, they found jobs in the local hospital. Now retired, they spent their time, waiting for grandchildren.

After her mother died, William visited frequently as did John David and Alex. Grant never spoke of their time in Hell. There was no reason to. Caroline and Tom now lived in Colorado. Pam and Diana had moved on, forgiving each other for not being the strongest and fighting back.

As the fall leaves fell, the sound of breaking glass pulled Winifred from her thoughts. Grant was on the kitchen floor. She knelt, touching his neck. Pulling out her phone, she called for help. But Grant had already left, probably following the path of her beloved friend.

Climbing into bed that night took all her strength. The sheets felt cold and uninviting. She prayed that time would flip, reset, take her back to when Kiran's spirt had merged with hers. But all remained quiet.

Their children returned home with wet eyes and shaking hands. The funeral was short and sweet. Once the visits ended and hugs were given, Winifred settled down on the front porch, watching the birds search for worms in the freshly mowed grass.

Her heart ached for what once was. But something was missing. She thought about her childhood, the farm, and the sex. She thought about the sacrifices, and how easily she was able to help kill those young men. Father Hurley's face entered her mind and she smiled. Was he someone that had participated or someone that had looked the other way? Did it matter?

The birds finally left and the crickets sang. Her hip ached from the cooling air. As the sun set over the distant ridge, she stood. It was almost time for bed. Walking through the empty house, she wondered.

What was Yeenoghu doing right now? Was he still in his city? Had he really been the one to visit her that day in Germany by the lake? If he was in Heaven, who would rule the city?

Standing at her bathroom mirror, she glanced at her husband's sleeping pills. Taking one's life was a sin. It would mean she would have to once again walk that Endless Maze. Would she be able to find Yeenoghu's city?

Pushing the thought from her mind, she curled under her blankets, allowing her dreams to wander.

The phone ringing jerked the sleep from Winifred. Pain shot up her arm and down her spine. Jumping from the bed, her ankle cracked.

"Ow!" Winifred grabbed her phone. "Hello?"

"Winifred?"

"Caroline?" Winfred had just visited with Caroline at Grant's funeral. "Caroline, what's wrong?"

"I need you."

The phone fell silent.

"Caroline? Caroline?" Winifred tapped on her friend's name but no one answered. Favoring her ankle, she sat in the chair, running through the familiar names. "It's five in the morning. Do I dare?"

She clicked on Tom's name.

No answer.

She would wait until sunrise to call their sons.

As the coffee brewed, her eyes fell to the floor where she had found Grant. It was strange, but a weird glow seemed to be spreading under the tiles. At her age, falling to her knees was not an easy feat. It was odd, but the tiles felt warm to the touch. Bending closer, her eyes refused to focus.

"Damn, need my glasses."

Pulling on the kitchen chair, she stood. The coffee was ready. Sipping on hot brew and holding her reading glasses, she knelt.

The twirling light seemed to be under the tiles.

"This is nuts."

From between the tiles, Winifred could see the faint glow of a city far below. It was as if she was high above the clouds.

"Am I going senile?" she whispered.

Struggling, she stood. Descending the basement steps, her heart pounded. The lower she stepped, the younger she felt. Wanting another cup of coffee, she frowned at the empty cup. The basement was cold, the floor chilly. A breeze flowed from somewhere inside the darkness.

"Hello?" she yelled. "Who's here?"

The lone light created a soft glow in the middle of the room. The shadows were deep and dark. The stench of rotting eggs filled her with a memory she had pushed from her mind a long time ago.

Taking a deep breath, she took a step.

All remained quiet.

"Hello?" she yelled again.

Her phone chirped from the kitchen.

"Damn." She hurried up the stairs.

The call was from Caroline.

"Damn!" Clicking on her friend's name, she waited.

"Winifred?"

"Caroline, what's wrong?"

"Oh my god," Caroline whispered.

"What's wrong?" Winifred yelled.

A low growl echoed up from the basement. The floor vibrated.

"You don't feel it?" Caroline asked. "You don't see it?"

The growl sounded again, rattling the basement door. Lights flickered from below.

"What's happening?" Winifred asked.

"He's back!" Caroline yelled.

"Who's back?" Winifred's heart pounded, her hands shook.

"Someone powerful."

Winifred's phone dinged several times. Another call was coming in. She glanced at the name and her eyes widened. "I'm patching someone in, hold on." She clicked *answer* and said, "Heleina?"

"Winifred? He's back," Heleina stated.

"Who's back?" Winifred asked.

"Baphomet," Heleina and Caroline yelled at the same time.

Winifred stood in front of the small church, allowing her gaze to follow the sidewalk to the entrance. The place seemed deserted. Inching her way up the slender path, she paused before entering. It had been months since she stepped inside a church to pray. The last time was for Grant's funeral. And at that time, she ignored the religion and focused on her *goodbyes*.

An older-looking woman was near the front, working on a computer that sat on a small desk. She glanced up briefly before concentrating back on her work.

Winifred made her way to the desk, sitting on the front pew.

"May I help you?" the old woman asked.

"Is the Father here?"

"We have not had a Father or a nun in this church for over ten years."

"Who does the services?"

"I do," the woman replied. "At least when someone shows up. I'm an ordained minister. As I said earlier, may I help you?"

"I need help." Winifred glanced around. "But I'm not sure you can help me."

"What do you need?" The woman clicked off the monitor.

Winifred took a deep breath and sighed. "About forty years ago, I entered Hell."

The woman's eyes widened.

"When I was fifteen, I was bonded with a demon. That demon refused to let me go. My friends and I entered Hell to travel the Endless Maze."

The old woman squinted and frowned.

"It sounds crazy, I know." Winifred shrugged.

"Quite crazy," the woman replied. "But ... I've heard crazier. How can I help?"

"There's a city under my kitchen floor." Winifred laughed. "Now *that* sounds crazy. But I can see it between the tiles."

"Did someone die there?" the woman asked.

Winifred paused before nodding. "Actually, yes, my husband."

"Then he is in Hell," the woman stated. "He is probably trying to reach out to you."

"My husband's in Hell?" Winifred stared at her hands. They were shaking.

"Many times, people believe their souls are saved. In reality, far from it. We pray for forgiveness. But do we ever wait to hear the answer? What did your husband do for a living?"

"He was a surgeon. A bone specialist."

"Not a bad profession," the woman replied. "Maybe it's something else."

"What do you mean?" Winifred massaged her fingers.

"There are times when our profession in life is actually a curse. But if he helped to heal people that wouldn't count. Did he walk through Hell too?"

Winifred nodded.

"Well … that explains it." The woman shook her head. "Those who walk through Hell are destined to return. Why did you go there?"

"To banish the demon that was haunting me."

"Stupid thing to do." The woman laughed.

"No … that demon dangled me off a cliff, raped me in public, did whatever he wanted to me. It wasn't stupid. It was our last resort."

The old woman stood. She walked to a bookshelf, returning with something old in her hands. Flipping on the pages, she paused. "Was this your guide?"

Winifred stared at the picture of Mother Hildegard. Her crooked smile, creasing her face, gave an allusion of a smirk. "Yes, how?"

"That is the demon Malus. The abyss or Hell plays tricks on us. Gives us illusions and warps reality. We can live a million lifetimes within seconds and not know it. Once on the Endless Maze, a human soul never returns. They are destined to search for the end for eternity. Winifred, you are still in that maze."

"I didn't tell you my name," Winifred replied, standing.

The room spun and the floor exploded. Winifred screamed as the pit below grew wider, denser.

"No!" Winifred screamed. "Not again!"

Eighteen

WINIFRED STOOD AT the balcony, feeling weak and helpless. Flames filled the sky as demons shouted from above. On one side of her stood Tom and on the other was Caroline. Winifred wiped her face as she stared into her friends' younger eyes.

"This cannot be happening," Caroline yelled. "Does this mean I raised kids again only to have them not exist?"

Laughter filled the room.

"This is bullshit!" Tom yelled.

Winifred sighed deeply. "I'm so sorry for introducing you to this." She shook her head, wiping her eyes again. "This is all my fault. I should never have tried to have friends. I should never have pulled you into this … this … world."

Again, laughter filled the air.

"They are so …" Winifred paused.

"So what?" Caroline asked.

"I've had enough!" Winifred closed her eyes and concentrated. Feeling herself rise high in the air and above the clouds, she glanced around. Her gaze landed on Baphomet who was sitting on a cliff's edge as if watching a sporting event. She studied his face. It was large with yellow-red, glowing eyes. His sharp teeth glistened with the firelight. Muscles bulged stretching the blonde fur to where it shimmered. A shiny-red breastplate decorated his huge chest.

Concentrating on only him, her mind flew her back to her youth. Back to her grandmother's attic. She squatted where he once squatted waiting for her. The moonlight draped across her back making the shadows deeper, more pronounced. Baphomet materialized, his form solidifying as the moon's rays lit the floor.

Winifred laughed. "You're mine, asshole."

Baphomet glanced around. His once giant stature now a third of what he once was.

Winifred towered over him. "I am the granddaughter of a High Priestess. Since the witch has died, her power is now mine. As was her grandmother before her, and her grandmother before her. You are nothing more than a demon. And I have the support of the bright one. My lord and savior." Winifred's body glowed, lighting the entire attic. The shadows disappeared. "You stupid, stupid, little thing. You have tortured me since I was a child. Why? A million humans would have gladly taken my place. But you demanded pleasure from a little girl?" Winifred sighed. "I understand that Hell is a terrible place. That demons are horrible creatures. But actually ... your job was to punish those who sinned against God, against the bright one. The Creator as you call him." Winifred walked around Baphomet, studying the demon as he cowered on the attic floor. "Give the man the respect he deserves, he is our Lord God." She slapped Baphomet across the back of the head.

He stumbled, his face hitting the floor. "With what you are doing now," he whispered, "your god will never forgive you."

"Maybe," she replied, "but I will be able to forgive myself."

"What do you want?" he asked.

"It's what I don't want," she yelled. "I don't want you meddling in my life or my friends. I want you out of my children's lives and their children's lives. I want you in the pits where you belong."

Baphomet moaned.

"Our bond is broken and the veil will be sealed. Whether I am on this side or yours will depend on my judgment day. But not on your whim."

Winifred stood in front of the small window and stared at the moon. "This old farm only exists inside my memories. If I erase those memories, perhaps you will cease to exist. What if I pull your insides out of you as you did to Malus? I remember that moment on the dome. It wasn't Satan, it was you!"

The demon sighed.

"What if I rape *you* with something sharp and long just like you did to me? What if I rip a life force from inside your body without you knowing?"

Baphomet shook his head. "It was fun while it lasted."

"Fun for you, maybe." Winifred raised her eyes to the heaven and sighed. "Lord, forgive me for what I'm about to do."

Baphomet's eyes widened.

Winifred raised her hand. "Bless you, Baphomet. May the lord have mercy on your soul." Waving her hand, the demon fizzled out.

She hovered over him as he opened his eyes. He cried and gasped for air. Many eyes stared at him as something harsh wiped his face. Cold air made him shake. His arms and legs moved on their own. He screamed and cried.

"You are a newborn, Baphomet." Winifred smiled. "You're parents are Catholics. Strict Catholics. They are poor. You live in the mountains. Enjoy your life. I've already written everything out for you. But you're not allowed to read it."

Baphomet screamed again as warm arms caressed his aching body.

Dawn broke at the same time as Winifred's fever. "Mom?"

"Shh," her mother cooed. "You're gonna be okay now."

"Where am I?" Winifred asked, trying to sit up.

"No, no, baby," her mother whispered. "Lie down. You've been very sick. Are you hungry?"

Winifred nodded.

"I'll bring you some soup. Be right back."

Winifred watched as her young mother left the room. Raising her hand, she stared at the tiny fingers. She stood and studied the very young girl who stared back at her.

"Young lady," her mother scolded. "I thought I told you to stay in bed."

"How yah feeling, sis?" her older brother asked from the door. "You still contagious?"

Winifred smiled. "Don't think so."

"Here." Her mother handed her a bowl. "Eat." Her mother pushed her son out of the room. "Come, I'll make you a bowl."

Now alone in the room, Winifred sat the soup on the floor. She knelt by the loose floorboard. Pulling it away from the wall, she reached inside. Nothing but dust. No colored pacifiers. Her hand was empty. She ran to the window and stared out. Her father was digging a hole with her younger brother standing nearby, steadying a young tree.

With her father at home, that would mean she was about six or seven years old. Years before her grandmother indoctrinated her into the coven, years before she was abused. But how could this be?

"Hey, why are you not eating your soup?" her mother asked, picking up the bowl. "Come and sit on your bed, young lady."

Winifred sat, opening her mouth as her mother fed her the warm, vegetable soup. It was just as she remembered, rich and thick with lots of chunks of potatoes and carrots.

"Mom?"

"Yes, dear."

"Am I gonna work on the farm this week?"

"What farm, dear?" her mother's eyes widened.

"Grandmother's farm."

"Grandma has no farm," her mother replied. "They sold that place years ago. Before you were born."

Winifred accepted another spoonful of soup. "Where are my jumpers?"

"What jumpers?"

"My school jumpers?"

"Your dresses?" her mother asked.

"No, my school uniforms?"

"Honey, Montgomery Elementary does not require uniforms." Her mother touched her forehead. "Are you feeling all right?"

"I feel funny."

"I can tell. You've been sick for many days. The flu. Maybe you're a little fuzzy from being in bed for so long."

Memories flooded through Winifred's little mind like an ocean crashing against a shore. Montgomery Elementary School had burnt down about twenty years before she was born and replaced with Hopkins Elementary. They refused to rebuild on the same lot because so many children had died.

"What year is it?" Winifred asked.

"Year? Why do you ask?"

"Just what year is it?"

"It's 1919, honey." Her mother stood. "Maybe I should fetch the doctor. You may still have a fever."

"Wanna play?" her middle brother asked, flipping the thin cards through his fingers.

"Sure."

He hopped on her bed, shuffling the deck. "Old Maid?"

"No, Go Fish."

"Fine." He dealt the cards.

"Can I ask you a question?"

"Sure, do you have a seven?"

"No." Winifred giggled. "Go fish. How much do you remember?"

"About what?"

"Do you have a five?" Winifred asked.

He slapped the five of hearts on the blanket. "Do you have a queen? And what are you talking about?"

"Here." She handed him a queen of spades. "Everything feels wrong."

"You've been sick," he replied. "Really sick, got an ace?"

"Do you believe in God?" She shook her head.

"Of course," he replied. "Don't you?"

"Yes, but can God change everything?"

"Maybe," he replied. "He is all-powerful."

"Yeah, maybe you're right. Do you have a four?"

Winifred floated above the crib, watching the baby sleep. Baphomet seemed so peaceful and happy. He yawned before sucking on his blue pacifier.

Soaring across town, she waited in the white building. As the robed members entered, she hid in the shadows. The crowd thickened, voices grew louder. When they silenced, she watched as four young girls entered. Each with wide eyes, their faces pale. Huddling in the back, they stood silent as a man with a bull's head walked in. Behind him was another man carrying a naked baby.

Winifred floated to the front. Her grandmother was on the floor screaming. The baby wiggled on the table. She stepped closer, making eye contact with the little boy. As the knife hit his chest, Baphomet didn't have time to scream as his spirit was ripped from the body.

"What the fuck!" He now floated next to Winifred staring at the deceased child.

"Did you enjoy that?" she asked.

"No!" he replied. "Damn, girl."

"That's what happened to that little boy when I was only a child. I had to watch. Look at those girls' faces. Look at them. They're terrified. That night still haunts me to this very day. And you're still playing your stupid games."

Baphomet rubbed his chest and laughed.

"You and Malus can pull me through time, change my family, change my life, but you can no longer change my soul. You have to stop this foolishness. You're playing with others' lives. As my life changes, so does theirs. I doubt if you'll ever get to Heaven."

"Who says I want to." He rubbed his chest again.

"We can repeat this life with you as a baby again if you'd like."

Baphomet shook his head. "No, I get it. I mess with you and you mess with me."

"Exactly," she replied. "I hate you and you hate me. Archenemies forever."

Baphomet nodded. "Agreed."

With her spirit back in her human body, Winifred rolled over, pulled the blanket over her shoulder, and slept peacefully for the first time in her hectic life.

A trip to Germany would take too long. Winifred, now in her late seventies, couldn't handle the plane ride. But she could handle a jaunt to California. Standing on her old street, she stared at the apartments that were built where her uncle's hill once stood. She shook her head and smiled. Walking up the driveway, she paused, remembering how her mother's house had looked nestled deep inside the lemon orchard.

But now, instead of one house and many trees, stood several houses and no trees.

She entered the apartment complex that had been built on top of the hill, trying to remember where they had found the entrance to the underground chamber. As a man swept the patio, she smiled.

"Hello?" she said.

"May I help you?" He paused, holding the handle just under his chin.

"This is gonna sound weird, but is there a basement here?"

He tilted his head. "Actually, yes. Not many know about it. How do you?"

"I grew up here," she replied. "My uncle used to own this land."

"That was a long time ago." He winked.

"May I enter that basement?" Her 'brows raised.

He paused, glancing around. "Are you one of them?" he whispered.

"One of who?"

"Them witches?"

Winifred laughed.

"A long time ago, there was a witch, the witch of the thousand oaks."

Winifred laughed again. "I don't know about the oaks, but maybe lemons?"

He frowned. "You never heard about the witches? At one time, a huge mountain sat on this very spot."

"Mountain?" Winifred shrugged. The land was not large enough for a mountain, just enough for the hill.

"Mountain." He nodded. "And witches used to dance under the light of a full moon. They sacrificed babies. Had all kinds of sex rituals … right here."

"How did you hear of these rumors?"

"In that basement …" – he glanced around – "… the one you want to enter, well, there are drawings on the walls. They tell a story."

Winifred thought back to the day her and her friends had found the stairs in the ground. She couldn't remember any drawings, just water. For years, she honestly believed it was an underground swimming pool. But now, with this man, perhaps there was something down there that she needed to know about."

"Can you show me the entrance?"

"It is locked. No one knows where the key is."

"Then how would you know if there are drawings?" Winifred asked.

"Good point. But the rumors."

Winifred pulled an old key from her pocket. "Please, if you'll show me the entrance, I'll let you inside if this key still works."

The man smiled.

Unlocking the door, the man pushed and the outside light lit the small room. "Utilities," he stated. "It's over here."

Near the back, a metal door in the floor was partially covered by several boxes. He scooted them aside and pulled. The metal hinges creaked, echoing through the small room.

"There's a ladder here," he said. "Where'd that key come from?"

"A box," Winifred replied. "After you?"

The man sat on the floor, dropping his legs into the small rectangle hole. As his head disappeared, Winifred struggled to sit. She scooted to the hole, allowing her feet to search for the ladder. At her age, her muscles were just not as flexible anymore. At the bottom, another door greeted them – a large metal door with an ancient-looking lock.

Winifred held the key to her heart before kissing it. Sliding it into the lock, a loud click echoed.

The man flipped on his flashlight, allowing the beam to light the path. "Water," he stated. "An underground swimming pool?"

"This way," Winifred replied, remembering her steps. At the stairs, she climbed, the stranger close behind. At the large door, she paused, gave the sign of the cross, and pulled the door open. No smell of sulfur, just a musty dampness.

The man flashed his light inside.

Winifred entered. Several rusting chains were on the floor. A table with only three legs sat crooked against the far wall. No bodies, just dirt.

"Nothing's in here," he whispered.

"There used to be," Winifred replied.

"What?"

"Dead bodies," she stated. "Lots of 'em."

"Bodies?" He chuckled. "Great story, lady, but no prize. There's nothing in here. No drawings on the walls, no nothing."

Winifred inched herself around the small room. It seemed larger when she was young. Something in the corner grabbed her attention. Picking it up, she sighed. "How about this?"

He held out his hand, and she dropped the small object on his palm.

"What is it?" he asked.

"Take it to the police," she replied. "I'll bet this was once a human finger."

"No shit!"

The police officer took her name and number. The apartment complex took the key. She didn't object because she had a duplicate made before boarding the plane.

"What makes you believe this is a human bone?" the lieutenant asked.

"My grandmother was the witch of the thousand oaks," she stated with a chuckle. "My uncle owned this land when it was a taller hill. We used to slide down it every fall. I found that underground well when I was about twelve or so. My friends and I explored all through those halls. In that one room, bodies were hooked to those chains that were once on the walls. Of course, no bodies anymore 'cuz there's no witch. But they were there once."

"Lieutenant Jenkins." The young sergeant was wide-eyed and out of breath. "We found something."

"What?" she asked.

"Smitty sprayed the walls with Luminol and the place lights up like an atomic explosion. Blood's everywhere. I think this lady is telling the truth. You can see the outline of where bodies were once hung on the walls."

"Are you serious?" she asked.

"How old are you?" Winifred smiled.

"Twenty-two," she replied. "Why?"

"You're young," Winifred stated. "All this happened when I was half your age. You would know nothing about the happenings in this town. But you just might learn fast."

"You're free to go," the lieutenant said. "A detective will probably call in a few days."

"I'm not concerned," Winifred replied. "Everyone involved is dead now. Let the demons judge them."

The lieutenant nodded.

The nights were growing longer and colder. Every time Winifred entered her kitchen, the lights under the tiles felt more and more inviting. She glanced in the refrigerator for a simple dinner. Nothing seemed enticing. Climbing the stairs, her hip ached. It wouldn't be much longer before these stairs would be unclimbable for her.

Standing in front of the bathroom sink, she studied the old woman who stared back at her – a woman with almost white hair who now resembled the old witch that helped to raise her. In the corner of her eyes, she could just make out Grandmother's twinkle. On the counter sat her husband's sleeping pills. Picking up the bottle, her heart pounded. She had just bought these the day he passed. Therefore, thirty pills were in the small container. Many years old, but probably still good.

Taking the bottle to her bed, she glanced at her phone. It was just a little past seven, but it was already dark. Texting her son and daughters, she asked if they were good and that she loved them. They replied with we're okay and we love you too.

"I wonder if this life is real?" she asked.

Removing the plastic lid, Winifred poured out the little white pills. They tumbled one after the other, hitting her skin with just the slightest of touch. With her glass of water in one hand and the pills in the other, she swallowed all thirty at one time. Finishing off the water, she smiled.

"Water is good for me …"

Resting her head on her pillow, she thought about Grant and wondered what he was doing. Was he still in Heaven or had he been reborn?

"I wonder how that works?" she asked. "Hey, God, are we reborn? Do we live over and over again?"

No reply.

Winifred shrugged as she didn't expect an answer.

The wind slapped the tree's thin limbs against the side of the house. Rain fell, creating a soothing rhythm. Pulling the blanket over her shoulder, she snuggled into the pillow. Yeenoghu entered her mind, filling her with that deep love that only he could provide.

"I still love you, Yeenoghu," she whispered as sleep snuck in for the last time.

Winifred stood on a baren shore next to a deep blue sea. She was hoping for red flames or the echo of horns, but all was quiet except for the sound of rolling waves. As her toes sunk deep, she immersed herself within the emotions of the sand caressing her feet.

"Where am I?"

No reply, just the ocean waves slapping.

A dim moon was cresting above the distant waters, a light's path flowing from eternity to her. The slight breeze felt cool against her arms. Glancing down, she sighed. She was naked.

"Where is my nightgown?" she asked.

Again, no one replied.

Behind her was nothing but darkness. The only light was from the heavens and even that was dim. No trees or rocks or animals. No birds twirped. No crickets sang. Just the tender rocking of the water. Winifred sat at the end of the lighted path, the ocean nipping at her toes. With nothing else to do, she waited. But for how long?

Her eyes focused on something that was moving at the end of the lit path. It was a silhouette of a man. A huge man. She stood, wondering how she could cover herself. How would she be modest? As the man inched closer, her heart pounded. She recognized the stride, the heaviness of the thighs, the hammer that dragged behind him.

"Yeenoghu?" she whispered.

Yeenoghu stepped on the sand, his hooves sinking deep. He smiled and reached out his arms. She ran to him, accepting his warm embrace.

"I have missed you so much," Winifred cried, allowing the tears to flow.

"As I have you," he replied.

"Was that you that day at the lake?" She glanced up at her demon lover. "Did you come to say goodbye?"

He nodded. "I wished to stay longer, but ..."

"I understand." She snuggled in deeper into his fur. The aroma of his essence filled her with a longing that felt pure and honest.

"Why did you take those pills?" he asked.

"I know I'm not welcomed past the gates of Heaven," she whispered. "If I cannot be with you and God, I prefer to live forever in your city. I can sleep in your bed. Be near you, but without you."

He sighed. "I understand." He chuckled. "Ironic ... if I had known you would return, I would have stayed. But I honestly thought it better if you married your own kind."

"What is in my heart surpasses what we are," she replied. "You were everything I ever wanted. Protection ... safety ... warmth. You never pushed our love, allowed it to grow naturally. When I kissed you ... I felt whole."

"My love," he whispered. "The Lord God granted me the honor to pass your judgment. If I could, I would ask for leniency. However, taking one's life upsets the written words, the path that is preordained, decided by our Creator at the time our souls are formed."

Winifred nodded. "Although I would love to live in Heaven with you, I still must find my son. I know ... the Soul Splitters said we merged. But a little piece is still missing. I feel connected to something that was left behind. I did raise another Kiran during my life. But that spirit will never replace the first."

"It is not Kiran you are missing," he replied.

"It's not Kiran?"

"No, Kiran, your son, will one day be in Heaven with the Creator," he stated. "It is *our* child that you must seek."

"Our child?"

"When we made love, it was real. It was not an illusion. However, Malus took the child from your womb. I tried to tell you. Many times I reached out, but you could not hear or feel me. And only a mother's love is strong enough to break the divide. I as the father would never find them. You … you share a life force. You will know when the child is near."

"Our child?" Winifred wiped her eyes. "My Kiran will be with God? Thank you … thank you, Lord."

"Find our child, Winifred … find our child …" Yeenoghu phased into the bright path, becoming a rolling wave.

Winifred ran to the water's edge and cried.

The horizon lightened before turning a deep red. As she watched, a large ship appeared. Pharsight waved from the bow. Winifred nodded. She understood. This was her passage back to Hell.

Winifred winked at the boat's large, yellow eye, before hugging Pharsight. It felt odd to be with him alone, just knowing that Yeenoghu was not with her.

"Welcome," Pharsight stated. "When I received the order to pick you up, I must admit, I was rather surprised."

"Why? I'm not all that pure."

"You are good in here." The demon pounded on his chest. "What happened? Why are you here?"

"I killed myself." She shrugged.

"Tired of life?"

"Not really." Winifred stood at the railing, enjoying the sights. Huge mountains reached into the cloudless sky, and fish, as large as cars, floated across the deck. "I need to find my child."

"How sad," he replied. "Know where he is?"

Winifred shook her head. "I just know that I have to find him."

"What's his name?" Pharsight raised a 'brow and his horn lowered.

Winifred paused, her eyes wide. "Oh, no ... he has no name."

"A no-named child?" Pharsight shook his head. "Not good. Perhaps you should name him before you arrive."

"Good idea." Winifred closed her eyes and tapped her chin. "David ... I will name him David. It means *beloved*. A gift from someone I once admired."

"Okay." He shrugged. "Yell it to the sea. Let the foreverness know."

Winifred grabbed the railing, and as her knuckles turned white, she yelled, "David ... I name you David."

"Just David?"

She shook her head. "David Yeenoghu Cranston."

The ship docked, and Winifred stared at the beautiful City of Tenarus, Yeenoghu's home. Taking a deep breath, she let it out slowly. For most of her life, she honestly wondered how much of Hell had been real and how much was just her imagination. Allowing her eyes to trail along the balconies and tall columns, she knew it was all real.

After thanking Pharsight and the ship, Umibōzu, she stepped onto the soil of the city. Following the familiar path, she entered Yeenoghu's castle. The same red demon with large ears, an inverted nose, white eyes, and wearing a dark blue uniform snapped his heels.

"I don't believe I ever asked." Winifred smiled. "I will now. May I have your name?"

The demon smiled which was obviously not easy for him to do. With two front teeth that were larger than Winifred's hands, his mouth was rather fixed. "Ukobach, my lord."

"Ukobach it is. I am not a lord."

"My lord!" Ukobach saluted her. "You are Lord Winifred, ruler of Tenarus. Yeenoghu passed this great city to you before he left."

"To me?"

Ukobach nodded. "To you."

"I have no powers to protect this great land."

"Oh, but you do, my lord. You have the power to be anywhere you desire and with just a blink of an eye. You also have the power to split a demon by pulling his insides to his outsides. A very powerful succubus you have become."

"A powerful succubus?" Winifred wiped her eyes. "Fine, if I'm a succubus, then I'm a succubus, but I still need to find my son."

Ukobach again slapped his heels together. "I will help."

Winifred stood on the tallest mountain peak. Turning around slowly, she had a full view. The circles of Hell were more than obvious at this height. If she faced Pandæmonium, the capital of Hell and where Satan ruled, there was a city at every hour of the imaginary clock, each with its own ring. The lights created an invisible dome, generating a map where an orange glow represented a metropolitan and where a congregation of demons lived. The darkness was the plateaus, valleys, and empty fields where nothing existed.

"Wow," she whispered.

"It can be impressive at times," Ukobach replied. "There are many more cities beyond the farthest that we can see."

"How far does Hell actually go?"

"Forever and a day," he replied. "The hours and minutes are meaningless, simply walking the visitor in circles."

"In circles?" Winifred smiled. "You mean the Endless Maze?"

"Exactly," he replied. "In order to traverse the Endless Maze, one must decipher the riddle which transports the individual to the next circle. The challenge is to not lose one's sanity before the riddle is solved."

"Really?" She tilted her head. "Do you have all the riddles?"

Ukobach glanced around before answering. "Yes, would you like the answers?"

With the secrets of the maze committed to memory, Winifred now held the knowledge she required to visit every city. One by one, she entered through their guarded gates. The beasts, sensing her presence, bowed, allowing her free passage. Not one demon tried to stop her or block her way. It was as if her arrival was pre-announced and no one wanted to experience her wrath.

There were so many cities for her to explore. Although she and her friends were never able to pass the rings of Dis, Winifred could now walk into Kasyrgan, stroll into Gehennom, skip into Acheron, or step into Naraka. It was easy as if she was touring the cities of Earth, a world that was a lifetime away and lost somewhere inside the shadows.

Hell was no longer a place of total darkness or confusion. Several times, signs posted statements such as, *He Went to Hades at Death and was Tormented* or *She Swam in the Lake of Fire Never to Return*. To Winifred, these signs were funny, almost a joke.

After the thirteenth city, Winifred stood at the edge of the *Pit of Corruption*. A place she would never wish on her worst enemies. Long chains dropped from the cliffs, falling deep into the ravine with glowing, yellow lava. The heat from the massive depths lapped at her from where she stood. Several recently deceased humans simmered as their skin melted from their bones. They screamed, begging the heavenly father for forgiveness.

"A little late, do you think?" Winifred shook her head.

A demon holding a long staff, probably ten times her height, nodded as she approached.

"Is there a path over this?" she asked.

He shrugged, grinning a devilish smile. "You, my lord, can simply walk across."

Winifred's eyes widened. "Walk?"

"You are Lord Winifred, the succubus from Tenarus. Are you not Lord Yeenoghu's replacement?"

Winifred nodded.

"Then walk across." He returned his attention to his clipboard.

Winifred stood by the edge, staring at the boiling lava. She glanced at those whose skin were melting. Holding her breath, she took a step. Beneath her it felt solid and firm. She took another and it was as if she was walking on a bridge. Throwing back her shoulders, Winifred walked through the air and across the huge ravine. When she reached the other side, she waved at the demon who nodded in return.

Huge fields of flames and bubbling soil greeted her for what seemed like forever. Glancing from where she had come, there was nothing. The city had disappeared, and the way was filled with brim and hailstones. She continued to walk, and the deeper into the inferno, the hotter the air. A small sign, she almost missed, displayed three words – *City of Chainlier*.

The answers to the puzzle did not list the City of Chainlier. How would she pass without the solution? The way slowly morphed from glowing embers to a shiny silver. The purest metal she had ever had the pleasure to see. As she walked, her psychic thought expanded, allowing her heart to analyze the situation. From somewhere not far, she could feel an inner light that equaled hers. An awareness that sparked memories.

She gasped. The feeling of her child leaving her womb pounded from the hidden recesses of her heart. The pain flowed, bursting, banging like a hammer against her back. Concentrating, Winifred pushed the waves from her mind, centering on that tiny spark of life.

Closing her eyes, her heart searched for her child. A vision of a female deity formed, rotating as if spinning wildly and out of control. Remembering what Yeenoghu had said, about how a mother's love was enough to break the great divide, she knew she was close to her destination. At the time, she didn't understand what the divide was, but now she knew. It was the distance between time, space, and existence. It was where past and present joined and became one. It was where dark and light no longer fought. A concept where the mercury ruled the moon and the stars. A brightness within the grasp of Hell.

Following the twittering echoes of her heart, Winifred entered the City of Chainlier. A town with crystals that glowed, lighting the streets. Small and large homes decorated the landscape, reminding Winifred of a winter wonderland on Earth. A picture from a fairy's dream.

Humans walked the streets, buying from merchants or selling their wares. They talked and laughed, experiencing the afterlife as if they were in Heaven.

"My lord," a soldier, wearing a silver guard, stated. "How may we help you?"

"I'm searching for my child. Have you seen him?"

The guard laughed and smiled. "We've been waiting for you. And *she* has been waiting for you too."

"She?" Winifred replied.

The guard waved his hand, speaking into a microphone on his shoulder, similar to how the police spoke on Earth. "David? Your mother is here for you."

Winifred's eyes followed the direction of the man's hand, and from across the street, a young girl of about ten or eleven bounced out, skipping. Her long, dark locks waved in the breeze.

"Mother!" she yelled, running to Winifred's warm embrace.

"It's a girl?" she asked. "A girl?"

"Of course, I'm a girl." David laughed. "I love my name, Mom. I doubt if any other girl will have the name David." She giggled.

Winifred held the girl's face with her hands. She studied the large eyes that matched her father's. Her thin nose and rosy lips mimicked Grandmother's, a woman Winifred had buried multiple times throughout her many re-runs of life.

"You're beautiful," Winifred whispered. "I've searched through almost all the cities of Hell for you. And now, I have you in my sight."

David shrugged.

"Many children on Earth go by their middle name." Winifred chuckled.

"Yeenoghu?"

"Maybe not the full name, but how about Yee?"

"Yee?" The girl thought for a moment, her eyes searching the netherworld. "Nope, I like David."

"Fine." Winifred laughed. "David it is."

"Wanna see our city?" David asked.

"Of course." Winifred followed her daughter through the streets to a small house. "You live here alone?"

David nodded.

"Will you be staying here or coming home with me?"

"With you, silly." David laughed. "Took you long enough to find me."

"Yes, it did."

"Will you tell me about my brother … Kiran and … my father?"
Winifred sighed. "Most definitely."

Nineteen

WINIFRED AND DAVID sat on the veranda of the castle that overlooked the city. The lanterns glowed a dim orange, creating a velvety cast over the homes and businesses.

"Your father built this place for the lost souls that are not that bad." Winifred shrugged. "He would wander the land and collect these spirits, bringing them here, where they could live in peace."

"Why did my father leave?" David asked.

"He was accepted into Heaven. He was forgiven by our Creator."

"Accepted?" David raised her 'brows. "You mean he was cast out of Heaven?"

Winifred nodded. "Yes. He challenged our Creator's rules. Argued and fought against the one who forms the souls from his very essence."

"Will we ever make it to Heaven?" David asked.

"You are a part of me and carry my sins." Winifred stroked her daughter's head. "I'm sorry. But I will try and make up for my misjudgments. Maybe one day we can be with your father and God."

"That would be nice," David replied. "Do I start school tomorrow?"

"Yes, but with no uniforms. I banished them when I arrived."

"How do we measure time, Mother?"

"We measure time with our breaths. With the silent beating of our hearts."

A century had passed. Maybe two. Winifred search the cities and fields for the lost souls with an innocent passion for death. The purity of these spirits fascinated her, providing her the strength to make it through another day. She longed for her demon lover. She wanted his warm embrace to comfort her. Several times, she had presented to Satan, who ruled Pandæmonium, in favor of these random souls. But he always shooed her, chastised her for not being a true succubus – a true demon.

She thought about the woman who had accepted the girls into her Florida home. How this woman had provided them with a safe warm bed, food, and clothing. With the help of others, identifications were issued, and the girls finished school and attended college. The woman died a few years after Winifred joined the army. She missed her and her guidance, her warm words of wisdom. The woman was the mother the girls never had as children.

Together they attended the local Catholic church. At first, the girls were hesitant to enter. But once inside, they soon learned that the nuns were real nuns, caring and non-judging, the Fathers accepting and understanding. A different world from what the girls had experienced.

She thought about the truck driver who dropped her off at the train station and his wise words. *'Religion is not evil, people are.'* But for Winifred, she was already tarnished, no redemption for her. The demon's violation and the abortion were more than what her weak soul could handle. The bondage too strong. Through her non-actions, she had sinned. The sacrificial deaths she had witnessed sliced deep scars into her soul, separating her from the freedom she had lamented for throughout her human life.

"Excuse me, my lord." It was Ukobach. He stood, waiting patiently, clasping his hands.

Winifred sighed, stepping away from the railing with the beautiful city that continued to shine. "Yes?"

"Something is on your mind, my lord?"

"In a way, yes." She nodded. "Why doesn't my daughter age?"

"Now, that is an easy one," he replied. "Those little sparks choose their age when they arrive. The mother must name them, or they remain nameless, easily absorbed by a demon. David chose to be a child forever. What a true blessing, even within this cursed existence."

"Indeed." Winifred pulled the hair from her eyes. "Was there something you needed?"

"Yes, my lord." He bowed. "We have human visitors inside the void."

"Humans?" Winifred tilted her head. "Visitors?"

"Yes, my lord. You must either escort them here or return them to Earth. The choice is yours."

"Yeenoghu had met me and my friends inside the void. It was *he* who saved us."

"Yes, my lord. Lord Yeenoghu saved as many human souls he could. All for a chance of redemption. However, he never loved a human as he loved you."

Winifred wiped her eyes and smiled. "Which direction is this void?"

"Across the sea. Pharsight will provide passage when you are ready."

"Thank you, Ukobach. You've been a true friend and companion."

"Thank you, my lord." The demon nodded and left.

Winifred glanced at the railing and smiled. She could spend an eternity staring at this city. The home of Yeenoghu, a demon she missed more than she missed her salvation. An inner argument she constantly battled and constantly lost.

The path into the void was not something Winifred was looking forward to. Although she was comfortable in the company of Pharsight and the ship, Umibōzu, the thought of entering the godless realm ransacked her soul. The void was an empty space, empty from emotions, pain, substance, and worst of all, the Creator – that little flicker that even demons felt was just not there.

Standing at the edge, she stared at the darkness that was past black, sucking in the light which instantly disappeared. Nothing glittered. Nothing moved. A person simply existed inside an empty bubble. No vibrations, no sound.

Since Yeenoghu dragged a hammer behind him everywhere he went, Winifred had a javelin made specifically for her. It was a little longer than she was tall. Zaffre in color, the brilliant hue brightened even the darkest of rooms. The staff made from cobalt ore and baked in a furnace had become her security blanket. Although not exactly a blanket, she carried it everywhere she went.

As she stood at the precipice of the expanse between her reality and the vast emptiness, her thoughts turned to Yeenoghu. What was he doing right now? And was Kiran with him? Was he still a baby or was he the adult she once loved as a son? The beautiful statue where she knelt as a child entered her mind, again presenting her with many challenges.

Winifred was here to rescue humans. Exactly how many, she had no idea. But was she even qualified to help? Memories flowed, filling her with a longing to fully understand the truth. The truth about her childhood, her grandmother, and her mother. Why was she singled out and her brothers left alone? It couldn't have been God's choice. Maybe life was like a lottery. If your number was pulled, then you either won or lost. Perhaps her number was simply pulled by her grandmother.

"Are you lost?" A beautiful demon with flowing, yellow hair and glowing red eyes approached. With skin the color of emeralds, her spirit didn't resemble wickedness, but something that was actually pleasant to look at.

"No," Winifred replied. "Just thinking."

"Thinking can be dangerous." The demoness laughed. "And you are?"

Winifred almost answered with just her name, but paused as she added her title, "Lord Winifred."

The demoness nodded. "I understand. You must be here for the humans that arrived a little while ago. I am Nyx, goddess of the night, the empty night."

"It is rather empty in there." Winifred sighed. "Nice to meet you."

"I was wondering when we would finally meet. Heard some good things about you and how you're handling Lord Yeenoghu's citizens."

"That is good." Winifred shrugged. "Satan wants me to toughen up. I guess he wants me to be evil. But I just can't."

"How's David doing? Is she adjusting?"

"After a few centuries, I would hope so. She enjoys being a child. I have no problem with that. An ever-lasting childhood with a loving mother. Now, that is a blessing."

Nyx smiled. "My city is just over that ridge. Would you like any help finding the humans?"

"The last time I entered this void, I was with several others, including a nun."

"A nun?" Nyx laughed. "In Hell?"

"Yep, I dragged a nun through Hell. It was an adventure. We never figured out if she was real or not."

"How odd." Nyx nodded at the darkness. "Come on. I'll show you around. It's not that bad once you understand how it works."

"How it works?"

"Come …"

They entered as a pair of demonesses. One a lord, the other a goddess from Hell. *What a combination.* Winifred laughed, silently enjoying the comparison.

"First, you need to pull in your emotions, figure out which direction your influences sway."

"Do what?"

"This is the void, right?" Nyx asked.

Winifred nodded.

"Blank out your feelings. Just become a stick figure. A nothing, like this void. Try it."

Winifred closed her eyes, listening to the pounding of her heart. Slowly, the sound faded as she pushed her most inner fears into a small area of her soul. Imagining a key, she locked the box. Opening her eyes, a path materialized and the void brightened, slightly. "This is weird," Winifred whispered.

"Yep." Nyx started their walk by taking a few steps. "Now for the influences."

"Influences?"

"Your powers," Nyx stated. "Pretend you don't have any."

Winifred thought about how helpless she was when she was with her grandmother. No power to do anything about what was happening around her. As her mind swirled, so did the void, lighting a little more.

"Well?" Nyx asked.

"I can clearly see the path, and the lost humans." Winifred smiled. "Wow, they are so bright."

"A human life force will burn your eyes and suck the energy from your soul," she replied. "Never stare at them for long. They are also hot."

"Then that is why when I first arrived, Yeenoghu wouldn't look directly at me. I was too bright."

"Exactly," she replied. "I think you've got this. Just return the way you came in and you'll be fine. Stay away from the demon who rules the void."

"And who is that?"

"Heeled Jack existed before the design of Heaven or Hell. An ancient entity that breathes fire, spreads hysteria, and tortures the imagination. He is half human, on the bottom, and the other half … I don't exactly know what it is. But if you run into him, you'll figure it out. Just wave and walk away."

Winifred nodded.

"Enjoy your humans, Lord Winifred. And … come visit sometime. We'll have tea."

Tea? Winifred chuckled.

"Yes, tea."

Holding her javelin slightly above her feet, she approached the humans. There were five in total. Two women and three men. As she stepped closer, their eyes widened.

Winifred paused, glancing at her reflection on the non-existent floor. She was definitely not human. Her demon core had morphed into something wicked but beautiful at the same time. Now standing over seven feet, her large thighs carried her muscular torso that she covered with a tight breastplate decorated with gold and silver lines. The symbol of Tenarus at the center. Long black hair clung to the dark fur that now covered her back and shoulders. Horns followed the curve of her forehead before swirling and pointing forward. Slender, multi-colored horns that she adored. Large hands with delicate claws were sometimes a little trouble. She still had issues trying to judge how far away something was. Constantly, she tipped over her drinks.

The humans stared at her. One backed away. A woman screamed.

"Why have you entered my domain?" Winifred asked.

"We're ... we're ..." The woman who had screamed wiped her eyes. "We're here to ask Lord Winifred for help."

"A human needs help from a demon?" Winifred laughed. "Now *that* is funny. What type of help do you seek?"

"She has a demon after her." One of the men pointed at the brunette who was crying into her hands.

"And who is that demon?" Winifred asked.

"Baphomet," the crying woman replied.

Winifred sighed. "At what age were you offered?"

"Fifteen," she stated.

Winifred shook her head, not staring directly at the humans for their life force was too bright. She raised her javelin and sighed. "Very well, follow me. For I am Lord Winifred, ruler of the ancient city of Tenarus. But it will cost you."

"We have no money," the man replied.

"I only ask for a good word to be stated in my name to our Creator, our God who resides in Heaven."

"We can all do that," the other man replied.

Winifred shook her head, following the path to the entrance of where she had entered. Baphomet was back at his old tricks. And witches were still alive on the Earth, tarnishing it with their foul rituals and sacrifices. Maybe helping these lost souls will help her daughter to return to her father. Maybe?

Ukobach greeted Winifred and her humans with a welcoming smile, offering food and a warm bed that they eagerly accepted. Not wanting any more challenges, Winifred excused herself and entered her room. David was waiting for her.

"What are those *things* downstairs?" David asked, rushing to hug her mother.

"They are called humans."

"A real human?" David jumped, clapping her hands. "We learned about them in school. Humans have a life force. Their souls actually glow. This is just *too* exciting, Mother. May I meet them?"

"Maybe tomorrow." Winifred sighed. "I'm exhausted."

"Our teacher said that a life force will pull at your energy." David helped her mother to her bed. "Maybe that is what's happening to you."

Winifred chuckled. "Now, I understand why your father left me alone that first night when he found us."

"You'll have to tell me about that, but for now, you sleep, my mother."

David quietly closed the door behind her, allowing Winifred to drift, her world no longer existing.

Winifred woke early. Her thoughts bounced between Baphomet and Yeenoghu, and how one was so kind and caring, and the other so harsh and cruel. After a hot shower, she slipped on a comfortable outfit to properly meet her humans. No longer in demon form, she wanted to greet them at a level they would accept. Therefore, jeans and a sweatshirt worked perfectly. With her hair pulled into a tight weave that flowed down her back, Winifred bounced down the stairs with the energy of a teen but with the wisdom of an elderly woman.

"Good morning," she said as she entered the dining room. "How was your sleep?"

In the bright light, she could hardly study the humans that were seeking her help – two young women, probably in their twenties, and three men. One of the men was much older than the others. To Winifred, he reminded her of a fatherly figure. Not a Catholic Father, but a dad or daddy. Sitting in her chair, she thanked Ukobach for the hot tea and sweet biscuits.

"Wonderful," the blonde replied, her eyes wide as she bit into the sweetbread.

Winifred smiled and nodded. "Do you have names? I understand that all humans are given a name at birth."

The blonde laughed. "Of course … I'm, Aeryn."

"Nice to meet you Aeryn." Winifred glanced at the brunette.

"Charlene, but, everyone calls me Charlie."

Winifred nodded and glanced at the men.

A young man, with wide eyes and rosy cheeks, frowned. "I'm Ulrich, this is my brother, Deckard, and my father, Hal." The men held the family traits of a thick nose, thin lips, and dark blue eyes. The father's hair was receding with gray along the temples. The boys' hair still dark and full, loaded with curls.

"Can you tell me again why you are here?" Winifred asked, keeping her eyes lowered.

"A demon is haunting Aeryn," Deckard replied. "We tried banishing him, but it only made it worse."

"Been there … got that t-shirt in my closet," Winifred stated.

"Excuse me?" Hal asked. "You don't seem like the typical demon."

"Do you know many?"

Hal smiled and shook his head.

"Don't believe everything you read." Winifred winked at the man. "Baphomet is very powerful. He is nasty and wicked … and this is speaking highly of him. His evil penetrates realities on various levels.

When I was in my twenties, a group of us tried to banish him. Didn't work."

"What did you do?" Aeryn asked.

"To banish him?" Winifred replied.

"No, to get rid of him," she said.

Winifred glanced around and sighed. "Ended up here."

Aeryn wiped her eyes. "I don't want to end up as a demon."

Winifred nodded.

"Mother?" A loud whisper echoed from the door. "Mother?"

Winifred took a deep breath and smiled, waving her daughter into the room. "I would like to introduce my daughter, David. David, this is …" – Winifred pointed to each human as she spoke their names – "… Charlie, Aeryn, Ulrich, Deckard, and Hal."

"You have a boy's name too?" David asked Charlie.

"How can you have a kid?" Charlie asked Winifred.

"I came here once for help. I received help, but I also received my daughter as a gift."

"You and a demon?" Aeryn asked.

Winifred nodded. "I still love him. He is now in Heaven with our Creator, our heavenly father."

Hal stood and held out his hand. "Hi David, nice to meet you."

David slowly reached out her delicate fingers, obviously not sure if it was safe to touch a human. She glanced at her mother who nodded. Their hands met and David smiled.

"You're so warm," she whispered. "And you glow."

"We glow?" Hal asked.

"We can see your auras," Winifred explained. "You are very bright, that is why we cannot keep our eyes on you for very long."

"Well …" – David took a step back – "I've gotta run … classes." She kissed her mother and darted from the room.

"She is a lovely child," Hal whispered.

"Thank you. May I ask how you fit into this equation?" Winifred asked.

"I thought I was a psychic, but after all of this, I'm not so sure," Hal replied.

"This world is much different. Paintings do us no favors. Hal, how did you find your way here?"

Hal shrugged. "A nun."

"A nun?" Winifred shook her head and frowned. "I may regret asking, but what was the nun's name?"

"Mother Hildegard," the man replied. "Why?"

Grinning, Winifred asked, "When you entered, where was this church?"

"In California ... an old mission," he answered.

"Did you enter through a large old door, and did she use a really big key?"

Hal tilted his head and widened his eyes. "Yes, how did you know?"

"Because ..." – Winifred sighed, loudly – "... Mother Hildegard is not a nun. She was one once ... a wise and loving one, about a thousand Earth years ago. Her likeness is now worn by a very mischievous demon by the name of Malus. He works for Baphomet. There was an ancient painting of the mother in our church. Malus has somehow taken over that painting. Malus uses the painting as a doorway to Hell. The Church must have moved the painting from Germany to California."

"Taken over?" Deckard repeated.

"Possessed ... haunted ... whatever you want to call it. Malus is able to pass through the veil into the realm of those given to Baphomet as a mate. Aeryn ... who is the witch in your family?"

"Not my family," Aeryn whispered. "A teacher at my school. We have a Satan club –"

"Satan club?" Winifred stood so quickly that her chair flipped, the sound echoing through the room. "Your school encourages a relationship with Satan?"

Charlie ran to pick up the chair, but Winifred held up a hand, pulling the chair back to the correct position.

"My god." Winifred sighed. "What are they thinking?"

"It's all the rave," Charlie stated.

"Rave?" Winifred swiped her arm through the air. "Does this look like a Rave? Is what Baphomet doing to your friend a Rave? What does Rave mean?"

"Craze, as in cool ..." – Hal shrugged – "... means you're hip."

"Hip?" Winifred repeated. "No ... a *God* club would have been hip, even a Jesus club, or a Mother Mary club." Winifred paced around the large table. "But to invite Satan or his demons into a school? My god, if that doesn't bring back memories. What do they think they are doing?"

"The principal said it's so we can have a place to socialize," Charlie replied.

"They socialize all right," Winifred stated. "Witchcraft is very social. Demonology ... a relationship with the Underworld ... unfortunately, you do not understand. I guarantee a coven is behind your ... club. There must be a high priestess involved. Do you or anyone there wear a cloak?"

Charlie shook her head.

"Any cloaks lying around?" Winifred frowned. "In a coat room maybe?"

"Wait," Ulrich finally spoke. His face ashen, seriousness running through his eyes.

"What did you see?" Winifred asked.

"It was on a hook," Ulrich replied. "Thought it was a costume or something. I reached to touch it once, but this man yelled at me. I mean, really yelled at me. Told me '*never* to touch the madam's cloak.' Thought it odd."

"What state do you call home?" Winifred asked.

"We're from Southern California," Charlie replied. "Why?"

Winifred shrugged and again shook her head. "What color was the lining of this cloak?"

Ulrich smiled. "Purple, why? Is that important?"

"Guidance?" Nyx laughed, taking a sip of tea. "You are funny. Where yah gonna find guidance down here? Nothing here is real. Everything is a mass hallucination. Demons play tricks with the mind. They can make one feel powerful … that one is succeeding, and then … splat … your back at the beginning doing it all over again."

Winifred held her cup, balancing the delicate porcelain with pink flowers between her yellow claws. "Experienced that already."

"Let me get my book." Nyx walked to a bookcase, running her fingers across the spines. Stopping on a dark green one, she pulled it out, flipped it open, and smiled. "I think I've found something."

"Oh?" Winifred placed the cup on the saucer.

"Yes." Nyx handed the book to her new friend. "Demon Lord Aequitas."

"Aequitas? Sounds Latin."

"It is." Nyx sat. "Aequitas is an ancient philosopher of life. One of Plato's great-great … something. You need to visit him."

"And where is *him*?" Winifred didn't want to speak the question for she knew the answer would be anything but simple.

"You could ask for an audience at the dome."

Winifred shook her head. "Satan already believes me to be too soft. He'd never allow that."

"I was there when you tried arguing with him about saving spirits." Nyx laughed. "You were pretty insistent on him listening until he zapped yah." She laughed again.

"Pretty funny. So where is this demon?"

"He rules the city of Advententia." Nyx flipped to the back of the book. "Look on this map. You are here … with me. But Lord Aequitas' city is way over here." Nyx's finger traced to the other side of the book.

"How do I get way over there?"

Nyx slapped the book closed, laying it on Winifred's lap. "You are naïve." She shook her head. "You really need to get out of your city more."

"What do you mean? Is there a rail system down here or something I don't know about?"

Nyx adjusted her top, giggling. "I'm not sure if I should just let you suffer and figure it out on your own or say something."

Winifred sighed, lowering her shoulders. Holding the book felt oddly uncomfortable, almost as if the thing was alive. Winifred stood and walked over to the bookshelf that didn't seem to ever end. Replacing the dark green *Book of Names* into the empty slot, her heart pounded.

Why was it that no demon could simply explain the rules of Hell? Why was it she had to learn on her own, by struggling and fighting and suffering? Winifred turned and smiled. "I understand that we learn more if we stumble through life. But I'm already dead. If I haven't learned it by now, I probably never will. I came to you for advice. Will you help me or not?"

Nyx waved her hand over the now empty seat. "Please?"

Winifred sat, allowing her memories to flow. Her grandmother, the demon, the sacrifices, her school, escaping, college, enlisting in the Army, meeting Caroline, marrying Grant, her children, Yeenoghu, and David. Love, hate, fear, knowledge, freedom, anticipation, friendship, love – all human emotions. From each, she learned a little appreciation. Even during the darkest of times, a little spark glowed somewhere between the shadows. Was that spark our Creator? Our God reaching out to her, offering help?

"I'm so stupid," Winifred laughed. "I can teleport myself directly to Advententia. I still have powers I don't know about. Don't use. How silly of me."

Nyx rested a small green hand on Winifred's knee. "It's okay, my friend. Existence does this sometimes. You must remember, you were human once. And because you were, your emotions control most of your thoughts. It's that *flight* or *fight* mode I keep hearing about. Emotions are a gift from the Creator. Demons do not have emotions."

"But Yeenoghu did and David does."

"Perhaps David is about to ascend? If her heart is pure, maybe the light will come for her soon."

Winifred froze. The thought of existing without her daughter sent daggers up her spine. *Lose David?* After a century or two, living with her daughter was her life, or what she pretended to be her life. How could she let her go? "I never thought …"

Nyx smiled. "If that time comes, I'll be there for you."

"Thank you." Winifred stood, wiped her eyes, and smiled. "It's good to have a friend."

"Just remember …" Nyx stated. "Demons play tricks. Never trust one."

"Even you?"

"Even me." Nyx winked.

Twenty

THE MOUNTAINS AROUND her city glowed against Heaven's lights. She stood on the ledge she had once shared with her demon lover, allowing her eyes to soak in the wonders. Was it even possible her daughter could be saved? It had to be. But what would she have to do?

Winifred knelt as she used to by the beautiful lady statue. She bowed her head and whispered, "Oh heavenly father, hear my plea. You have my lover, who worked so hard for your grace. You gave him that. Now, I beg the same for my daughter. Please, spare her this existence. Please come for her. She did nothing wrong. She is innocent. Please, do not punish her for my sins."

The cliff remained silent, heaven's light shined, and the mountains glowed. She stood and wiped away her tears. Taking a deep breath, she closed her eyes and concentrated on the city of Advententia. In the middle was a tower, taller than the other buildings, darker than the void, and surrounded by a fiery lake. A bridge on each side led to gigantic double doors. No windows. Just an extremely tall, black building.

"Well … doesn't this place look inviting." Winifred sighed. "Maybe, I deserve this."

Winifred stood just outside the city, studying the large gate. The huge stone entrance was most intimidating. Tall pillars greeted a visitor where large creatures guarded each side. Winifred was an ant to these things. One toe would be enough to annihilate her existence. The city of Advententia was surrounded by tall mountains, almost like hers. Only with her city, Tenarus, the large lake was on one side.

She approached the creature on the right. He stood maybe fifty feet above her head. How could she talk to the thing? Toes as tall as her were only a few inches away. The thing reminded her of a cross between a trunkless elephant and a monkey.

Tapping on his toe, she stood back and waved.

The creature glanced down, before stomping his foot.

Winifred flew from the pressure, landing back across the bridge. "You wanna play that game?" She stood, brushed herself off, and huffed. Boldly, she stepped up to the foot, stabbing the toe with her javelin.

The creature yowled and the ground shook.

"What do you want?" a voice yelled from behind the now sobbing creature.

"Who's there?" Winifred asked.

"I am. I'm the guardian of Advententia." It was a little purple thing. About half of Winifred's size. He was bald, reminding her of her butler, Ukobach, almost.

"I'm Lord Winifred." She glanced at the sobbing creature, praying he wouldn't crush her. "I must meet with Lord Aequitas."

"Lord Winifred?" the purple thing replied. "We've heard rumors."

"What kind of rumors?"

"Not too kind rumors."

"Who are you?" she asked.

"I am Marcus … guardian of this city …" – he glanced around – "one of four. But I guard this entrance."

"Are these your pets?" Winifred raised her arm. "This one is crying and favoring his sliced toe."

"That wasn't very nice," Marcus stated.

"It wasn't nice that he stomped his foot. He could have killed me."

"I hate to break this to you, but you're already dead. Now, you have asked for an audience with our lord. Let me see what his schedule is like."

Winifred peeked past the golden gates. The tall, black, windowless building towered above all the others. Just as Nyx had said, no windows. Just a pure blackness that threatened even the darkness.

"He said he would meet with you," Marcus said from behind.

Winifred jumped. "You frightened me."

"Why? You know I'm here." Marcus laughed. "He's sending a guard to escort you."

"Thank you."

The gates slowly opened, allowing enough room for just her to enter. As the gates locked behind her, the ground shook. She nodded to Marcus, before following the guard.

The guard was of normal height if anything was normal in Hell. He wore black metal armor that reflected the streetlights. A large sword swung from a leather belt that ran across his chest. This creature was not something a person would want to fight.

Walking through the city streets, no one spoke. No children played. The shops seemed cold and empty. A couple of people stood on the corners with their heads bowed, a cloak covering their faces.

"What is this place?" she asked.

"Lord Aequitas reigns over the damned. Those souls who once used their knowledge against others and not for the better good of all."

Winifred stopped and glanced around. Her eyes widened as a thought flickered behind her eyes. "Oh, my."

"What is it?" the guard asked.

"Grandmother is here," she stated.

"Grandmother who?"

"Not who. What."

"Grandmother What?" The guard shrugged. "Never heard of that demon."

"Well, I did." Winifred stepped over to where three spirits stood. Their eyes lowered. A look of pure sadness decorated their putrid faces. "Do any of you know …" Winifred paused. *What was her name?* The last name, Oxford, she new. Grandma and Grandpa Oxford. But what was her first name? Winifred only referred to her as Grandmother. Others called her Your Highness or Your Majesty. "Shit," Winifred whispered.

"Who are you looking for?" A woman reached out her bony hand, brushing her fingers against Winifred's arm.

"My grandmother," Winifred replied. "But I don't remember her name." With her heart pounding and her mind reeling, the conversation she once had with a beautiful black girl flew through her mind. "Wait, Grandmother was the High Priestess of the Kalevala coven. Kalevala means *Daughter of Death.*"

The woman nodded. "I know of this woman."

"You do?" Winifred glanced around. "Where is she?"

"She stands beside Lord Aequitas at his throne."

Winifred's mind froze. Taking small breaths, she tried to understand. Was her grandmother so powerful that she now stood at the side of a lord demon? *How can this be possible?*

"Come," the guard ordered.

Winifred walked meekly behind the man, feeling helpless. Would she once again be under that woman's spell? A woman, that if it had not been for her birthing her mother, Winifred would not exist. People walked as if in a trance. A few limped as if in pain. Their faces pale, sickly. No city windows were open. All doors closed. Only a lingering aroma of rotten eggs and urine whiffed through the air.

"The ghettos of Hell …" she whispered.

"It is what it is," the guard replied.

Winifred now stood at the doors of the large, building. She looked up, and the blackness seemed to flow on forever. Double doors with silver hinges were open and two guards protected the entrance. She thanked her escort and took a step.

"Halt!" A guard held up his sword.

"Lord Aequitas is expecting her," the escort stated.

The guard waved at someone inside.

A young woman still in her teens stepped out. Wearing a pink flowered dress that barely covered her dirty feet, she smiled. "Follow me." Her voice was soft, her stance sweet and innocent. "You are Lord Winifred. I would love to live in your city."

"Why are *you* here?"

"My mother was the great-granddaughter of Hammurabi."

"Who's that?"

"He was the king of Babylon. Killed anyone who opposed him and not in a good way. Tortured them, ripping them apart, eaten by rats, burned by fire. The stories I heard." The girl sighed. "I'm glad I never met him."

"But why are *you* here?"

"My mother and aunt started a coven. I lured in men for sacrifices. I'm being punished for my sins."

"You've been here a long time," Winifred replied. "What is your name?"

"Hatshepta."

"Hatshepta … that's a pretty name."

They stopped at a double set of metal doors. The girl pushed on a button, tapping her fingers in her hand. When they opened, Winifred laughed.

"An elevator?"

Hatshepta nodded.

"In Hell?"

"You have to get up there somehow." The girl shrugged. "How else? I wouldn't want to climb that many stairs."

The ride was quick. Within a moment, the doors opened, and the hallway resembled any corporation in the world. Except, offices with glass windows seemed to run into eternity. Black carpeting with white walls was quite the contrast. People with their heads lowered walked somberly between rooms, carrying what looked like documents. No one spoke. No one smiled.

Winifred followed Hatshepta down the hall to door 77667766. She laughed as she stepped inside.

"I'll be back when you're ready to leave." Hatshepta nodded. "Wouldn't be a good thing if you were to get lost in here."

"Thank you," Winifred replied.

"Lord Winifred?" A woman wearing a dirty and tattered, tan robe reached out her hand. "If you would please follow me?"

The thought of running into her grandmother made her stomach churn. Each step sent tiny sparks of memories down her spine. The pain between her legs. The bruises. The cuts. The deaths. The odors – rotten eggs mixed with rusting iron.

The woman opened the door and Winifred stepped inside. The room was an office. A corporate executive's office. Nothing devilish nor evil. No hail or brimstone. Just an ordinary office.

"Please, sit," the woman whispered. "Lord Aequitas will be right with you."

Winifred sat. As soon as her muscles relaxed, a man appeared in the chair opposite her. He wore a black suit and red tie. His face resembled any aging corporate executive with graying temples. Wire-rimmed glasses decorated his slender nose and lips.

"It is nice to finally meet you, Lord Winifred." He smiled, leaning to one side. "Why are you here?"

Winifred shook her head as the tears fell.

Lord Aequitas handed her a box of tissues. "A good death ... requires one to have a healthy disposition. A harmony that bonds the three parts of our soul. I believe it was Plato who first stated it on Earth."

"Stated?" Winifred blew her nose.

"The three parts of the soul ... reason, spirit, and appetite."

"Appetite? You mean food?"

"Food for thought, my dear. We long for reason ... a reason why. Why are we here? Why did this or that happen? Why me?"

A rush of warmth flooded Winifred with a sensation of acceptance, an awakening that felt fresh and mimicked freedom. She held the box of tissues, allowing her fingers to run down the side. She understood now that reality was more than just an existence. There was something else.

"We all have an inner nature," he stated. "It is what allows for self-discipline. Our character grows and matures. But if there is a disturbance, a break in the chain of life, then that inner nature is damaged and demons can enter. Our souls are very much connected to the veil that separates our worlds. The cardinal against the spirit. A very delicate and thin separation."

"But ..."

"Playing with evil only damages the human inner nature. Creates bruising, pain, and suffering. Sometimes, it can be repaired. Many times, it cannot."

"That is what turns people evil?"

Lord Aequitas nodded. "Mostly, it's the pain."

"Then what happens to us means nothing," Winifred whispered. "What matters is how we see ourselves within a situation."

"That is correct." He smiled. "We learn from the challenges. It is why our Lord God created the universe and the planets. They are schools of learning. On Earth, it is emotions. There are so many human feelings that I doubt if anyone could list them all."

"Wow." Winifred wiped her eyes and dabbed at her nose.

"Wow is quite right. For our spirits to grow, we must be able to walk freely. Not be sheep or little ducklings that follow the crowd. We must be able to think for ourselves."

"Fads," Winifred said.

Lord Aequitas laughed. "Yes, fads. It is that yearning to be part of the whole."

"Whole?"

"Our Lord God flakes off a little piece, and it is that piece that becomes an individual soul. It travels the dimensions, living various lives, learning valuable lessons. When a cardinal life ends, the spirit returns, sharing everything experienced with the Lord God."

"Then what happens? Is that Heaven?"

"No." Lord Aequitas laughed. "A place before Heaven. A soul then decides, makes a choice. It can stay with our Creator or return to their training and adventures. Just depends on that soul."

Winifred blew her nose and smiled.

"You are wise, Lord Winifred." He waved his hand through the air. "You have courage and you hold a deep appreciation for life. You simply lack temperance."

"Temperance?"

"The art of self-discipline," he replied. "You are trapped in a world of illusion. One based on appearances. Look past the blooming flowers and into what flows through the stem. See through the clouds. What is deep inside?"

Winifred smiled. "I believe I understand."

"I believe you do," he replied. "And yes, your grandmother is here. Her name is Marabel. Marabel Agusta Oxford. She was born Marabel Agusta LeVey. Her mother was Gertrude Agusta and her father was Michael LeVey."

"Why is that important?"

"Anton Lavey, as he was called, is your grandmother's eldest brother. He was born Howard Stanton Levey."

"And what does that mean?"

"Howard was the founder of the Church of Satan," Lord Aequitas whispered. "A very angry and deadly soul."

"Then evil flowed for centuries throughout my family?"

Lord Aequitas nodded.

"And it is continuing to this very day, lifetimes later?"

Lord Aequitas nodded again.

"Then I must be the one to break the chain. The chain that binds ... that means Aeryn is one of my future ancestors?"

"Your youngest brother's line. Many times removed, but the curse does not break with just time. It also takes courage, patience, and a never-ending search for the truth."

"Does my grandmother reside by your side?" Winifred asked.

"Only as a suffering soul," he replied. "She has no power here, no authority. She suffers the constant duties of servitude. My slave, so to speak. Go, freely, Lord Winifred. Rest assured that your grandmother may hurt you no more. Feel vindicated, redeemed."

Winifred frowned. She didn't feel redeemed nor vindicated. Only pity.

Twenty-One

AS THE HEAT grew and the flames flared, Winifred placed one foot in front of the other. Not wanting to transport and suddenly appear, she preferred to walk valiantly into the demon's lair and without hesitation – the *Goat God* of many and the savior of none.

The gates were glowing red, hotter than a thousand suns. She bravely pushed the gates open, no guards stood – no one paid her any attention. In front, a wasteland loomed, lost souls who walked aimlessly, suffering, dead, but then again somehow alive. A few were bleeding, swinging a single arm or hopping on a single leg. A few, wrapped in blankets, leaned against a large rock or broken tree stump, crying. Many were begging and praying for God to forgive them.

Winifred took a deep breath, gathering her strength. She forged up the winding path to the *Tower of Death* as if death didn't exist.

"What are you doing here?" Malus asked, grinning. His grotesque face reminded her of a cow's hind end.

"Where is he?" Winifred demanded, her voice loud and stern.

"Where is whom?" Malus laughed.

Winifred stared at the lower demon. Shaking her head, she searched past his outer reflection, penetrating his dark, bloody skin that seemed to fade the deeper she searched, replaced with a normal-looking human male. The man was probably in his late fifties, boasting a receding hairline and dark stubble that was streaked with white. His eyes held a sadness – a dark secret.

Concentrating, her gaze dug deeper, searching for the demon's soul. It was locked away, inside a large chest, a million locks holding the miles of chains.

"You liked little ones when you were human," Winifred whispered. "So many to atone to ... but you'll never ask for forgiveness. Will you?"

Malus' eyes widened. "How'd you –"

"I can see through you now. You have no power over me or my citizens. Behind the strength of *my* knowledge, I'm now protected by the weight of *our* Creator."

Malus took several steps back, holding up his hands. "This is impossible." He fell to his knees and cried. "Forgive me, my lord."

"You can feel my power?" Winifred laughed. "Admit it."

"Release me, my lord." The demon cried. "Forgive me, please."

"Go, screw yourself, Malus. Take a long walk off a short pier. I think Pharsight could help you with that."

Malus kept his head low, weeping.

"Asshole!" Winifred entered the tower and glanced around.

With no elevator, it would be just her and the winding stairs to the top. No floors. Just steps, many steps, that continued and continued.

"This is bullshit!" she screamed. Closing her eyes, she materialized before Baphomet and smiled. "Hello, old friend."

"You come for me?" Baphomet laughed. "Have you missed me?"

Winifred stared past his thick fur and directly into his soul which was inside a small box with a million locks, inside another box with a million locks, inside another box and another. "Wow, you really screwed up once ... or twice."

"What are you talking about?"

"Your soul is so deep, you'll never leave this place." Now, Winifred laughed.

"My dear, what are you talking about?"

Winifred released her soul, and as it traversed into time and space where no spirit lived, she pulled Baphomet's remaining life force from the center box. Now, standing in the void, the realm between God's kingdom and the Underworld, nothing existed.

"Where are we?" Baphomet asked. "What have you done?"

"I am in control now," Winifred replied. She walked around the lord demon, tapping her chin with her finger. "No demon or man can cross from either realm directly to us. We are in-between realities, inside the veil that separates our worlds."

"In between?" Baphomet's eyes widened. "There is no such place."

"Then where are we Bap?" Winifred crossed her arms. "Huh? Go ahead, run in any direction. Go …"

Baphomet ran to the right, entering the blackness that was darker than the deepest hole on Earth. Winifred could hear his footfalls and his grunts of panic. Then, from her left he appeared, panting.

"What the fuck!" he yelled. "How did you do this?"

"There are a few basic laws that govern us." Winifred laughed. "The *Grand Key* for one."

"Grand Key?" Baphomet pounded his fist in the air. "You are making no sense. Come to me, I will enter you, as I did before, over and over again. Explore every inch of you, inside and out."

Winifred held up her hand, and the demon froze. "There is no escape. These laws are from God and direct how our lives walk the paths of fate. Your power lies only in your ability to hold souls hostage. I refuse to be one of your slaves. I refuse to give you the power over me. My soul is mine. You will never touch it again."

"What started all of this?" Baphomet asked. "I thought we had a truce."

"We did," she replied. "But you broke that truce. You are attacking another human. Does the name Aeryn ring a bell? One of my future nieces?"

"They summoned me," he stated.

"Children summoned you?" she repeated. "Do you realize that girl is only seventeen? Still in high school. She joined a club to socialize. Not to be raped by a demon."

"Stupid humans. They should know better than to summon a demon." Baphomet laughed.

"You're correct, they should know better. But that doesn't give you the right to take advantage. To use their innocence against them."

"And what are you going do about it?" he asked.

"I can lock you in here forever." Winifred raised a 'brow. "What if I sail you down the Phlegethon, the river of fire, to the depths of Tartarus? Where demons feel pain, sorrow, regret, loneliness, and fear. They scream and beg God for forgiveness. But I'll drop you below the bottom of Hell, where our Creator will never hear your pleas."

"You wouldn't dare," he yelled.

"Why not? How can you stop me?"

Baphomet took a step, but again, Winifred held out a hand and the demon froze. He couldn't move, not even a finger. "I am more powerful than you, for I have the understanding of how this works." Winifred laughed. "It is so simple. Should have figured it out earlier. Quite basic, actually."

Baphomet's eyes glared at her.

"Cat's got you tongue, Bap?"

Baphomet murmured, but his words never passed his lips.

"Oh, sorry." Winifred flicked her fingers, releasing his mouth.

"What the fuck?" he yelled.

"Watch your mouth!" she scolded. "Or I'll lock it shut again."

"Who the fuck do you think you are?"

"I am Lord Winifred, ruler of Tenarus, wife to Grant, lover of Yeenoghu, mother of Kiran, Katara, Kennedy, and David, granddaughter of a High Priestess. Who are you?"

"I am Vlad the 1st, my grandson was Vlad the Impaler … Vlad Dracula, a Voivode of Wallachia."

"Bullshit."

"What?"

"I call bullshit. You are older than the Vlad's. Much older." Winifred shook her head and sighed. "I think you've told so many lies that you no longer know the truth. Perhaps, you can't read your lineage, but I can."

"Then … I am related to –"

"Silence, powerless demon … you are one of God's original fallen angels. You fell from grace before time … before the Earth was formed. I know who and what you are. With your disguise lifted, you become nothing. I will banish you to Tartarus for a million eternities. A place where the veil will escape your touch. Never again will you rape a human. Never again will you feel the pride of making others suffer."

"And what of my souls?"

"Your souls are now my souls. I will bring them to my city where they will live in peace until the light comes for them. They will serve out their punishment without you tormenting them."

"You can't –"

Winifred nodded at the demon who had just vanished. In her mind, she watched as he landed hard on the ship floating on the river of fire. Sentries, larger than the span from the Earth to the Moon, grabbed his arms and legs, chaining him to the ship's bow. He struggled as the flames lashed at his fur, his horns sizzling from the intense heat.

"Enjoy the ride," she whispered in his ear, before leaving the demon to his misery.

David ran to greet her mother at the docks. She waved at Pharsight and Umibōzu. Pharsight waved, but Umibōzu could only blink. However, David understood that he was waving too.

"Mother? Who are all these people?" David asked.

A billion souls were following behind Winifred. With lowered heads, they shuffled their feet.

"They need a place to live and heal," Winifred replied. "Perhaps, I should expand our city."

"I think so." David laughed. "I will help."

David ran to the first few limping souls, assisting them to the nearest bench. Other citizens noticed and they too ran to help. When Winifred and David fell on their couch, the last few souls had finally been settled into their new homes.

"That was a lot of work, Mother." David crossed her arms.

"Yes, it was. Thank you for your help."

"I enjoyed that."

They sat in silence, resting their aching bones. A light appeared in the middle of the room. Winifred stared at it, wondering where it was coming from. She glanced around, and no lanterns were lit yet.

"What is that light, Mother?"

"I'm not sure." Winifred stood.

The light grew wider and more intense.

"I can feel it," David whispered.

"Feel it?"

"Yes, can't you?"

"No." Winifred shook her head. "No, I cannot. Ukobach! Ukobach, come quick."

The butler entered, eyes wide. "What is wrong, my lord."

"What is that?" Winifred asked.

Ukobach stepped closer and smiled. "Which of you can sense the presence?"

"I feel nothing," Winifred replied.

"I can feel it," David said.

"Then the light has come for you, my dear," Ukobach replied. "Your last lock has been released."

Winifred understood. She stepped closer, and a large figure of a man with broad shoulders loomed. He reached out a hand and Winifred could sense his essence. "David, your father is here for you. Go with him, my love."

"Mother?" David stood.

"It is okay." Winifred hugged her daughter. "It is your time to leave this place."

"But this is my home. I want to stay with you."

"This is not our home." Winifred kissed the top of her daughter's head. "Where your father lives, that is our home. Go … I will arrive one day and we will be together."

The light grew larger and brighter.

"I cannot resist, Mother."

"Do not resist, my love." Winifred wiped her eyes. "Go now."

David stepped into the light, and two strong arms immediately embraced her. As father and daughter stood together, Winifred smiled at her demon lover's beautiful face as it once was, when he was first created. A beautiful angel of a man with dark hair and a strong build. No fur, no horns. David waved and blew a kiss. As the kiss hit Winifred, the light dimmed, fading into the mist.

"Oh, Ukobach." Winifred cried. "I'm all alone again."

"You have me, my lord …" he replied, "… and your new souls to attend to. There is still a lot of work to be done."

Winifred sat on the couch with the tears refusing to stop. She sat there for what felt like a century, reliving her life and examining her sins. As the emotions rolled through her like waves on an endless shore, she prayed for the salvation of each spirit that had followed her to her city. Only Nyx and the butler could comfort her with their words.

"It's time to rescue more," Winifred whispered. "I will save all the lost souls I can find."

Nyx patted Winifred on the back and smiled.

Winifred spent centuries traversing the Endless Maze, searching for lost souls. The way was clear to her now. No longer did the shadows frighten her, for they were a place of familiarity. Her city grew in both depth and spirit. She preached the goodness of the Creator on a daily basis while counseling those in need of relief from their guilt or pain.

As she stood at the entrance to the great dome, her mind drifted back to when she had stood there with her friends. Such a long time ago, but just as fresh in her mind as the day it actually happened. Something moved between the disgusting trees, grabbing her attention. The guards shrugged. She frowned. Again, something moved.

"What in the …?" Winifred took a step.

Malus jumped out. "Are you following me, witch?"

"Malus? You scared the crap outta me." Winifred waved her hand through the air. "What are you doing here?"

"My home is gone," he yelled. "I am alone. I have no one to tell me what to do. I just walk and walk and walk. I can't do this anymore."

"Can't do what?"

Malus stomped his foot and the powdery dirt puffed into the air, surrounding him with a brown haze.

"What can't you do?" she asked again.

"I can't exist like this."

"But why are you here at this dome?"

"I will ask Satan to send me to the depths of Hell, where I can burn forever."

"Malus …" Winifred sighed.

"I can't do this."

Winifred allowed her thoughts to wander. If she forgave Malus, would that be pointing the blame at herself? Would the Creator consider it an act of mercy? But her thoughts would have to be pure. God would see through any deception, and that was something she could not have against her. "Malus, maybe I can help."

"Help?" Malus sat on the powdery dirt. Again, a puff of brown surrounded him in a makeshift halo. "How can *you* help me?"

"You can come with me to my city," she replied. "I will train you."

"For what? To be your slave?"

Winifred shook her head. "To be self-sufficient. To be able to think for yourself. Never again would you be alone and lost. You could learn to console yourself."

"I wouldn't have to walk the Endless Maze anymore?"

Winifred reached out her hand. "No more Endless Maze."

"No more pain?"

"No more pain," she whispered.

Malus glanced up at the guards and frowned. "I don't know."

"We are in Hell," Winifred replied. "We were sent here because of our sins. You did terrible things to children once. You murdered many. Now, you have a chance to help others. To make up for those sins. Do you want that chance?"

Malus nodded as a tear finally rolled down his bloody and rotting cheek. The first tear he shed in over a million centuries.

Malus stood on the balcony overlooking the city. The citizens were living their deaths, existing, developing, growing in spirit and wisdom.

Winifred approached, placing a hand on his shoulder. "Yah know what?"

"No, what?" Malus asked.

"You're not as hideous as you were before."

"What do you mean?"

"Look at your hands," she replied. "They are no longer a deep red. More of a pink in color. You are slowly returning to your human self. You're also no longer inside out."

"How can this be?" Malus asked.

"As the evil leaves your body and another lock is opened, your soul purifies a little more. Each spark of goodness moves you closer to your redemption."

"I had a wife once," he whispered. "I remember now. A wife and two boys. I don't know what happened, but suddenly, I had the urge to rape and kill others. I was a rather small man. Kids were weaker and easier to find. The last one, I cut his throat and watched him bleed. Why did I enjoy that so much?"

Winifred shrugged. "Why does anyone do anything? Maybe stress? Anger from our past? Afraid of the future? But those are only excuses. Take responsibility for your actions. Accept what you did. Then repent."

"Repent?"

"Will you walk with me?" Winifred asked.

Malus nodded.

They walked through the city to the central plaza with the beautiful fountain. Winifred whistled, and two large bat-like creatures larger than a house, swooped down, each with their claws ready to grab. As they soared over the city, Malus screamed several times.

Winifred laughed. The creatures gently left the two on the ledge of the mountain that separated Tenarus from the lake.

"Look up, Malus," Winifred whispered. "The entrance to Heaven."

"It is beautiful," he replied.

"You see … you appreciate beauty now. Something you could never do before." She patted his shoulder.

"God, the Creator, is in there?"

"As is your wife and two boys, along with many offsprings. Your ancestry line is long. They are waiting for you."

Malus allowed the tears to fall. "I remember my home. I remember my parents. Lord Winifred, I remember being a child."

"What happened when you were six?"

"Oh, my." Malus slapped a hand over his mouth.

"You were raped by a teenager. Were you not?"

He nodded.

"Evil spreads, Malus. It is a sickness that grows. But you are receiving the cure from our Creator. It will take time, but I think that eventually, the evil will leave your soul and you'll return to our Creator."

"Thank you, my lord." Malus knelt.

"Stand up, Malus." Winifred laughed. "I'm no one to bow to."

"You are wise, my lord."

"There is someone you should visit. Perhaps if you remain with Aequitas for a while, one day, you can rule Tenarus as I do now."

"Oh, I don't …"

"Shh, never say never, Malus." Winifred whistled for the bat-like creatures to return them to their city of lights.

Winifred waved as the ship left the dock. Malus stood at the railing, his eyes showing his apprehension. She shook her head and smiled. Walking the streets, Hatshepta ran up to greet her.

"Lord Winifred," the soft voice echoed.

"Hatshepta?" Winifred hugged her. "How did you get here?"

"Aequitas sent me," she replied. "He said I could come here to be with you."

"Wonderful." Winifred hugged her again. "Come, we will find you a home."

They stopped at the fountain decorated with flying creatures and large flowers, water trickling into the deep blue.

"It is beautiful here," Hatshepta whispered. "I have half a century left before I can enter the light. Aequitas said I should be happy while I wait. Asked where I wanted to go and I thought about you."

"I'm glad you did," Winifred replied. "You are welcome here. Sometimes, you remind me of my daughter. It will be a comfort knowing you are safe."

Winifred sat on her couch, staring into the large, dark hearth. "I should make a blazing fire one night." She laughed. "Too bad it's never cold enough." She shrugged, stretching out her legs.

As her eyes followed along the seams of the rocks, a bright light hovered above the small table. Her heart felt a tug. A warm, welcoming tug. The urge to step into the light felt overpowering.

"Ukobach!" Winifred yelled. "Ukobach!"

The demon butler entered. He stepped closer to the light and smiled.

"What do I do?"

"As you once said to your daughter, go," he replied.

Winifred hugged Ukobach which wasn't easy as he was half her height. "I will miss you."

"As I will you."

"But my citizens?" she whispered. "Who will care for my lost souls?"

"I have word from Lord Aequitas," Ukobach replied. "Malus is almost finished with his training. He will protect and love this city as did you and as did Yeenoghu. Now, go." He chuckled.

Winifred stepped closer to the light. The pull strong and inviting. As she stared into the swirling mist, a large figure of a man reached out his hand. Next to him, stood a young girl of about twelve.

"Mother?" David yelled. "Come, Mother. Grant and your friends are here too, so is your family."

Winifred stepped into the light as warm arms surrounded her. She leaned into the embrace, feeling the love. As the darkness faded behind her, a brighter light beamed in the distance.

"The Creator," Yeenoghu whispered. "And you are simply Winifred here. No longer a lord. You can release the responsibility and relax."

"Just Winifred?" she replied.

"Not just Winifred," the Creator stated, holding out his arms. "You are *my* Winifred. A little spark of my eternal flame. Welcome home."

www.ingramcontent.com/pod-product-compliance
Lightning Source LLC
Chambersburg PA
CBHW061645190726
48289CB00006B/1747